Gil Scott-Heron

a father and son story

Leslie Gordon Goffe

First Edition
10 9 8 7 6 5 4 3 2 1

Editors: Kenisha T. Duff & K. Sean Harris
Cover design: Monique de Latour
Typeset & book layout: Sanya Dockery

Published by: LMH Publishing Limited
Suite 10-11
Sagicor Industrial Park
7 Norman Road
Kingston C.S.O., Jamaica
Tel.: (876) 938-0005; Fax: (876) 759-8752
Email: lmhbookpublishing@cwjamaica.com
Website: www.lmhpublishing.com

Printed in the U.S.A

ISBN: 978-976-8202-89-5

NATIONAL LIBRARY OF JAMAICA CATALOGUING IN PUBLICATION DATA

Goffe, Leslie Gordon

Gil Scott-Heron : a father and son story / Leslie Gordon Goffe

p. ; cm.

ISBN 978-976-8202-89-5 (pbk)

1. Scott-Heron, Gilbert "Gil", 1949-2011 2. Blues musicians – United States – Biography
3. Blues(Music)
I. Title

781.643092 dc 22

for Elsie

Contents

Acknowledgments

There are so many people I would like to thank. I would like, of course, to thank the late Gil Scott-Heron for talking to me about his Jamaican pa and his Tennessee ma, and talking to me about being born Up North but growing up Down South, and explaining how he never thought of himself as a complex man or someone who was really that hard to understand. I would also like to thank the late Gilbert St. Elmo Heron who, though he was encircled in a dense Detroit fog, talked to me about Portland Street, Kenilworth Street, beating Herb McKenley, playing for Celtic and being the 'first black'; Brian Jackson for taking me back to how it all began and to how it all ended and for writing the foreword to this book; Monique de Latour for the lovely book cover and photos and for all her interventions; Gayle Heron for the family photos, documents and stories she shared with me; Denis Heron for helping me understand the father and son relationship between Gil and Gillie and between Gillie and himself and the brother to brother thing, too; Roy Heron for talking to me about running the Sack Race at Kingston College and for talking to me about chasing whales in the Antarctic; Albert Porter for talking to me about driving Lillie and Scotty to the Berean Baptist each week and driving them to see their kin in Alabama and talking to me about lending Scotty a typewriter because he knew Scotty had something special about him; Madeleine Walker who, with Scotty and Gillard Glover, de-segregated the Jackson, Tennessee school system on January 25, 1962 and who wishes she could now find that poem he wrote for her while they were at Tigrett; Brenda Monroe-Moses, who contributed her own part to civil rights history in Tennessee; Melvoid Estes Benson, who told me why Tennessee isn't like Mississippi and why Madison County isn't like Haywood County; Tom Campbell, who as a 13 year old was among the 40,000 people at Celtic Park on August 18, 1951 to see the 'Black Flash' make his debut for Celtic; Sean Fallon, Gillie's Celtic F.C. team-mate who took him out on the town when he first arrived in Glasgow; the late Audrey Fearnie, secretary to Celtic manager Jimmy 'Mermaid' McGrory and the person who paid Gillie his weekly Celtic wage; Lloyd Lindbergh Delapenha, who played on that 1952 Jamaica team with Gillie and was the first Jamaican to play professional football in Britain; Walter Bahr, captain of the US National Soccer team; Jack Wood, Jackson-Madison County Library; Lan Wang, Lane College Library; Maura McColgan, Celtic Football Club; Bert Bell, Third Lanark A.C. archivist; Matt Wall, Kidderminster Harriers F.C.; Jez Hamblett, Kidderminster Library; Brian Gallagher and Cecelia King of the *Daily Record* newspaper; Colin Jose, US soccer historian; Jack Huckel, US National Soccer Hall of Fame and Museum. I would also like to thank everyone at LMH and thank the artists Mark 'Markdraws' Hammermeister, Gian Paolo La Barbera and Nat Creekmore for allowing me to use their work in this book.

Finally, I would like to thank my daughters Tao and Gaia for all they do and thank my wife Judy for being Judy.

Foreword

Who knew?

We were the black odd couple, an odd couple that never expected that one day people would be saying that Gil Scott-Heron and Brian Jackson were important bits and pieces of the American musical tradition; that we were in the tradition and that we helped make the tradition. Who knew?

Some say we had something to do with how hip hop began. Some say we had something to do with urban blues and jazz and with neo-soul, too. Some say, some say. Some say that what we did on *Pieces of a Man*, him and me, was simply sublime. Some say that what we did on *Winter in America* had never been done before. He brought the lyrics and I brought the music. Sometimes, sometimes, I brought the music and the lyrics: *A Prayer For Everybody, It's Your World* and I brought musical hooks and verses and lines to other songs, too.

Read on, read on and you'll find I say he's "one of the greatest writers of the 20th century." Read on, read on and you'll find he says I'm "the best composer" he knows.

We were brothers from other mothers who both had father-son dramas. But I am sad to say us brothers from others are not brothers, anymore. Read on, read on. You'll find out why. You'll find out why.

Before I tell you about all the whys and the whats and the wherefores, let me tell you about all of the places we've been and where we are coming from.

He was coming from 17th Street by way of the Bronx, by way of Jackson, Tennessee, by way of Chicago, Illinois and I was coming from Jay Street in Brooklyn Heights by way of Flatbush by way of Bedford-Stuyvesant. He was coming from Herons and Gentles from Jamaica and Scotts from Tennessee and Hamiltons from Alabama. I was coming from Bouies and Blacks and Slaughters from Georgia and Jacksons from South Carolina. These are all of the places we've been and all of the places we're coming from.

Read on, read on and you'll find out why we stopped being brothers. But first a word about fathers and how fathers make sons and sons become fathers and how though we try to do better we do not do better, but often do worse. We, brothers, have gotten good at it. But other men are pretty good at it, too.

A lot of men – young ones and old ones – struggle with this, with lives like this. Sometimes it sends us early to prison, or late to prison like my brother. These men, these boys, punish those who get close to them, who remind them of not being close when they needed closeness. Read on, read on. Read about a man here who believed in nonviolence but ignored the fine print which says, "Violence towards yourself counts as violence, too, and you can also be violent in your thoughts and actions towards others without lifting a finger."

If you read on, you will meet a young man who mostly held it together till he was an old man, but then could not hold it together anymore.

And he is not just any man, but at his best, a very special man. His accomplishments are epic. His work made him an icon of a generation. He turned his sick soul inside out so that the world could watch him die, and did it in a way that was pure poetry. Who better to speak of the alienation and rejection we were feeling as young black men and women in America? He didn't preach about killing people. The songs are about love and good vibes, not destruction. The only person he actively sought to destroy was himself. And along that road to destruction he gave the world timeless gifts. Not bad for a guy who, had he not found a way to channel some of those self-destructive urges, at least for a while, could have easily been a poster boy for the local FBI's 'Most Wanted' list.

Read on, read on and you will find out about brotherhood and betrayal and about brothers from other mothers trying to be more than just musicians but bluesicians. You will find out about sons failed by fathers becoming fathers who fail their own sons, and their daughters, as well.

Read on, read on and you will find out what is behind the microphone, behind the music, behind the man, behind the men, you will find out that the artiste, the artistes, don't always know what we are saying and sometimes we can hardly understand that we are only pieces of a man. Read on, read on.

Brian Jackson

Brian Jackson
New York City
May 16, 2011

The Flight of the Heron

(for Gilbert St. Elmo Heron)

When Duke was in the Lebanon
Grooving for the human race
Gil flew high in the Western sky
On a mission full of style and grace

From Jamaica to the Kingston Bridge
He was inclined to roam
Drawn to the flame of the beautiful game
Here was a brother who could not stay home

Higher, raise the bar higher
He made his way across the sea
So that all men could brothers be

When Miles was on the juke box
And Monk was on the air
Gil crossed the ocean to the other side
To play for Celtic with a noble stride

The arrow flew, he's flying yet
We state his name so we don't forget
What it means when his name we hear
The hopes and dreams of every pioneer

Higher, raise the bar higher

He made his way across the sea

So that all men could brothers be

The arrow flew, he's flying yet

His aim is true so we don't forget

What it means when his name we hear

The hopes and dreams of every pioneer

Michael Marra

Gil Scott-Heron, illustration by Mark Hammermeister

"My life has been one of running away just as fast as I can. But I've been no more successful at getting away than was my old man."

Gil Scott-Heron

Prologue

a father and son story

> "We might be through with the past, but the past ain't through with us."
>
> ***Jimmy Gator***

I'll begin at the beginning.

The other day – I'm not sure what day exactly – I went to the Motor City, somewhere between the Six Mile and Seven Mile sections of town to see Gilbert St. Elmo Heron. I thought he might be able to tell me what was wrong with his big son, Gilbert Scott-Heron, the one who wrote those songs about the protest and the rage and the people who gave a damn. You know, the one who wrote those songs about plastic people with plastic minds on their way to plastic homes.

He used to be the voice of the sane, used to be the voice of the sane. But that was before his house was filled with pain, filled with pain. For a long time, he had been living in darkness and the sun had not been shining through. For a long time, he had been lost in his white powder dreams and had taken to turning his sick soul inside out so that the world could watch him die, watch him die. Somehow, somewhere, he lost his way and we all watched and wondered if he would make it through the day. To understand how his day turned to night, we need to go back, back a long time ago and to a galaxy far, far away.

When the son was born, the father was on his way down after a long time of being up. Back then, back before the bloodshed and the break-up, the father had been playing soccer for Sparta A.B.A in the 'City of the Big Shoulders.' Sparta had won everything; but it won nothing with him, the first black man allowed among the Bohemians. So Sparta got rid of Gillie and Gillie got rid of Bobbie and got rid of Scotty, too. It was as if the son had not been named for the father and as if the father had not understood that the sins of fathers are always, always, visited upon their sons.

But Gillie Heron – he's flown away now as all birds do – had not read Larkin and could not say whether it was true that they fuck you up – your mum and dad – because they were fucked up in their turn by fools in old-style hats and coats. He had not heard Home Is Where The Hatred Is and so could not say whether home is, indeed, filled with pain and white powder dreams and if it is an empty vacuum filled with silent screams. He couldn't say whether home was a place that could heal a broken heart or whether it would, in fact, not be a good idea, a very good idea, not to go home again, home again.

Gillie Heron was fourscore and five years when I went to see him and was beginning then to forget what he'd eaten for lunch and what he'd watched on TV and forgetting who he was and who he had been. Gillie told me, as best as you can when worms have feasted on your cerebral cortex, what it had been like to be the first black person to play professional football in the United States and one of the first black people to play professional football in Britain. It's worth saying that Gillie, in common with others of his time, regarded himself less as a 'black' man and more as a man of many colours, a thing that has no sense and certainly no sensibility.

Besides, this 'first black' thing didn't amount to very much really in the way of much. Being first would, I guess, have been alright had it amounted to something, to anything. Gillie told me what it had been like to make nothing from it, this kicking of the ball, his species-essence alienated from itself, eking out a living on an assembly line in the Motor City where sometimes in his role as estranged proletarian he affixed single barrelled carburettors on Falcons and sometimes he attached tinted, transparent plastic roofs to Fairlanes and sometimes he affixed 'Swing Away' steering wheels to Thunderbirds. Our Gillie was a model of estranged labour, estranged from himself. He was estranged, too, from nature and from the mighty sensuous external world. In other words, his reality was lost and so he was lost to himself, completely lost. Lost to yourself is no way to spend the transcendent end of history. But that's what Gilbert St. Elmo Heron did, which is a big surprise when you think how he started, his will and consciousness, his species-being, very firmly in place.

Anyone who had grown up or even spent a little time in the place he had, had their species-being intact. That was just the way it was.

⁂

He grew up across the road from Kensington Park, where all sorts of splendid cricket matches took place, and grew up across from Nelson Oval, where all sorts of merry dancing and bright speeches went on. He grew up, also, at Hartlands, a modern day Jamaican plantation with modern day slaves and a modern day slave driver. His father, Walter Gilbert Heron, had been a slave driver, an assistant overseer, a man who liked and knew how to push and press, how to bully and beat, how to cajole. He taught them all, his spawn, how to push, how to press, how to bully, how to beat and how to cajole till they got good, real good at it.

⁂

Gillie told me, as best as he could encircled as he was in a dense Detroit fog, what it had been like to have to leave his home in Kingston, his Grandpa Gentles' home actually, at 6 Portland Road, a comfortable house on a large lot of land abounding in bearing fruit trees, for ugly old, cold old Cleveland as the rockets' red glare and bombs were bursting in air elsewhere. He told me what it had been like to leave his father – the amateur arboriculturalist, apiarist and professional slave driver – behind.

Walter didn't want to go to America, which was okay because Lucille, his wife, didn't want him to come with them, she and the kids, to America. They were no more one flesh but twain. What God had joined together they, by their own works, had put asunder. She blamed him. He blamed her and took out an ad in the *Gleaner* to tell everyone in the land of wood and water so:

NOTICE

> **"HAVING BEEN DRIVEN AWAY AND DESERTED BY MY WIFE LUCILLE ISABELLE HERON FOR OVER THREE YEARS, I DO NOT HOLD MYSELF RESPONSIBLE FOR HER OR ANY DEBTS SHE MAY CONTRACT. IT IS MY INTENTION TO MARRY AT AN EARLY DATE."**
>
> ***Walter Gilbert Heron,***
> ***Hartlands, St. Catherine***
> ***August 10, 1936***

Walter, in common with other Heron men, was a sinner who thought himself more sinned against than sinning, more wronged against than wronging. It's just as well he stayed behind; a family man without a family. He acted as if he'd never had five sons named Roy, Gilbert, Gerald, Cecil, Leopold, who everyone called 'Poley', and a daughter named Elsie, whose middle name was 'Isabelle.'

A family man without a family, Walter gave all his love to his flora and to his fauna and squandered what little he earned on the *Daily Double*. The rest of the time he spent besotted with bees or grafting one fancy plant onto another on his one acre retreat in the high elevations of Jamaica. Walter did other grafting, too. Like the cultivator he was, Walter sowed his seed and so up flew a new flock of Herons who knew nothing of the Herons who'd flown away, long ago, over the rainbow, at least so they thought, to Cleveland and then on to Detroit.

Gilbert St. Elmo Heron, when he was here, told me a lot of things. What he could not tell me, though, was what was wrong with his big son, Gilbert Scott-Heron, who has flown away now. I figured the answer lay in one of those father and son stories that stretch down through the ages.

Black Flash in the Pan

"One that appears promising but turns out to be disappointing or worthless."

Webster's Dictionary

Gilbert St. Elmo Heron had a lot of the African and a little bit of the Scot, the Caledonian, in him; his great-great something or other having left Scotland for Jamaica hundreds of years before. But looking for Celtic roots, collecting clan colours, and that sort of thing was not why he ended up in Glasgow in 1951.

When he got to Glasgow, people were still picking themselves up after the war. Soap and petrol had been rationed. Meat and fish had been rationed. Eggs, too, were hard to come by. Neither bon bons nor buttermints could be had without a nod or a wink. Cloth, too, was rationed and without the proper ration card someone wearing the kind of wide-legged zoot suit, with its reams of wasted cloth that Gillie Heron turned up in at Glasgow Central Station on July 30, 1951, could have found themselves in real trouble with the authorities. After all, turn-ups on trousers had already been deemed, years before, damaging to the war effort and banned. Yet, there Gilbert St. Elmo Heron stood in front of the Central Hotel on Gordon Street, just off the train from London, dressed in a broad-brimmed hat, multi-coloured shoes and a "killer-diller coat with a drape shape, reet pleats and shoulders padded like a lunatic's cell." There was nothing like the Jamaican in all of Scotland.

Celtic Football Club hadn't been looking for him when it found him, a down on his luck footballer who'd given up football, the full time kind, for full time at a car assembly plant in dismal Detroit. He'd put football, which was no longer an occupation and was now only an entertainment, behind him by the time Celtic, while touring the US in the summer of 1951, encountered him and bid him, without seeing him play, come to Scotland for a try-out.

"Gee, I was tickled. Glasgow Celtic was the greatest name in football to me." In Jamaica, Gillie had played in front of only a few. In America, he had played in front of fewer still. Here, in Glasgow, he would play in front of tens of thousands and see how the game was loved and how those who wore the green and the white were beloved. In Jamaica, the game had been second to cricket. In America, it had been fifth behind baseball, basketball, American football and behind even ice hockey. There, football had been merely fringe. Here, football was their North, their South, their East, their West, their working week and Sunday rest. But there was little rest in Glasgow, a divided city of Catholics who supported Celtic, who played in a green and white strip, and Protestants who supported Rangers, who played in a Union Jack-like red, white and blue kit. Football there was an entirely sectarian affair.

Scotland was not as the Jamaican had imagined it. It was dirty and damaged; but not from bombs, really. It was always that way: dirty and damaged, grimy and grey. The sun struggled to split the clouds that hung always over Glasgow. On winter evenings a thick fog, full of pea soup, caused the city's one million or so citizens to perpetually hawk and perpetually spit. Daniel Defoe had lied. Glasgow was not "the cleanest and beautifullest, and best built city in Britain, London excepted." Nor did its nickname, 'Dear Green Place', make much sense either.

When Gillie got to Glasgow in 1951 people were keener than ever on God. Billy Graham and other born-agains came often across the oceans to offer salvation and save souls. But if hell and brimstone were not to your liking, there were other amusements. The 'samba' was in at the time and the Alhambra, the Citz and the Empire were where one went on a Saturday night to dance. There you could see the Flying Cromwells or the Balmoral Four or, if you were really lucky, Lena Horne or the Ink Spots, all the way from America.

Though Glasgow was as grimy and grey as it had always been, there was now, after the war, more colour in it. Jews had long been there. Italians had come because they could not get along with Mussolini. Poles and Czechs came because they had been displaced. A Jamaican by way of Detroit joined them in 1951, the same year Salvador Dali's 'Christ of St John of the Cross' was bought and brought to Glasgow to give the city a bit of colour. Like the Christ in Dali's painting, Gillie Heron would be Celtic's saviour or would be crucified on its cross and in Glasgow's newspapers, of this he could be assured.

The Prisoner

"Well, I'm doing fine, thank you, but I could've been pulling time."

Angola, Louisiana
Gil Scott-Heron

When we are out making history, there are things that fall by the wayside, people who fall by the wayside. While the father was out making history, and the mother was just out, the son – Scotty – was falling.

You couldn't tell, at first. He had always been, when he had been a boy in Jackson, Tennessee, so seemingly solid. He always looked so fragile but had always seemed so solid. It was the same when he arrived at Hampden Place and the same when he arrived at 17th Street and the same when he arrived at 3901 Fieldston Road and the same, even, when he arrived at 1570 Baltimore Pike. He always looked so fragile, but seemed so solid. He was the one folks leaned on when they weren't feeling strong. He was the one folks leaned on when they needed a friend to help them carry on. Who could have known that it would not be very long before he was going to need someone to lean on?

It's all there in the songs, in the poems, hidden among the umbrage and the outrage. But he would have none of it. They were all just songs and poems, he said, just songs he sang and poems he read loud and proud; not things to be read into.

You couldn't pin him down. He knew how to push it down and keep it there, at least in the early years he did. Besides, back then a lot of people's people were away somewhere. Dropping your loved ones off here and there had, I think, something to do with slavery. Back then, no one asked where your father was. They knew where he was. He was with their father and with all the other fathers who'd gone out for sugar and not come back. There was no shame in that. The shame was in trying to explain where your mother was and why she was there and why she was not here. His mother, he'd been told, was an aspiring librarian and there were not nearly enough books in Jackson, Tennessee, a place of sawmills and cotton fields, for someone like that.

His falling apart was gradual and imperceptible. It could not be detected by the ordinary eye. You'd have to have had superhero sight like Superman to have seen it, noticed it. Those around him couldn't see it. They didn't have super sight. They were a short-sighted lot, them and their excessive positive diopters. They saw only themselves and could not see that the boy was falling apart and that this would, some day, lead him to becoming a common con, doing time and serving time for being in possession of the stuff of his white powder dreams.

Prior to his white powder dreams he had sung about prison and feeling imprisoned, but he had not, back then, been, yet, to prison. He had, of course, been to prison to support political prisoners and been to prison to entertain the imprisoned with liberating music and songs of freedom, but he, in and of himself, had not actually been to prison.

One time he went to prison, Memphis State Penitentiary, to scare straight and turn around a boy who threatened to go far wrong but who, in the end, didn't. Back then, back when the *New York Times* included him in that 'Superstars of Tomorrow' article, he went to prison because he wanted to, not because he had to; not because he'd been sentenced to 18 to 24 months or to 4 to 6 years or because a judge, New York State Judge Carol Shenkman, told him he'd had lots of opportunities to be better but didn't seem to care to be better.

Back then he went to prison because he wanted to, not because he had to. Back then he wrote and sang about men who were pieces of men. The truth was, he was pieces of a man himself and he had a lot of pieces missing. His pieces were missing, in part, because there had once been a home he had called home and his ma and his pa had called it home too but one day his pa walked out of that home and then his mother walked out too and then he, only a baby boy, was sent South while his ma, an aspiring librarian, and his pa, a fanciful footballer, went on their merry way – each in their own individual way – without him.

We could talk here about the protest and the rage, about the people who gave a damn. But we won't. Let's talk about the son, Scotty, in prison; not political prison; just plain old prison. Sixty four, forty six was Toots' number. Zero 6R3165 was Scotty's number.

At Collins – Collins Correctional Facility – a medium security prison in New York's Upstate, he was one among 1,576 inmates. Most were common-or-garden criminals: burglars, larcenists, car thieves, fraudsters. There weren't many rapists or paedophiles there. There were, however, many record company executives guilty of pressing artistes too hard for hits and many music critics who though they don't write music nor do they play music, get, somehow, to say what music is and what music is not.

Most of Collins' inmates were, like Scotty, the drug addicted, found out of control in possession of a controlled substance. Some say his thing was heroin. But he said he never touched the stuff. He saw too many insulin-dependent Scotts with needles in them to easily put a needle in his arm. His thing was cocaine, the freebase crack form of it, which, like him, has jagged edges, and, like him, can be hard and brittle and, like him, snaps when broken. He was pieces of a man.

This Heron, though, was not the first Heron to fall foul of the law. Herons had been to prison or got caught up in the law and its workings before.

Gillie Heron, had occasion to find himself up against the law. Unhappy with what Father Christmas had brought him in 1935, 13 year old Gillie went out, like Rhyging, and took what he really wanted from a Kingston shop without paying for it: a Walter Winterbottom-style regulation football. Deputy Constable Coombs caught him. But all they could charge the boy with was a criminal love of football. So, as I said before, Herons have got caught up in the law before. This takes me back to Scotty and how he found himself at Collins Correctional Facility.

Collins is not San Quentin, nor is it Sing Sing, nor Angola. Convicts don't boast about having done time at Collins and, as far as I know, the prison is not mentioned in any poems or rap songs and Scotty didn't pen anything about the place, either. It's just not that sort of prison. In Collins, Scotty was a sort of celebrity. Some of the older inmates remembered where they were when they first heard his 'Johannesburg' or his 'Save the Children.' The younger inmates found it hard to believe that *this* Gil Scott-Heron was *the* Gil Scott-Heron whose 'Home Is Where The Hatred Is' one rapper sampled and whose 'Revolution Will Not Be Televised' everyone is always talking about. Back then, he had only sung about prison and feeling imprisoned but had not yet been to prison.

To try and get him off $Coc\text{-}H^+Cl^- + NaHCO_3 \rightarrow Coc + H_2O + CO_2 + NaCl$, Collins Correctional Facility recommended he report each day of his incarceration to the prison's Alcohol and Substance Abuse Treatment

Center. Those who saw him inside say he looked pretty much as you might have expected: eaten up and eaten out. But don't be fooled. Prison didn't do this to him. He looked much worse when he arrived at Collins, ate up by the big disease with the little name. In Collins, he put on more flesh on his bones than at any time since Stick left and since Brenda left and since Clive asked him to leave. He was the weight of a teenage girl when he got to Collins. When he left, he was the weight of a teenage boy.

It would be easy to believe that because he believed in his convictions that he was convicted for his beliefs. It would be easy to believe it but it's not true. He is, was, a junkie walking through the twilight.

You keep saying, kick it, quit it, kick it, quit it
God, but did you ever try
To turn your sick soul inside out
So that the world, so that the world
Can watch you die

Home was where he lived inside his white powder dreams. His home was once an empty vacuum that's filled now with his silent screams. It might not have been such a bad idea if he had never gone home again. After all, there was no one there. There never was anyone there; his kith and kin being so expert at the getting up and the going. They both left, not just the one. They both left, not just the one. For the son, that the mother left, too, made his narrative, his song of himself, problematic. Around here, no one dare say that a woman's tender care can cease toward the child she bares. It is not allowed. But it can cease, her tender care. Fathers are stones. Fishman said this and everyone knows this. They are like granite. Their voices like gravel; their lips granite white. But mothers are not stones or at least they are not supposed to be. Mothers are made of sugar and spice and everything nice. That's what mothers are made of. They are made of sunshine and rainbows and ribbons for hair bows. That's what mothers are made of. Tea parties, laces and baby doll faces. That's what mothers are made of. What then are fathers made of? They are made of snips and snails and puppy dogs tails. That's what fathers are made of! His father was, as it was in his nature to be, a stone. This is how, though you don't intend it, you end up being corrected in a place like the Collins Correctional Facility.

Go away
I can't stand to see your face
Cause you've seen the weakest me
And now you know I'm only human
Instead of all things I'd like to be

He Was New There

"What was silent in the father speaks in the son, and often I found in the son the unveiled secret of the father."

Nietzsche

Gillie Heron wanted to be all of the things he wanted to be. So he went. What was he to do, not go? There wasn't much for a black man in 1951 besides the factory and the foundry, the foundry and the factory. He got the chance at football and fame, fame and football. So he went. The way he saw it, the way Gayle sees it, the way Denis sees it, if he hadn't gone to Glasgow, and to Celtic, someone else would have gone and become the first black man to do this or the first black man to do that. So he went. He felt he had gone far wrong in Chicago, in Detroit, and so went off to Glasgow to turn it all around. He thought he could be new there and that he could turn it all around there.

He packed up his old kitbag with suits of many colours and shoes of that colour and this colour and wished his friends, and his foes, a fond farewell and set off in July 1951 from Detroit by train for Montreal. From there it was on to England aboard the *SS Columbia* with the 3rd class tourist ticket Celtic Football Club had sent him so he could see what he could be.

Travelling, too, were 61 British subjects and six aliens. Gillie was numbered among the aliens as he had, two years and two months before, given up his British passport and citizenship of the United Kingdom and Colonies and become a citizen of the United States and its colonies. He gave up the lion and the unicorn for the bald eagle and E Pluribus Unum.

None of the passengers was as glamorous as was our Gillie. There was among them a barber, a mechanic, a housewife, a secretary, a watchman and an American Express executive. Two of the aliens were from the US like him; one was from Canada; the remaining three were stateless Poles made homeless by the war on their way to new lives in north London.

He had with him the Brownie camera he took everywhere. He snapped this passenger and snapped that passenger and snapped the captain and the first mate and the tinker and the tailor and the candlestick maker. They thought him strange. He thought them stranger. It had to do with ways of seeing.

After six days and change at sea, the *SS Columbia*, with Captain Demetrios Sigalas at the helm, arrived without incident at Southampton on July 30, 1951. He steeled himself for the immigration officers. They liked people like him. They liked to pick at and probe people like him. It was the same all over the world. He remembered one time when he was returning to Detroit from Toronto in 1942, during the war, and how he had been picked at and probed. Then the immigration officers had looked the Jamaican over and decided he was 5 foot 9, around 140 pounds, dark of complexion, had black hair, had brown eyes, and had a scar on the back of his left hand. The only thing they got right was the scar on the back of his left hand. He was invisible to them. Anyone with eyes could see he was closer to 6 foot, weighed 170 pounds, was light of complexion, had brownish reddish hair and hazel green eyes.

They threw him a piece of paper and told him to fill it out. He wrote that he had been born in Kingston, Jamaica on April 9, 1922 and that he had left the island aged 17 for the United States on September 10, 1939, landing at Miami, in Florida. His residence, he said, was his mother's house at 67 Kenilworth Street, Detroit and said his employment was 'stock selector.' He hated immigration officers. They hated him; people like him.

In front of the English immigration officers at Southampton, Gillie looked forward to being picked at and probed. Maybe being picked at and probed was only a bother when you'd not become what you'd hoped to become and didn't want to be reminded of it by a petty official. It was his turn next in front of an immigration officer who had seen too many of Heron's kind come 'home' to the 'Mother Country' in the six years since the war ended. When asked what his calling was, the footballer said, proudly, 'footballer.' His once-ago wife, Bobbie, had told him once-ago that football was an entertainment but would never be, for him, really an occupation and that he should grow up and face life. Football, she said, was getting in their way. He agreed and asked her and Scotty to stand aside. Now, when he was asked whether he was accompanied by a wife or by a child, he could say without fear of contradiction: 'No, absolutely not.' When asked by the immigration officer what his last country of residence was, he said 'USA.' When asked if his future country of residence would be some country other than Great Britain he said 'yes.' The immigration officer, not understanding his part-Jamaican, part-American patois, misspelled the footballer's intended address in Glasgow. He wrote 'Kenichworth Hotel' when he should have written 'Kenilworth Hotel'. For Gillie there would, when he finally got there, be a kind of symmetry to it all. He'd begun his journey by saying goodbye to 67 Kenilworth Street, his mother's house in Detroit, and would soon say hello to the Kenilworth Hotel in Glasgow, which, at 12 shillings and six pence a day, provided lodging and a full Scottish breakfast of black pudding, haggis, and tattie scones for travelling salesmen and Celtic footballers, alike.

At last out of the clutches of the immigration officer, Gillie got on the train to London. There, with time to spare before his train to Glasgow, it seemed to the Jamaican that he was the only black man in Britain. But this was not true. There were others there, too; men like him of substance, and flesh and of bone, of fibre and liquids who might be said, too, to possess minds. They had served as he had served and they had come home to the Mother Country. Enoch Powell (British Parliamentarian) had encouraged them; the same Enoch who would later be filled with such foreboding. There was not yet a flood nor yet an influx nor had their coming in swamped the British character or caused the River Thames to foam with much blood. But then this was after the war and before the war.

But our Gillie was not in Great Britain to fight great wars – race or class ones. He was not there to enlist himself in anything but football. So he went on his way to Glasgow, London receding in the distance.

The Babe Ruth of Soccer

"The glory of children are their fathers."

Proverbs 17:6

Gillie Heron knew how to make history. He knew how to be in the right place at the right time and when, on occasion, he found himself in the wrong place he knew how to leave, quickly, as if he had never been there, at all.

He arrived on July 30, 1951 just in time to see Celtic get in one last kick-around before the team played Aberdeen in the final of the St. Mungo Cup on August 1 in front of 100,000 people at Hampden Park.

Sure it's a grand old team to play for,
Sure it's a grand old team bedad,
When you read its history,
It's enough to make your heart go sad.

Gillie Heron's heart was not sad. With tickets provided by Celtic, the Jamaican got to see up close how the game was played there and how he would fare if he got to play there. He saw Celtic fall behind in the first half to goals from Aberdeen's Henry Yorston and Tommy Bogan. He saw Celtic come from behind with two goals from Sean Fallon and a winner from Charlie Tully. A come from behind victory was just what he needed to see. He had come from behind himself and knew he would have to impress in a few days, on August 4, at the so-called 'public trial.' It was public but it was not really a trial. The public got the chance to see Celtic's first team play Celtic's second team. If a player on the second team played well enough, he got the chance to replace a first team player and become a first teamer, himself. A public trial was quite a sight: a first teamer trying to hold onto his job and a second teamer trying to take it from him.

Gillie had come to Glasgow to make history, to make something of himself. His mother had always implored him to do that, make something of himself. He'd made something of himself before this, five years before this, on June 7, 1946 when he became the first black person to play professional football in the United States. That was the first of his firsts.

The team on which he made his first 'first' was the Detroit Wolverines of the North American Professional Soccer League. This 'first black' thing, though, was more by accident than by design. After all, he'd never really thought of himself as 'black' when he'd been back home in Jamaica. There he'd been 'brown', a place of contentment in the Caribbean between 'black' and 'white.' It was only since he'd been in America – the seven years, eight months and 21 days he'd been in America to be precise – that he'd come, reluctantly, to see himself, as all others did, as 'black.' Still, being called "brilliant" and "beautiful", "great" and "glorious" by the American newspapers made up for them calling him 'black.' In 1946, a newspaper called him one of the game's "greatest players" and said his "scoring power and speed" had combined to make him "the biggest individual soccer attraction in the country." One magazine, even, called him the 'Babe Ruth of Soccer.'

The comparison was truer than the magazine realised. Both the Babe and the 'Black Flash' liked wine, liked women and liked song. Both, too, allowed their indulgences to interfere with and diminish their talents. Both hated their fathers: feckless men who were harsh taskmasters but who rarely followed the rules themselves.

The Babe's father deposited him in an orphanage when he was seven and hardly saw him again. The Black Flash's father, Walter Gilbert Heron, who loved drink and horses more than he loved his own flesh and blood, hardly saw him again after the boy turned 12 and decree nisi became decree absolute.

Both nursed their hurts expertly; hiding them beneath fake hale fellow well met personas. Both could be bright and cheery. Both could also be dark and brooding. Their families knew this of them. Their rivals knew this, too. Pitchers threw at the Babe's head and full-backs and centre halves aimed their studs at the Black Flash's groin. The Babe took it, mostly. But the Black Flash could not. He defended himself against centre-halves, full backs, against siblings, and against all slights, the only way he knew how; with fists and feet. He'd been raised not to take anything and so he did not take anything, which was, of course, a problem as he was a black man in a time when black men had to take a lot and not say anything.

He could have learned to take things, take things in his stride. But Walter had not been there to teach him how. He remembered that his old man had put on his training wheels but had not been there to take them off. He remembered that his old man had shown him how to bait the hook but had not been there when he caught the fish. Where is it that these men like his old man go? They go out for sugar and never return. They go out for ice cream – Gouz' Cherry Vanilla – and never return. Where is it that these men like his old man go? Do they go all at the same time? How do they go? Is there a signal that announces the time of the going or is their going individual and entirely special to each of them? When they have gone, these men, Walter Gilbert Heron and George Herman Ruth, do they meet in a secret place and discuss how it was that they went and why and whether they will return, someday?

There is no return from this, no putting it behind you. It's always in front of you. All you can do is use it, use it to do something useful with yourself like hit a ball or kick a ball as if it were your old man.

Life treads on life, and heart on heart,
We press too close in church and mart,
To keep a dream or grave apart.

Fathers, Fishman says, are not stones. But Gillie Heron's father was a stone, a naturally occurring solid aggregate of minerals and mineraloids. His outer layer, his lithosphere, was made entirely of rock. He was a rock in his composition, in his texture, and he was a rock by all the processes that formed him. He was igneous rock, made of molten magma; plutonic and volcanic. He was rock on the outside and rock on the inside. His archipelago was all rock, all ancient volcanoes that rose millions of years ago from the sea. Coming from rock, in time, Gillie, too, became rock.

He became so, he said, because his old man came to see him play but was not there at full-time. He became so, he said, because his old man had read him a bed-time story but had not been there to see how it had ended. Where is it that fathers go? His father – Walter Gilbert Heron – went out for sugar and never came back. All you can do is use it, use it to do something useful with yourself like kick a ball as if it were your old man.

He kicked a ball, kicked it like it was his old man and put all his troubles, all his moanings and groanings, behind him; for awhile at least. He put it all aside long enough to have a go at making a man of himself the way his father had never really managed to make a man of himself. Though he was, essentially, a self made man – a man indebted to himself for himself – Celtic promised him it, too, would make a man of him. So he decided to let Celtic at least try.

It was the job of the Celtic trainer Alex Dowdells to run him into foot-balling shape and make a man of him, a footballer of him. It would be the job of Celtic manager Jimmy McGrory, too, to make a man of him by explaining to him that because he was a black man, that in Glasgow, and in the rest of Scotland and the rest of Great Britain, too, he would not really be treated as a man. This done, it would be the job of Celtic chairman Bob Kelly to make this man a man people would pay money to see. But before people would pay money to see him play, he would need some brushing up. That was the view of manager McGrory. The boy is very promising, he said, but needs a little brushing up.

To succeed here, Gillie Heron would need to do what he was told. But Gillie Heron rarely did as he was told, even though he had been brought up by hand. Though he was beaten when he was born and caned at school and hit at home, he was not a disciplined child. Neither Kingston College nor St. George's College nor the Canadian Armed Forces had made him a disciplined child or a disciplined adult. But here at Celtic it would take discipline to make it. He knew when to stare discipline down and when to cower in front of it. He had, after all, been brought up by hand in the land where everyone is brought up by hand.

Gillie Heron wasn't a great reader but he had read his Marx and so knew that men make their own history, if not exactly as they please. He knew that men like him did not make their history under circumstances chosen entirely by themselves but under circumstances directly encountered, given, and transmitted from the past. His past – him and his ancestors too-ing and frow-ing across the Atlantic – had caught up to his present. Here, now, laid out in front of him was his future. He knew he ought to have been stuck on some assembly line somewhere across the Atlantic. He had come from a city – Detroit – where there was nothing for a footballer to a city – Glasgow – where there was everything for one.

We Almost Lost Detroit

"The past is always a rebuke to the present."

Robert Penn Warren

Detroit had been the first of his firsts. It was in Detroit that, before he came to Glasgow, he first made something of himself and made a little bit of history, too. It was back then, on June 7, 1946 while playing for the Detroit Wolverines, a team in the North American Professional Soccer League, that he became a 'first black' the way Jackie Robinson became a 'first black' and the way Lucius Twilight had been a 'first black.'

The league he played in was a kind of first, itself. Made up of four Midwestern teams and one from nearby Canada, the NAPSL was the brainchild of Fred Weiszmann, a Chicago waiter who wanted to become a sporting impresario. Weiszmann set up the league after the American Soccer League, the largest and oldest of the semi pro soccer leagues in the US, would not allow a team owned by Weiszmann, the Chicago Maroons, to join its league. The ASL said the Midwest was too far from the East Coast, where the other ASL teams played their games. The American Soccer League proposed instead that Weiszmann set up a division of the ASL in Chicago. Wesizmann accepted the offer but soon changed his mind and began his North American Professional Soccer League. He convinced four amateur teams from the US and one from Canada to go pro and join his new professional league: the Detroit Wolverines, Gillie Heron's team; the Pittsburgh Strassers; the

Chicago Vikings; the Toronto Greenbacks and the Chicago Maroons, which was owned by Fred Weiszmann and Reg Varney.

Fred Weiszmann's league was launched in June 1946 with Gillie Heron as the only black man in a world of white, hyphenated Americans: Italian-Americans, German-Americans, Polish and Czech-Americans. Heron was a hyphenated American, too; a Jamaican-American from Detroit. The hyphenated Americans took him as they found him. They could see past colour when it came to football. But home-grown whites just couldn't. Try as they might, they just could not abide a darkie and certainly did not want one rubbing shoulders and bruising shins with white boys.

Fred Weiszmann was no activist; but neither was he one to allow isms and schisms to interfere with profits. He told the home-grown whites that Gillie Heron wasn't a Down South or Up North Negro. He told them that Heron was, in fact, not one of their Negroes, at all. He was an overseas Negro, a Jamaican boy, a black boy born under the flipping and flapping of the Union Jack.

Black people, too, seemed not to know exactly what to make of Gillie Heron. In a feature article about the Jamaican that appeared in *Ebony* magazine in 1947, the words 'Negro' and 'black' were never used. The magazine described him, weakly, as "tannish." This was foolishness, of course, as only a few years before this, in 1943, the U.S. Immigration and Naturalization Service had described him as a 'Negro.' He was, an immigration officer scribbled on an entry form, a Negro with black hair, brown eyes and a dark complexion. On the matter of colour, *Ebony* was only willing to concede that the Jamaican would quickly become a fan favourite and that "a big turnout of negroes from Chicago's South Side" would be on hand when the footballer came to town to play.

Gilbert St. Elmo Heron was a hyphenated American. So were all the others who played with him in 1946 on the Detroit Wolverines.

They were like a pack of Bassett's Liquorice Allsorts. The manager John McInness, a Scot, was smitten with the Jamaican. The Jamaican was, he said, as good as any player he'd seen in Europe and maybe as good as any centre forward anywhere. "He's smart, just like a cat". McInness signed Heron in 1946 after the Jamaican had scored 44 goals in 1945 for the Detroit team Venetia and helped it win the Detroit District Soccer League championship.

The North American Professional Soccer League season was launched on June 7, 1946 with a game between the Chicago Vikings and Gillie Heron's Detroit Wolverines at Chicago's Comiskey Park. It was the first time football, the kicking kind, was played under electric lights in the United States. One paper described the game, which ended in a 4-4 draw, as the return of "Big Time Soccer" in America. At one time, soccer had been more popular than either baseball or American football in the U.S. In the 1920s, it was not unusual for 15,000 people to attend a soccer match in the Midwest or on the East Coast.

Gillie Heron settled down well to being a 'first' and being a football star in the USA. He scored twice for the Wolverines against the Vikings on his debut. Then he scored a spectacular winning goal against the Maroons a few weeks later. The newspapers were impressed. "The second goal was a solo effort by the fleeting Gil Heron who weaved his way through the entire Chicago eleven in a burst of speed to set up a shot the Maroon goalkeeper had no opportunity to prevent."

But though he was the star of the Detroit Wolverines, team owner Martin Donnelly was not a particular fan of Gillie Heron. Donnelly, the US born son of Scottish immigrants, wouldn't use the Jamaican to promote the Wolverines. The Chicago Maroons' Yugoslavia-born star, Pete Matevich, appeared in all his team's promotions and the Chicago Vikings' Scandinavian star, Roscoe Anderson, appeared in all the Vikings' promotions. But Heron, the Wolverine's star, did not appear in his teams'. His picture did not stare back at you from Detroit billboards or from Detroit newspapers. The Jamaican's Wolverines teammates – the two journeymen Mexican Jose Alegria and Scot George Hay – were instead the faces of the franchise. "SEE AMERICA'S FINEST TEAMS IN ACTION", a Wolverines' poster with Alegria's face on it said. "AMERICA'S FASTEST GROWING SPORT PLAYED AT ITS BEST", a Wolverines' newspaper ad with Hay's face on it said. The Wolverines' owner, Donnelly, was convinced a white, Scottish face, or a brown, Mexican face, would sell more tickets than would a Negro one. Donnelly believed putting Gillie Heron's black face on a Wolverines' poster would be bad for business and would convince whites who saw soccer as a sport controlled by foreigners, that the sport was not for them. But Fred Weiszmann was not bothered. He was convinced Americans would pay to see what he called "the world's fastest outdoor game" presented in the right way.

"It never has been presented to the public properly" Weiszmann told the Associated Press. "It has been played on sandlots and controlled mostly by foreign elements who don't realize that American fans want a proper setting and efficient presentation at their favourite events."

The North American Professional Soccer League debut season was a good one for Gillie Heron. He was the league's top goal scorer and his Wolverines won the league title. It was a bad one for league founder Fred Weiszmann. There had been lots of goals and lots of coverage in the press but attendance had not been good and wealthy sponsors had not materialised.

Ignoring the grim financial evidence, Weiszmann went ahead anyway with a second NAPSL season though several of the league's teams had declared bankruptcy. Before the new season began, Gillie Heron's Detroit Wolverines went bankrupt. Heron was sold to the Chicago Maroons.

This is how Gillie came to meet Bobbie and how a country girl in country-girl college clothes from the Hog and Hominy state and an island guy in yellow shoes from Jamaica, by way of the Motor City, came to meet in the Best in the Midwest, a real down city full of good folks from home. These were the now years and maybe years in Chicago, that great iron city, that impersonal, mechanical city, amid the steam, the smoke, the snowy winds, the blistering suns which caught whispers of the meanings that life could have.

A Revelation of Opposites

> "...the forces of two bodies on each other are always equal and are directed in opposite directions."
>
> ***Newton's Third Law***

Theirs was one of those brief encounters, like that film with Celia Johnson and Trevor Howard in that foggy rail station. He was in from Jamaica by way of Detroit, a fast train that frequently left the tracks. She was up from West Tennessee, a sensible, but fragile locomotive that chugged, chugged along. Both had been reared to steer clear of people like themselves. She was the wrong colour, or at least the wrong shade, for him, caramel kinda fella that he was. He was the wrong class for her. He had no college or pedigree to speak of. Neither he, nor his people, had gone to Fisk, to Tuskegee or to Meharry. His people weren't Alpha Phi Alpha or Delta Sigma Theta nor were they Alpha Kappa Alpha nor Kappa Alpha Psi. They weren't Divine Nine nor, really, divine, at all. Still, he was proud of Kingston College and of St. George's. "I had fairly good grades." He was proud, too, of Glenville, the high school in Cleveland he attended after arriving from Jamaica, before he and his family moved to Detroit. Then, they had been living with mean Aunt Minnie who had made it big in America and had become a black society maven in Cleveland. He ran track there at Glenville High School and earned a few dollars driving, loading and unloading The Gentles Flower Shoppe delivery truck. He was athletic not academic.

He got to the semi-finals of the Golden Gloves Middleweight boxing competition in Cleveland but was easily defeated when asked to conjugate a verb or asked if x is an integer, what is the solution set of $-1 \le x < 2$?

Bobbie, by contrast, had no such troubles or struggles. She was academic not athletic and could not comprehend that 'footballer' could, for example, be an occupation and not just an entertainment. She wasn't from the Antilles, not the Greater ones nor the Lesser ones, and did not know that Jamaica was grouped into three counties and divided into 14 parishes or that its capital had once been St Jago de la Vega. Still, and for all of that, they got along, got along real well and as if I need to spell it out, fell hard in love, there in Chicago, him in from the Motor City and her up from the Hog and Hominy state.

They met at a bowling alley over on the South Side where he liked to hold court; a place where the guys and girls from Western Electric liked to hang out after their day was done.

The footballer was as excellent at bowling a ball in those alleys as he was at everything else athletic. But Bobbie wasn't athletic and wasn't much of a bowler and had no idea what soccer was. He didn't know what an aria was and hadn't had a good read since his Pitman's Primer. She liked nothing so much as a good book and anything sung by Marian Anderson. He loved high-waisted, wide-legged pants, broad-brimmed hats and Louis Jordan, especially his 'Is You Is or Is You Ain't My Baby?' She was his baby and he was to her a credit to the race. He was a credit to the race, she felt, just for playing, as he did, among so many people who hated him and kicked him to show him so. He always got up, though; most times with a balled fist.

It had been Big Sister's fault the two met, at all. In 1942, or something like that, Gloria left the South for the South Side of a city which was a real down city, full of good folks that come from home. The week Gloria arrived in Sandburg's 'City of the Big Shoulders', 3,000 other sojourners with similar spiritual strivings arrived there, too, from all parts South. The newspapers noticed:

"HALF A MILLION DARKIES FROM DIXIE SWARM TO THE NORTH TO BETTER THEMSELVES."

That's why Big Sister, who was planning on becoming a teacher some day and some day travelling to Vega Baja and Bangkok and Bandung, came; to better herself.

During the war, girls like Gloria, who had studied awhile for a Master's at Michigan, and boys like Gillie could work just about wherever they wanted. A temporary halt had been called to discrimination in employment while the country was at war. For the first time – their colour, their creed, their race, their religion – was not an ongoing impediment. There was a war to be won, after all. Afterward, things could return to the same. And they did. When Johnny came marching home again, hurrah, hurrah, the darker races simply had to step aside. Things returned to normal, if you can call this kind of thing normal.

It had been Abbott's *Defender* that had made the Scotts leave the land of yellow-poplars and dogwoods and the place of trees with blood at the leaves and blood at the roots. The Scott home in South Jackson was a *Defender* home. Homes were either *Chicago Defender* homes with 'Black Metropolis' on the night table or they were New York *Amsterdam News* homes with 'Black Manhattan' on the night stand. The Scott home at 453 South Cumberland Street was a *Chicago Defender* home. '*Defender*! *Defender*!' shouted the man rolling the red wagon down Cumberland each Thursday. 'Get Your *Chicago Defender* here!' Thanks to the man with the red wagon, Gloria, Bobbie and Sam Ella would choose State Street over 125th Street and St Clair Drake over James Weldon Johnson. True, Harlem had had its Renaissance. But Chicago had something, too.

For my people lending their strength to the years, to the Gone years and the now years and the maybe years...

These were the now years and the maybe years in Chicago for a country girl in country-girl college clothes from the Hog and Hominy state and an island guy in yellow shoes from Jamaica, by way of the Motor City.

She was there to work and he was there, in the 'City of the Big Shoulders', to play; play football.

Chicago was a bigger city than was Detroit and his team there, the Maroons, was a bigger and a better team than was his old club, the Wolverines. Gillie didn't feel out of place in the city or on the team. The Maroons starting 11 was composed entirely of foreign born players, players paid better than all others in the North American Professional Soccer League. The year before Gillie got there the Maroons had paid their leading scorer, Pete Matevich, 100 dollars a game. Gillie, by contrast, had earned only 25 dollars a game playing for the Wolverines. Heron figured as he had been the league's top goal scorer in 1946 with 16 goals and Matevich had scored only eight, he would be in line for a big pay raise in Chicago. He was wrong. He made only five dollars more than the 25 dollars he had earned in Detroit. He wasn't happy about it. But he took what he got, consoling himself that at least he did not actually have to work for a living, but instead played for a living.

In Chicago, he settled down to life in the 'Black Belt' on the city's South Side. He had lived in nothing but ghettoes since coming to America from Jamaica, so one more ghetto wouldn't make much difference. He had lived in a ghetto in Cleveland with fancy pants Aunt Minnie and her so siddity husband Uncle Ben and he had lived in a ghetto in Detroit, at Oakland Avenue and at Kenilworth, too. This was his very own ghetto, his very own Bantustan.

Gillie got himself a kitchenette, a one-room with bedbugs, with a funky washbasin, and with a grimy hot plate. For this he paid six dollars a week. It didn't have a bathroom or a toilet. That was down the hall. Here, near State Street in Chicago, was where our Gillie called home sweet home. He wasn't the only one in a kitchenette. Richard Wright had lived in one, too. This simple kitchenette could, Richard said, distort an "individual personality, making many of us give up the struggle, walk off and leave wives, husbands, and even children behind to shift as best they can."

By night, he was a resident of the Black Belt. By day, he was a footballer free to mix and mingle on the field of play with the palefaces as he pleased. Football was his freedom, was his diplomatic immunity. It took him places; allowed him to go places he would not have been allowed to, without a ball. As long as he had a ball, he was allowed to venture far from the South Side to the white world of Winnemac Park, where his team, the Maroons, played. There he played alongside the Wolanins and the D'Orios, the Poles and the Italians.

He hadn't met and married Bobbie yet when the Maroons played their first game of the North American Professional Soccer League's second season on April 6, 1947.

Pitted against the Pittsburgh Indians at Bridgeville Field in the Steel City, Gillie earned his team a draw with a clever kick from the corner flag. A week later, he was among the scoring again when the Maroons drubbed the St Louis Raiders 4-0. A few weeks later *Ebony* featured him in its pages: "*ROOKIE GIL HERON AMAZES PROS IN FIRST YEAR*".

The *Ebony* feature spread Gillie's name and fame far and wide. Up till then he had been mostly a marvel of the Midwest. Now his name was sprinkled here and there across the country in the black press. He was mentioned in Sam Lacy's 'A to Z' column in the Baltimore *Afro American*. He was mentioned in the Los Angeles Sentinel and he was also mentioned in the New York *Amsterdam News*.

"Soccer Babe Ruth Is Jamaica Negro" the *Amsterdam News* said. "The Old World game boasts its greatest star in a New-World Negro." Gillie was a black star and black people wondered whether whites would treat him fair. "The Negro rookie wonder will not get much more from the Windy City booters." They were right, of course. He did not get much more from the Windy City booters, the Chicago Maroons. After all, he wasn't white. He wasn't Pete Matevich. No matter how many goals he scored, Gillie was not going to get Matevich money, 100 dollars a game, white man's money.

It didn't matter though, as in September 1947, a month before the end of Gillie's second season with the Maroons, the club announced it could not pay their black nor their white players and so would cease operations and file for bankruptcy. A month later, the North American Professional Soccer League, which had only been around a year and six months, shut down, too. Most of those who had played in the league gave up the game for good and returned to the factories and the mills from whence they had come. Others, the best of the bunch, found places on semi pro teams on the East Coast and in the Midwest. Gillie Heron found work with Sparta ABA, a Czech team in the National Soccer League of Chicago that was at one time the most successful semi pro team in the United States. SPARTAS SIGN GIL HERON FOR SLOVAKS GAME, the *Chicago Tribune* reported. Hearing their team had a new addition to the forward line, a larger than usual number of fans turned out to see the Jamaican play on Septmember 28, 1947. But Gillie Heron had misjudged the time and was far from Sparta Stadium when the whistle blew. He arrived before the end of the match and was allowed to play the final few minutes.

"Gil Heron, the widely heralded importation from Jamaica became involved in transportation difficulties and arrived late" the *Tribune* said. The game ended 0-0, a point for each team instead of the two points Sparta had expected. The fans blamed the scoreless tie on Gillie Heron's tardiness. The *Tribune* however, was even-handed and said though the Jamaican had come late he had proved his worth when he got his chance. "His presence made a remarkable difference, and with Heron playing from the start Sparta probably would have won as they pleased."

In Gillie's defence, he was new to the part of Chicago where Sparta's stadium was located. He lived in the Black Belt, near State Street on the South Side of Chicago. Sparta was in Cicero on the outskirts of Chicago, in the White Belt; a No Man's Land for a caramel kinda fella like Heron. Lost in space, he drove from one hostile suburb to the next in search of Sparta Stadium.

Gillie Heron wasn't late for Sparta's next game against Schwaben at Skokie High School stadium. Skokie was another of those Greater Chicago suburbs so scary Stagger Lee himself would not have gone out there. Heron did, and he made it on time this time. He scored 4 times in a 5-2 whipping of Schwaben, Sparta's chief rival for the title. This is what Sparta believed it was getting when it broke its colour bar to bring Gillie Heron to the club.

Celebrated on the white side of Chicago, Gillie Heron was celebrated on the black side, too. The *Chicago Defender*, a black newspaper, made sure black folk knew who he was. The paper pointed out that he was "the only member of his race" to be included in a Chicago All-Star football team and that he had played football at the very highest levels in the United States. He was "a veritable sharp shooter" and a "menace to every defense". The paper said he had played centre-forward during the war on an otherwise all white Detroit All-Star team that defeated a Royal Canadian Air Force team. The paper said his success in the white world of football was down to his "go-get em spirit" and that Heron was "one of the best all around athletes in sport today" and should "be given a tremendous amount of credit for helping soccer." Heron's exalted condition came, the *Chicago Defender* newspaper said, with its burdens. "Being the only Negro in soccer in Chicago all eyes are on him, he is a work-horse and a marked man."

It's true, he was a marked man; marked by lesser men whose one job was to kick him, block him, stop him. Kicked and pushed and abused in a game against Hansa, a German-American team known for its brutish half backs, Heron struck back against the team's centre-half, who had kicked the Jamaican up and down the field for much of the game as if he were the ball. Heron struck and was sent off for brawling and suspended.

Gillie Heron was a proud and hot headed man who never, never let things go on the field or off it. Being a 'first' was a burden for him. He was no Jack Roosevelt Robinson who could take a licking and keep on ticking. He hit back. The theory of nonviolence as a strategy for social change hadn't yet caught on with Gillie Heron back in 1947. Gillie always had blood in his eye. Everyone from where he was from had blood in their eyes. He was used to having his name taken by the referee and being sent for an early bath. He was sent off in schoolboy matches at St. George's and sent off in army matches at Camp Borden. He was sent off in Detroit when he was with the Wolverines and sent off in Chicago when he was with the Maroons. He had been sent off in peacetime and in wartime and sent off in Jamaica and in Canada and in the United States and in Scotland. He'd been sent off all over the world.

Gillie Heron's season with Sparta – really a couple of weeks – had not gone as he would have liked. But not everything in the footballer's life was a disappointment. There was, of course, Bobbie Scott.

His and Bobbie's relationship was a strange one. Gillie did not believe in introspection and leaving things unsaid. Bobbie was a watcher, a contemplator, a meditator, a student of what was right and what was wrong. This is how it is when you have been raised pious in the Christian Methodist Episcopal ethic. You'd have never known 'Free Will' was among her tenets. She did nothing without thorough examination and complete contemplation. They were an unlikely pair. Still, though she didn't see the sense in it she came to game after football game, sitting in the stands with her sister Sam Ella.

One thing led to another thing and that thing led to a baby on the way and a quick ceremony on August 20, 1948 in front of the Reverend J.P. Palmer on Washington Street with one or two friends and Gloria and Aunt Annabelle McKissack to witness it. Though her Lane College siblings still did not accept that 'footballer' was an occupation and her mother did not know what a 'Jamaican' was, they gave her their 'okay.' So, he, aged 26, said "I do" and she, aged 22, said "I do", too. In sickness and in health, for better, for worse, for richer, for poorer, to love and to cherish. They would try, they said, to be together till death do them part. But theirs was a very brief encounter. She tried to make it work. He tried to make it work. Lucille, 'Mother Heron', prayed it would fail.

Lucille knew how to stitch a sackcloth of sorrow and cover it in ashes. She had come herself from an awful patchwork, an uneven piecework of history and so she like a lot of people from her land was a badly put together thing with jangly bits that poked you if you got close. Let's not make excuses for her; she knew what she was. "Then Jacob rent his garments, and put sackcloth upon his loins, and mourned for his son many days."

Though her son Gilbert had not been thrown into a pit as Joseph had by his brothers or taken as Joseph was into captivity by the Midianites or sold into slavery by the Ishmeelites, Lucille mourned him all the same now her caramel-coloured boy was married, married to a darker skinned girl from the Hog and Hominy state. He'd married into colour rather than out of it as any Jamaican with sense knows one must do.

When they, Gillie and Bobbie, married on August 20, 1948, they were so filled with joy it did not matter then who was there and who was not and who sent gold and who sent incense and who sent myrrh and who sent not. It did not matter then who neglected to send anything at all. Back then, when things were not just good but splendid, she had decided to cleave to him and he had decided to cleave to her, too. But it was difficult from start to finish. A surviving picture from this time shows the young couple, the footballer and the aspiring librarian, to be okay with one another if not exactly thrilled by one another. He is all style, as usual. He is wearing a white Panama hat, a light-coloured two piece with his shirt collar flopped over his jacket collar. He has a cigarette squeezed between the first and second fingers of his right hand. She's dressed as if taking a break from some desk job. In sharp contrast to his light suit, her suit is dark, grave, all business. The photographer could not coax a smile. The look on her face seems to say 'footballer' is not an occupation. It is only an entertainment.

Still, she liked that three weeks after they were wed the *Chicago Defender*, the newspaper she had grown up on in Jackson, featured her fine new husband in its pages. All her kith and kin in Jackson and in Russellville were ordered to buy a copy of the paper which shows her husband handsome in the dark shirt and white shorts of Sparta ABA. Bobbie was pleased; as were her kith and kin. These were the now years and the maybe years for a guy in yellow shoes from the Motor City via Jamaica and a country girl in country-girl college clothes from the Hog and Hominy state.

They shared the shivers of passion and eight months after their August 1948 wedding Scotty – Gilbert Scott Heron – was born in the

Windy City on April 1, 1949. It was an eventful time. I'd like to tell you that Baby Boy was a bonny baby boy. But he wasn't. He had bad bones and all sorts of ailments. This is just what he got from the Scotts. What he inherited from the Herons, who could say. Theirs was too brief an encounter for that.

The Herons caught their first glimpse of Scotty when he was two months old. Already by then his developmental and behavioural outcome was being determined by those who cared, or cared not, for him. Stimuli such as stressful experiences that could result in neurochemical changes that could lead to structural changes in the brain were kept to a minimum. There were all sorts of things that had to be navigated and negotiated like attachment and separation, autonomy and mastery and recognition memory and habituation of attention. The Herons – 20 year old Cecil Heron and 21 year old Poley Heron – caught sight of Scotty because they had come to the Windy City from the Motor City to play football. Cecil and Poley, decent amateur footballers, were there to play for the Detroit Corinthians in an exhibition match against Gillie's Sparta ABA.

"The loyalty of the Heron family was divided yesterday in a soccer manner of speaking as three brothers were in the line-up of Spartas and Detroit Corinthians in Sparta Stadium", the *Chicago Tribune* reported. Gillie scored 3 goals in a 5-1 win for Sparta. It wasn't all bad for Cecil and Poley. The newspapers said they had "heart" and had acquitted themselves well. "Brothers Cecil, who provided Detroit's only goal, and Leopold turned in excellent performances for the visitors who couldn't halt the fleet Gil."

They were fleet, too. When Cecil and Poley got back to the Motor City they were quick to report. How, the Herons demanded to know, did the baby look? What was his hue and what is his complexion?

Does his hair sit straight upon his head or does it look as though it will disappoint us and kink up and need a hat to hide it? Who does he favour? I hear he favours the girl and has her mouth and nose but, thank God, I understand he has our boy's tone and general shading.

Gillie could have told his mother this himself. He would, after all, be back in the Motor City sooner than Bobbie or the Baby Boy could have realised. His dream had become deferred. It had dried up like a raisin in the sun and festered like a sore and then run. It began to stink like rotten meat and crust and sugar over like a syrupy sweet. And then, it exploded.

He'd had a poor year in 1948 for Sparta ABA and was having a poor year in 1949 for Sparta ABA. Sparta fans complained the black boy was not what they thought he would be. They thought he'd score more goals and help win more matches. It's not easy being a first. So much is expected of you. He failed, too, to be invited to participate in the US Olympic soccer team trials, which were held that year, that 1948, right there in Chicago at Sparta ABA's stadium. It was clear his time as a top flight footballer in Chicago was coming to a close. He didn't know it then but his last game for Sparta was against the Sterlings, a team from Canada on November 6, 1949. Sparta won 4-3. He scored the winner in the last minute. Sparta had not won what it had hoped to when it asked the Jamaican by way of Detroit to come play for it. So, it told him it had fallen out of love with him and fallen in love with a new striker, Karel Tomanek, a Czech centre forward.

He, too, had fallen out of love; with Bobbie and Scotty. He told her he was leaving because she said 'either' and he said 'either' and because she said 'neither' and he said 'neither.' He told her she said 'potahto' and he said 'potato' and so they should call the whole thing off. It was clear these two would never be one and that something had to be done. So, they called the whole thing off.

So that was that. Just as he had come to Chicago, Little Jimmy Rushing egging him on, now he was going back to Detroit, and he would be all alone.

It's not as hard as you might think, turning your back on kith and kin, leaving them in the distance in the rear view mirror. Herons have been flying away, wading away from and leaving loved ones behind in the country with grandmothers or in town with a friend for years. Charles Gilbert Heron abandoned his son, Walter Gilbert Heron, and went off to Panama. Walter Gilbert Heron, in turn, abandoned his son, Gilbert St. Elmo Heron, and retreated to Manchester. Gilbert St. Elmo Heron, naturally enough, abandoned Scotty and went back to Detroit, and in time on to Glasgow and to Celtic.

In 1950, Detroit wasn't a home sweet home; but it was a home. In 1950, before Celtic came along, Gilbert St. Elmo Heron was no longer a professional footballer able to earn his keep entirely from what he did on the field. He was not even a semi-professional, able to earn part of his keep from what he did on the field and part from gainful employment. He was just an amateur playing for the sheer love of the game, or something like that. In Detroit, where the Herons had come when they flew away from Jamaica, he went back to his old life, to his old job at the car factory and he went back to his old team, the Detroit Corinthians. Four of five of the Heron brothers – Gillie, Poley, Cecil and Gerald – played for the Corinthians. The Herons were the only four brothers playing in 1950 on a single team in organised football in the US. It was another Heron first.

Gillie's life, then, was football and the factory, the factory and football. He had packed up his old kit bag and returned home to Detroit like one of the dregs from a Wilfred Owen poem. He did not return to the beating of great bells nor to drums and yells. He crept back, silent, to the still village well. He earned his everyday living painting cars at the Hudson Motor Car Company for 50 dollars a week, which wasn't a bad wage back then. A Hudson was a good car. Kerouac and Steinbeck thought so, anyway. While he painted Hudsons and kicked a football around with amateurs, our Gillie fashioned for himself another living, too: taking pictures of the newlywed and the nearly dead.

Gilbert St. Elmo Heron
Photographer
Weddings, Christenings, Funerals

It was the best he could do now he was back, broke and beat, from the Windy City, a place he had gone to make it big. He squeezed himself in at 67 Kenilworth Street, the 4-floor house Mother Heron turned into a place for roomers and renters, and family. Being here brought Gillie's self and his consciousness into conflict. This was home but this was not a home sweet home. He'd had a home with Bobbie and Baby Boy in Chicago. But like Laura and Alec, it had been an all too brief encounter.

Up on top of this not so home sweet home, the Herons – Elsie; Poley; Gerald; Cecil and Gillie – squeezed in. The eldest, Roy, had flown the coop to Canada and become a citizen in the Great White North. Later, much later, Elsie's Richard, Margaret, Denis, Gayle and Kenny would all squeeze in, too, here in the family manse in Motown.

Down below, on floor two and floor one of Lucille's rooming house, were those who'd paid to stay, the tenants. There was the night worker, the day worker, the woman with a gaggle of kids who, like Mother Heron, once had a husband who'd stepped out for sugar and not returned.

It was a tight fit at Kenilworth. I guess, in retrospect, it was a good thing Gillie had gotten rid of the wife and the kid he'd picked up along the way. But it wasn't long before he was wondering why he'd come back to this place and to these people. They were a complicated lot, these Herons. They could not live without each other but could not live with each other. Detroit had been the second stop in America for the Herons after leaving Jamaica. Their first stop had been Cleveland where they had lived and worked for mean Aunt Minnie, who owned a famous flower shoppe and ghetto tenements and made life miserable for her sister, who helped around the shop, her niece, who was a flower girl and her nephews, who drove the flower shoppe trucks. Wilted, they left Cleveland for Detroit. They went to Detroit not just because Aunt Minnie was mean to them and the two Gentles sisters had fallen out, but because Detroit is where automobiles were made and where black people back then, and brown people too, who wanted a chance at a good paying job at Ford, at Chrysler, at Hudson, went.

In Detroit, at Oakland Avenue, Lucille opened, as Minnie had in Cleveland, a flower shoppe. A fine floral arrangement is more important than you might think in the ghetto. But her sons weren't interested in flowers. Gillie was, of course, keen on football and Roy – they called him Ishmael – was interested in whales, great white ones. So in 1941, Roy got a job on a British whaler, the *HMS Lancing*, and set off, with the men that go down to the sea, to catch himself a Great White. And he did catch himself a whale; several of them in fact. He returned from six months in the Antarctic with whale eyes, whale ears and whale teeth, one of which he carved a foot long knife out of.

Gillie liked adventure, too. So around that time, with the world at war, he, like Roy, set off on an adventure. On March 3, 1943 he walked across the US-Canada border from Detroit to Windsor to the #1 District Depot and signed up for service in the Royal Canadian Armed

Services. He didn't get to fight; at least not the Nazis. The Canadians had heard of his sporting exploits and so asked 20-year old Trooper A-117586 Gilbert St. Elmo Heron to go, instead, from army camp to army camp in Canada and teach the troops how to play football, softball, baseball and how to box. Trooper Heron was a hit and the newspapers took notice of him. "Are your parties dull? Invite R. Gilbert Heron" said the *Winnipeg Free Press*. He had hoped for more. So he joined the Canadian Air Force. But it didn't have anything for him to do besides washing down and fuelling planes.

In time, the world no longer at war, he came back to the world, and to Detroit, and to his little job on the assembly line at Hudson. In the evenings he played a little for an amateur outfit called Venetia.

"Gilbert Heron, alert Venetian centre forward, is being acclaimed today for the outstanding individual scoring feat in many years of city soccer competition" the *Detroit Times* said of the Jamaican. The newspaper called him a "fast stepping West Indian" who had "by his lone efforts" scored all 5 of the goals in his team's 5-1 defeat of their opponents, Thistle. In his first season back he scored 44 goals in 14 games and helped Venetia win the Detroit city championship. In another city, this might have led to something. But Detroit didn't have a very strong footballing tradition. The teams in the Detroit District Soccer League – the All Scots, the Swedish-Americans, German United – were not very good. Detroit was where a footballer went to die. There was nothing there for a footballer. Detroit was a place the great foreign teams that toured the United States each summer flew over and flew past. Gillie Heron wasn't in Chicago anymore. He was stuck in Detroit, and it looked as though he would be stuck there forever on an assembly line in a big city that was a very small town when it came to football.

The Makings of You

"Human frailty; it makes me sick sometimes."

Christopher Moltisanti

No sooner had the husband and father said bye bye to Bobbie and their baby boy in 1950, and headed back to Detroit, than did Bobbie say bye bye to Baby Boy, too. The husband and father had packed his bags and gone, so the wife and mother packed, too. She wasn't leaving. Baby Boy was. It was the Great Migration in reverse. He was going South, to South Jackson, Tennessee to Lillie and to a house that was not filled with hatred but had recently been filled with pain.

Nothing ever happened on South Cumberland Street in Jackson, Tennessee. Sometimes stuff happened on North Cumberland Street. But nothing ever happened on South Cumberland Street. So Baby Boy's coming caused a stir. People had seen people leave the Scott place, but had never really seen people come there. Gloria, who was little and light like Lillie, had been the first to leave, in 1942. Bobbie, the sullen and very serious one, was second, in 1946. Sam Ella was next, in 1948. William left in 1951 for Paris and the Air Force but ended up, eventually, at Hampden Place in the Bronx. Robert 'Bob' Scott left, too. He didn't go far; just the 27.6 miles south-west of Jackson to Bolivar and the asylum there.

Bob Scott wasn't crazy. He was crazy with syphilis which, because it lay untreated inside him, ate away at his eyes and ate away at his bones and ate away at his brain. Syphilitic Meningo Encephalitis made him lose his sight and general paresis made him lose his mind.

He'd been in his right mind when he'd become a barber in 1910 and had been in his right mind when he had got himself a wife in 1919. He was in his right mind, too, when in 1929 he decided to take a risk and put his all and all into the National Benefit Life Insurance Company. Bob managed the Jackson branch of the Benefit but after awhile neither he, nor the big bosses of the Benefit in Washington D.C., could manage. Wall Street crashed and the National Benefit Life Insurance Company crashed, too, and took a lot of good folks' cash with it. Wall Street recovered, eventually. Bob Scott never did. He ended up a custodian swabbing floors and cleaning toilets at Merry High School in Jackson.

They weren't very merry – Gloria and Bobbie and Sammie, star students one and all – to have their old man sweeping and swabbing as they went on their way to science, sociology and scripture. The Scotts had come up from slavery but had slid down again. They had nothing. Then they had something and then they had nothing again. Then Bob brought home syphilis.

Tuskegee 626
Somebody done got slick
When deadly germs are taking turns
Seeing what makes us tick

People guessed but didn't know the diagnosis and Lillie, being a confidential kinda person, didn't let on. She told South Jackson that diabetes was the criminal that had robbed her husband of his mobility and stolen his sight and misappropriated his mind. The deadly disease made him a raging bull in its late stage. Lillie couldn't cope. So the men in white came to 453 South Cumberland on May 29, 1948, days before Sam Ella graduated from Lane, and while William was in freshman year there, to take Bob to the Western State Mental Hospital in Bolivar. He was housed there, in the 'Coloured Only' ward, for 79 days before succumbing to syphilis. The funeral was held in Jackson at the Mother Liberty C.M.E. church on Chester Street and he was buried in Elmwood, Jackson's coloured cemetery.

Bob's deadly disease did what it pleased and so the results were not hard to predict. Bobbie Scott was as happy and as sad as she had ever been. Married on August 20 in Chicago, on August 22 she buried her father in Jackson.

"Robert Scott died at Western State Hospital Aug 18, survived by his wife Mrs. Lillie Scott, father of Misses Gloria, Bobbie, Sammie Scott, all of Chicago, and Mr. Wm. Scott of this city."

The world was not his home. He was just passing through. His treasures were laid up somewhere beyond the blue. The angels beckoned him from heaven's open door and he could not, eaten up by his deadly disease, feel at home in this world anymore.

The Misses were happy to be done with it; the funeral, not the man. They loved him, adored him, but he always cast a shadow over them. His death, of the deadly disease, is a clue as to why they were as they were, the Scotts; why they were so siddity; why they were so utterly against the wrong and so utterly for the right. It was no consolation to the Misses Gloria, Bobbie and Sam Ella Scott, and to Master William Scott, all of whom adored only the highest of the arts, that Shakespeare and Voltaire had written of the deadly disease or that Schubert and Schumann actually had the deadly disease. It was no consolation that the Italians thought of it as the 'French disease' or that the French called it the 'Italian disease' or that the Turks called it the 'Christian disease.' The Scotts thought of it, and had been taught to think of it, as the disease of the darker races, those who lived their lives beneath the veil.

The Scotts had always been a god-fearing, Old Testament-reading kind of people. Their favourite bits of the Bible were the bits with prescripts, prohibitions and proclamations. They liked the bits rich with rules and regulations. They liked dictates and dictums. They liked summons and subpoenas. Most of all they liked commandments. You know, you shall not this and you shall not that. They liked that there was no room for moral equivocation. They liked the bits of the Bible where those who feared God, and kept his commandments, got great blessings and those who failed him got great punishments and great pestilences fell upon them.

"The Lord will smite thee with the botch of Egypt, and with the emerods, and with the scab, and with the itch, whereof thou canst be healed. The Lord will smite thee with madness, and blindness and astonishment of the heart."

They disliked forgiveness until they needed forgiveness, the Scotts. They disliked charity until they needed charity. They disliked mercy. They needed mercy because Bob Scott was a good man in a very bad way and they – Lillie, the Misses, and the Master – were in a bad way, too. They waited to see if they would get it. They didn't. What they got instead, the Misses, was lots of fear and loathing, self loathing. They had come up from slavery and now because of this deadly disease their days were anxious days and their nights sleepless. They frowned on those who said bricks could be made without straw and scorned those who lay in their beds before they were made. They shunned fun and frivolity. They didn't marry. If they married, they didn't stay married. Their children were only children; brotherless, sisterless, fatherless, motherless. They were self-made people, people who did not like how they had been made so made themselves over. They were New Negroes. They were ex-coloured people.

They were competent and capable people. But they were not, as claimed, a family that contradicted the concepts. They were competent and capable. But they were not, as claimed, a family that heard the rules but wouldn't accept. They did accept, all too easily and this is why though they should have resisted, the Misses left as soon as they could leave. This is why even though Lillie needed someone to lean on when she was not strong, someone to help her carry the load, she had to depend upon someone – not family – who was right up the road. The Misses only came back when they absolutely had to; for funerals mostly or, in Bobbie's case, on the occasional visit to Scotty. Who knows if she gave him up willingly or if she gave in to greater might, to a mother, to a grandmother, who claimed she knew what was right.

What we do know is Bobbie, like Stanley Ann, had a man's name and was, in this, very like a man. She, like Stanley Ann, visited only when she had to. She, like Stanley Ann, did only what she had to. We know already that there was no paternal bond between Barack and Barack Snr. or between Gilbert and Gilbert Snr. But what about the maternal bond? The maternal bond between a human female and her biological child usually begins during pregnancy with her adapting her lifestyle to suit the needs of the developing infant, Winkler says. Later, through touch, response and mutual gazing, a bond, the maternal bond, develops. But if there is no touch, response, and mutual gazing, a bond does not develop.

People had seen people leave the Scott place. But people had never really seen people come there, to the Scott place, to stay. There had been a lot of going but very little coming at that solid, single storey house at 453 South Cumberland Street till Baby Boy got there in December 1950.

He was there because Bobbie, who was well on her way to becoming a librarian and singing alto in a big Chicago choir, wanted to be what she wanted to be. She was setting up, she said, for single parenthood. She needed, she said, to organise and re-organise. She had, she said, to get this together and she had to get that together and, most importantly, she had to get herself together. She needed time; a lifetime in fact – 10 years – to adapt, to be exact, to the rigours and demands of parenthood. She had been a quick learner in all things but this. Her transcript shows she was good at sociology and psychology and all the other ologies and good at geometry and trigonometry and all the other ometries, too. At parenting, though, she was barely passing. Bobbie can and should, her report cards say, do better.

But this is not fair, this damning of women. After all, women existed not for themselves but for men. Sometimes they were named after the men to whom they were related. Always they were named after the men to whom they were married. Never did they live their lives according to the fashion of their own souls.

With the man who named her dead, and the man who married her disappeared, Bobbie determined to live her life, with little concern for the remaining man in her life, according to the fashion of her own soul.

They arrived – Lillie and Scotty – on the overnight train from Illinois. Before he can grab a good night's sleep, he is unveiled on the porch in his Windy City diapers. In time, he stops crying for the Big Onion. Tears, he realises, will not win him a reprieve and a quick return home.

For better or for worse, his mother now, and his father too, is this little light-skinned lady named Lillie. He was not alone. Jackson was full of babies with no ma or pa; babies whose ma and pa had gone North, leaving the Big Mommas and Big Daddies to do the rearing and the raising.

By the time he got there, when he was nearing his second birthday, he would already have experienced the emergence of sociality, you know, social smiling, mutual gaze, that sort of thing. He would have already experienced transition sociality and he would have, in the second half of his first year, already experienced stranger anxiety and been both amused and made anxious by the performance of the Peek-A-Boo. He struggled with object permanence. It was hard for him to accept that an object existed when he could no longer see it, hear it, or touch it. That's the way it was with his folks. He looked up and they were gone. He should have said something. But what would have been the use of words anyway? No one would have listened to what he, a perfect idiot and one great blooming, buzzing confusion, had to say about all the comings and the goings. No one had asked him, for example, if they could leave Chicago and go back to Detroit and then on, later, to Glasgow without him. No one had asked him, for example, if because they were newly single they could, or should, stay on in the Windy City without him and then go onto Santurce, where Schomburg had come from, and then go up to Barranquitas, where Cacique and Munoz Marin had come from, without him. No one asked him if he, for example, wanted to leave the North for the South; if he wanted to leave his Windy City kitchenette for a Hog and Hominy house with porch and back hall 600 miles away. No one asked him anything. If someone had asked him he might have said that it was wrong of them both to go off into the world on their individual own without him. That's what he would have said. It was as if because they had ceased cleaving to one another that they had decided not to cleave to him anymore, either. It was as if they – Gillie and Bobbie – were the thought and he only the after-thought. He would have told them, had he been able to find the words, that he would have preferred they both stayed around and played around with him, awhile. He would have said all sorts of wonderful things, if only he could have found the words. But who listens to a 20-month old April's Fool, anyway?

Hush now, don't explain.
You're my joy and pain.
My life's yours love,
Don't explain.

Later, when he was older and afraid she could leave even then, he told her don't explain. He told her just say that she would remain. He told her hush now, what's there to gain, don't explain. She was, he told her, his joy and pain and he didn't need for her to explain. Later still, when he was able to find the words, he wouldn't use them, for this at least. He used them, instead, to tell us the revolution would not be televised and tell us why there ain't no such thing as a superman and tell us why we ought to be willing. But he wasn't willing, really, to sing a song that was truly a song of himself. He insisted that your daddy loves you, your daddy loves his girl and implored us to do something, yeah, to save the children. He asked us to join him in a toast to all black fathers who lived their lives in vain and join him in a toast to all black mothers who shouldered this life in pain. His Black father did not live his life in vain, not really. His black mother did live much of her life in pain; peripheral, autonomic, proximal pain.

Scotty lived a lot of his life in pain, too. He gets meningitis, a bad case. He gets tuberculosis. He has scoliosis; a life-long tribulation. He has bad eyes: congenital cataracts. But he has good brains, very good brains; the sort of brains that make him good with words. In this he is like his Scott kith and kin. They are good with words, too. They have an ear for music. He has an ear for music, too. The Herons did not have an eye or an ear. The Herons are not artistic nor are they academic. They are athletic; almost supermen in fact. They have boxing. They have tennis. They have football. He is a Scott. But he is a Heron, too.

The Scotts don't talk about the Herons and, presumably, the Herons, wherever they are, don't talk about the Scotts. When they do talk about Gilbert St. Elmo Heron, the Scotts don't say much. The boy is told he looks like his old man. But he does not remember ever meeting his old man. There are pictures of them – him and him. But he does not remember anything of his old man: what he smells like; what he looks like; how he walks; how he talks. Lillie says he looks like his old man, says he has his lips and swivels his hips like his old man. He knows his old man is a Jamaican. But he is not sure what a Jamaican is. He knows his old man plays soccer. But is not sure what soccer is. He knows his old man was, for a time, away in Scotland. But he is not sure where Scotland is. He's told his old man is a football legend. But that is not true. He is told he was part of a championship team. But that is not true, either. He is happy that when the women gather – his grandma, his ma, his aunts – that they do not, when they do talk about his old man, crucify him, the absent black man, though he bashed, bludgeoned and finally broke Bobbie's heart. He's only a baby boy but he hopes if some day he ends up like his old man, that people won't crucify him, either.

Hope in the Belly

"You gotta get yours, but fool I gotta get mine."

Snoop Dogg

On August 4, 1951, Gillie Heron played in Celtic Football Club's 'public trial', which was not really a public trial, at all. The public trial was a game played a week before the beginning of the Scottish 'A' Division football season. The game was a chance for those assigned to the reserve team or those promised a contract if they impressed, like our Gillie, to impress. In the 1951 public trial game the 'Green and Whites' team, which featured Gillie, played the 'Green' team.

Thousands turned out for the game. They were thrilled at what they saw from the Jamaican. He scored a "wonder" goal, one of the best goals ever scored at Celtic Park. "Every Celtic player congratulated the Jamaican, clapped him on the back and ruffled his hair and Giles just smiled shyly", a newspaper said. Gillie got a second goal, too, from a penalty. Bobby Collins, a Celtic regular, stepped forward to take it. But he was waved aside by Celtic star Charlie Tully. Tully wanted to give Gillie a chance to shine and win himself a place on the first team. "At first Giles wouldn't think of it, but after a little persuasion, he did – and scored." Gillie's two goals, and all-around performance, looked to have won him a one year contract. "It is almost certain that Celtic will sign Heron, who was an instant hit with the Parkhead faithful." He was a hit, too, with Celtic chairman Bob Kelly and with Celtic manager Jimmy McGrory, who said the Jamaican boy by way of Detroit had something very "special."

For his part, Gillie was impressed with Celtic Football Club and with Celtic's fans. He told the *Daily Express* newspaper, "Nowhere else in the world—no matter what sport you follow—will you find anything to compare with the enthusiasm of these Celtic fans." He was, he said, "overwhelmed." The *Express* reporter asked the "coloured centre forward from Detroit" what he thought of Glasgow and of Glaswegians. "Great, great", Gillie said over and over again. "Great." He said a team mate, Sean Fallon, had shown him the city's sights. "It's a fine place. I'm sure I'll love it." The reporter asked if he was worried Glasgow might not, after living in a big American city like Detroit, be too quiet for him. "Not at all. Over in the States I worked as a photographer in a Detroit night club on Sundays, usually till 2am on Monday. I am quite looking forward to the restful Sundays of the future." He was asked if the inclement Scottish weather and the rationing of food might not grind him down. "So far, I have not had to change one item of my diet. The food suits me fine—and the weather, I can stand plenty of heat and plenty of cold." He told the reporter the temperature in Detroit was often below zero and he was used to weeks of snow each year. Besides, said Gillie, he was a little bit Scottish himself. He told the reporter his forbears had been born in Glasgow so Scotland was in his blood. "Today I have been writing to the motor company I worked with in Detroit, saying 'Find somebody to take my place.' I won't be back."

Things couldn't have gone any better for the Jamaican. After his fine performance at the public trial, many thought he would immediately be given a place in the first team and would play in the first game of the new season against Third Lanark, Celtic's Glasgow neighbours. As the first game of the season would be played at Celtic Park, it seemed the ideal occasion for Celtic to unveil their 'Black Flash', their exotic new import. Heron's inclusion would have grabbed all the local newspaper headlines. It would also have made sense too, to play Gillie in the Third Lanark game as Celtic's regular centre forward, John McPhail, was injured and could not play. But Heron did not play.

He did play, though, a week later, on Saturday 18 August, 1951. That Gillie Heron was to make his debut against Morton at Celtic Park had been a secret only from Gillie Heron. The whole of Scotland knew. The *Daily Record* knew about it and told everyone so. "It is almost certain that the Jamaican Gillie Heron will make his first team debut." The *People* newspaper knew about it, too, and declared it a "publicity stunt" designed only to sell tickets.

The news was spread by Celtic chairman Bob Kelly. It was Kelly who decided Gillie would be Celtic's gimmick and came up with what he thought a catchy moniker for Heron, the first person of African descent to play in the green and white. He didn't know Heron had in 1949 been known as 'The Black Hawk' when he had played football for the Chicago Maroons team in the North American Professional Soccer League. As far as Kelly was concerned, Heron was black and was as fast as a flash so he was the 'Black Flash.' Kelly stole the name from Roy 'Black Flash' Ankrah, the British Empire Featherweight champion. Ankrah, an African boxer, was given the name in 1950 after he arrived in England from the Gold Coast. His handlers decided as Ankrah was black and as he was fast as a flash he should probably be known as the 'Black Flash.' It was better, I guess, than being called 'Kid Chocolate' or 'The Boston Tar Baby' or something else racial like that. So, Gillie Heron was, like Roy Ankrah, the 'Black Flash.' Celtic fans also called him the 'Black Arrow' because, they said, he was as fast, as sharp, and as deadly as an arrow, and, of course, he was black.

On Saturday August 18, 1951 they came in their thousands to Celtic Park to see if Gillie Heron, the 'Black Flash', would be as advertised or if he would, as some joked, be nothing but a flash in the pan, a black flash in the pan.

As was the practice back then, the players took part in a brief kick-around before the game began. Dozens of young autograph hunters seized the opportunity to run onto the pitch to meet the 'Black Flash' and get him to scribble his name into their autograph books and such. It was an amusing and awkward moment for both Gillie Heron and for another Celtic player, Jimmy Mallan.

Instead of making a beeline for Heron, the autograph hunters headed instead for the player they judged to be the darkest, left back Jimmy Mallan, a swarthy Scot who was darker than the caramel-coloured Jamaican. "I think Jimmy Mallan was a bit mortified at that", said author Tom Campbell, who attended the game.

The newspapers had predicted the 'Black Flash' would bring out the fans in large numbers. "The decision of Celtic to introduce Heron, the Jamaican footballer from Detroit, to their forward line against Morton today will no doubt add considerably to the attendance at Parkhead."

Gillie Heron took all the fuss in his long, elegant stride, and, like a flash, scored a wonderful goal on his debut against Morton within two minutes of the kick-off. He made Morton goalie Jimmy Cowan, who tended goal also for Scotland, look foolish. But the goal was called offside and disallowed. It didn't matter. Heron scored a goal that "flew like a rocket" into the Morton net soon after. This time Cowan managed to get a hand to the ball. But so powerful was the shot, the goalie was helpless to stop the ball rolling into the net. Heron won the game "almost singlehandedly" for Celtic, 2-0, a newspaper said.

In the end, only 40,000 people turned up on August 18, 1951 to see the 'Black Flash.' This was well short of Celtic Park's 90,000 capacity and well short of Celtic chairman Bob Kelly's great expectations. The *Glasgow Herald* had suggested there would be a "drift of neutral followers of football to the novelty of a coloured player leading the Celtic attack."

It was a novelty that made news all around the world. "Detroit negro scores goal in Glasgow debut", read a headline in the *Chicago Tribune* on August 19, the day after the debut. "Gilbert Heron, American born photografer (sic) became the first Negro player to take the field in Scottish senior football." The *New York Times* mentioned Heron's feat, too, but with a mind to racial sensitivities, avoided mentioning the Jamaican's colour in its headline. "US Player Helps Celtic down Morton in Glasgow Soccer, 2-0." The headline "First negro" appeared in the *Lethbridge Herald*, a Canadian newspaper. The paper managed to get Gillie's nationality, his age and just about everything about him wrong. "Gilbert (Black Flash) Heron, an American-born photographer from Detroit, Mich.," the paper said getting his nationality wrong, "on Saturday became the first negro player to take the field in Scottish senior football." Gillie Heron was not the first black person to play football at the professional, or senior level in Scotland. The first black person to play professional football there was John 'Darky' Walker, who played for Edinburgh's Heart of Midlothian club in 1898. The first black person to play for the Scottish national team was Andrew Watson, who was born in British Guiana but grew up in Scotland. Though Watson was described by Scotland's Football Association as "one of the very best backs we have", he only played for his country three times between 1881 and 1882.

As for Gillie Heron, his feat was noticed not just by American papers like the *New York Times* and the *Chicago Tribune*. His feat was noticed, too, by black papers in the US, which, naturally enough made much more of Heron's achievement than did the other papers.

In the black papers, banner headlines declared proudly that racial sporting history had been made in Europe. "Negro stars in Scottish soccer; gets goal in bow," said a headline in New York's *Amsterdam News*. "Another milestone in sports democracy passed here last Saturday as a Negro for the first time played as a member of a big league Scottish Soccer team. Gil Heron, of Detroit, USA, played with Glasgow Celtic as that team defeated Morton 2-0. Heron is not only the first Negro to play in big time Scottish soccer but also the first American to make the grade. This makes his feat doubly significant."

Gillie Heron was not unknown to the black papers. They remembered how he had made history, too, five years before in 1946 when, playing for the Detroit Wolverines, he became the first black person to play professional football in the US.

Gillie Heron had made history in the United States and had gone over to Europe and made history there, too. He was a racial pioneer and a racial role model so the black newspapers said and so they made what use they could of him. Using Gillie Heron as a model, the *Amsterdam News*, New York's biggest selling black paper, insisted the black man in America, too, could succeed as Heron had done in Europe if the shackles of discrimination were removed from him at home. The *Amsterdam News* was thrilled that Heron, a black man, had "led the attack" and that this black man's footballing skills had been judged by whites to have been "smart" and that this black man's "maneuvers drew repeated applause from the crowded stands" filled with whites of one sort or other. So excited was the newspaper, it reported, incorrectly, that Heron's Scottish debut attracted one of the largest crowds in football history. "Over a million fans were present" the *Amsterdam News* said, "for the precedent setting debut." In fact, only

40,000 were in attendance. Pride had overcome facts. So proud was the paper of Gillie Heron, it dedicated its Weekly Salute column, which honoured Negroes of note, to the Jamaican. Heron, the paper made abundantly clear, was a river to his people:

> **"TO GIL HERON – What a trailblazer you are, Mister!**
> **Not only do you pull one of the prize coups of the year by winning a trial with a big league Scottish team but you do it in a field that few Negroes operate let alone excel.**
> **And then to score a goal and star afield your first time out tops everything.**
> **Wow!"**

Other black papers were, too, wowed by Gillie Heron's footballing feat. Baltimore's *Afro-American* newspaper reported that soccer fans in Britain were "thrilled and astonished at the brilliance of a colored American soccer star Gil Heron of Detroit." Excited at what the event suggested, the paper became hyperbolic. Gillie Heron could well become "the most popular sports figure in the British Isles, since soccer as a national sport has a bigger hold on the sporting public than any other".

The Broth of a Boy

"An outstanding person; produced as if by boiling down a savoury broth."

The Free Dictionary

Everyone wanted to know about the black man who'd made history at Celtic. They wanted to know about him in America and wanted to know about him in Scotland, too.

"Right now he is Scottish football's Golden boy. Fifty thousand supporters hail him as the greatest thing seen at Celtic Park since goal-posts." This is what Glasgow newspaper the *Daily Record* had to say about Gillie Heron in an article titled 'The Broth of a Boy from Detroit.' Calling the Jamaican a 'broth of a boy' was a compliment. Gillie Heron was, to the Scottish way of thinking, like the savoury broth produced by boiling a piece of meat – vital and powerful.

The *Daily Record* arranged for Heron, whom it called "the coffee-coloured boy", to meet one of its reporters and one of its photographers at a Glasgow billiard hall. There, the footballer posed for pictures playing snooker and told the reporter the story of his life. He had worked, Heron said, as a 60 dollar a week painter in a Detroit car plant and had earned money, too, as a part-time portrait photographer while also playing for the semi-pro Detroit team the Corinthians. He had before that, he said, been in Chicago where he had played for Chicago Sparta and for the Chicago Maroons. He had before that, he said, been back in Detroit, where he had played for the Detroit Wolverines and for Detroit Venetia. He had before that, he said, been in Jamaica and played centre forward for St. George's College and run track for Kingston College.

"Next year he might be back where he came from last month" the *Daily Record* reporter predicted. "That also will suit Gilbert...He just never worries." This wasn't true, of course, but it fit with the portrait the reporter was constructing. Gillie Heron was not, the article went on, "what you would call a 'steady young man'" nor would he, it said, "thank you" for thinking of him as "responsible" or "disciplined."

The photographs that accompanied the article – photographs showing the Jamaican playing snooker with the skill of someone who'd passed too much time in smoky pool halls – contributed to the image of Heron as a feckless fellow. In the first picture, he is attempting a trick shot. In the second, he is sinking a difficult one and in the third he is looking sleepy. "Those eyes: Sleepy...but confident."

The article recounts how Celtic discovered Heron while the team was on a tour of the US in the summer of 1951 and how Celtic manager McGrory had asked the Jamaican to come to Glasgow for a trial. Heron said "Yes", the reporter wrote, "just as if he had agreed to go across the street." Gillie was thrilled and didn't hide his enthusiasm. "Gee, I was tickled, Glasgow Celtic was the greatest name in football to me." He did, though, say that had he been issued the same invitation by Glasgow's other leading football team, Rangers, he might not have been as quick to come across the Atlantic. "Yeah, I guess I heard of Rangers, too – sometime" he said, dismissing the Protestant favourite, which though it had signed several Catholic players in its time had never signed any that were black. But to Rangers' credit, the club had tried but failed to sign the black British player Walter Tull back in 1914. Tull, who had played for Tottenham Hotspur and for Northampton Town, had been approached by Rangers but decided against it. Instead of making history with Rangers, Tull decided to enlist in the British Army when war broke out in 1914.

It's certain that Gillie Heron's comment that he would not have been as quick to come across the Atlantic had Rangers and not Celtic showed interest in him offended the Protestant two-thirds of Glasgow. Many of them wrapped themselves in the Union Jack and some had even allied themselves during the war with fascists. One of them had been behind, some said, the setting up of a branch of the Ku Klux Klan in Glasgow after the war. Heron probably meant only to please the Catholic minority with his comments and not to inflame the Protestant majority. He was, after all, a Church of England man himself and had as a boy attended All Saints' Church on West Street in Kingston, the same one his parents had married in. He was a Protestant who was just fine with Catholics, he said, and wanted folks to know that his secondary school, St. George's, had been "loaded with priests", priests whose teachings, he said, he tried to "overlook." Still, he didn't have anything against Catholics and when he had been in Chicago, with the Maroons and with Sparta, he had spent his Saturday mornings travelling around Chicago's South Side with the Catholic Youth Organisation teaching black youngsters how to play football.

Truth be told, he didn't care a jot about religion and didn't know a thing about Glasgow's sectarian divide. Besides, both Protestant and Catholic in Glasgow were unhappy with the Jamaican when they read what he had to say in the *Daily Record* about Scotland, its lifestyle, its women, and men in kilts.

"Look," he said sticking his neck out. "I don't want to stick my neck out, but why don't you guys enjoy yourselves a bit more?" It was a foolish comment. In Scotland, as elsewhere in Europe in 1951, people were still mourning their dead and trying to rebuild their bombed-out houses and battered lives. "Here is a city about the size of Detroit, and it drops dead at 9pm" Gillie complained. "Why, over there (the USA) that's just late afternoon; you start out to enjoy yourself about then." He had something to say, too, about the weather. "I catch a cold awful easy, especially in the rain" he said, poking fun at a city where it rains more than most places in the world. "I'm told it can rain here sometimes."

Gillie had something foolish to say, too, about how poorly people were paid in Scotland and how people there made ends meet. He seemed not to know that economic hardship there, a place where the rationing of food, drink, gasoline and clothing was still, six years after the war, making life miserable for most.

"Another thing is the number of magicians you have here – guys trying to live and raise a family on 6 or 7 pounds a week. They must be magicians." Most Glaswegians would have been happy to have earned seven pounds a week in 1951 in a country where two pounds a week was typical. Gillie Heron was rich by comparison. The footballer earned 12 pounds a week. He earned one pound extra for a draw and two pounds extra for a win. For a win in a big game against an important rival like Rangers or Hibernian, Celtic players were paid a hefty bonus, too. For a victory in a Scottish Cup match, a quarter or semi final match, a Celtic player could expect to earn a 30 or 40 pound bonus. There were other perks, too. Heron stayed, for a time, at the Kenilworth, a small hotel in Glasgow city centre, at Celtic's expense. When he moved from the hotel to a rented room at 333 Paisley Road, in West Glasgow, Celtic helped with his costs there, too. He wasn't a magician but he was having a magical time playing football and being well paid for it in Glasgow.

Not content with what he had already said, Gillie Heron had something to say, too, about rules and regulations in Scotland. "Everybody seems stuck on rules and regulations" he protested. "Do this and don't do that." In Scotland, Heron complained, it was mainly, "don't do that."

Speaking his mind had gotten Gillie Heron into trouble before and it would get him into trouble again. However, the *Daily Record* reporter, George Martin, did let Glaswegians know, though, that the Jamaican by way of Detroit had found things he liked about Scotland.

"There were things about us, though, that made Gilbert happy" the reporter wrote. Among these were, "the friendliness and the eagerness to make him feel at home." He also liked, Gillie told the reporter, Scottish women. He couldn't have admitted publicly to such a thing – that he had a liking for white women – had he been back in the USA. Still, though he liked Scottish women, Gillie said he wished they would show what they had instead of hiding what they had.

"And the girls – Gilbert gets warmed up – the girls here are just as pretty as any place else. If they let you notice it. But, no! They dress up to please their grandmothers and nobody else." Gillie knew a thing or two about girls. He did, after all, have a wife back home; a wife named Bobbie who had given him a baby boy who would, as soon as he was grown, start running away, too.

For now, Gillie Heron wasn't running anywhere. He was having too much fun in Scotland. "Where", Gillie Heron asked the reporter, are all "those guys in kilts I heard about?" Racially stereotyped and caricatured in America, Gillie found it strangely liberating to be able to stereotype and caricature others. He was, after all, a kind of Scot, an Afro-Scot, himself. Some of his father's people, the Herons, had come from Wigtown, and some of his mother's people, the Gentles, had come from Kirkcaldy. He was pieces of a man.

A Man's A Man For A' That

"I've always had a weakness for lost causes; once they are really lost."

Rhett Butler

Gillie Heron had a little bit of the Scot, the Caledonian, in him, one great-great something or another having come from Stirlingshire and another great great something or another having come from Wigtownshire – which is bounded by Ayrshire and by Kirkcudbright – to the land of wood and water. But looking for Celtic roots and that sort of thing is not why he ended up in Glasgow in 1951.

He knew that Herons, distant ones from a distant side of his Jamaican family, had been often in Scotland. He knew, for example, that Alexander, his second cousin once removed, had cut up cadavers at Glasgow University in the 1870s and that Darcy, his third cousin once removed, had gone to Glasgow Academy in the 1880s to prepare for a life at sea and that cousins Louis and George, second cousins once removed, had gone to Glasgow High School in the 1890s to learn how, in time, to become first class breeders. He knew, too, that a great Aunt Fanny had left Jamaica for Glasgow long ago and was living there still in 1891 at 237 West George Street. He knew, too, that other relatives, the distant kind, had lived in Helensburgh on the north shore of the Firth of Clyde and that other Herons, distant cousins from a distant side of his family, perhaps still lived in Crail, in the East Neuk of Fife.

There was a lot of Jamaica in Scotland and a lot of Scotland in Jamaica. This Gillie knew. He knew, too, that not far from Celtic Park there was a 'Jamaica Street', a 'Kingston Bridge', and a 'Kingston Docks', where the sugar sweated from slave labour was unloaded, its profits making Glasgow rich. Gillie Heron knew, too, that Scotland's King Kenneth had, it was claimed, black blood and that this was why he had been given the name 'Niger, the Black.' Gillie knew, too, that in 1936, when he was a 14-year old and running the 100 and 220 yard dash for Kingston College, that a black Jamaican with Scottish ancestry, George Duncan Robertson, had been chosen to become chief of one of Scotland's ancient clans and that this black Jamaican was a descendant of Scottish kings.

Gillie Heron wasn't descended from Scottish kings but he knew he had more than a little bit of the Scot, the Caledonian, in him and that his great-great grandfather, Alexander Heron, had left Wigtownshire in 1790 for Jamaica, "the grave of Europeans" Smollett called it, to make his fortune out of the slavery business.

Alexander Heron was not alone in this. His compatriots – the Camerons and Cholmondeleys and Clemetsons from Argyle; the McKenzies and McDonalds from Perthshire; the Grants and Gordons from Lanarkshire – did the same. Together these Scotsmen spread their seed liberally about the place, ensuring there would be more Campbells per acre in Jamaica than in Scotland.

Alexander Heron found employment in Jamaica as a slave driver for others till he could save up enough to do a bit of slave driving for himself. In 1793, three years after arriving from Wigtownshire, he purchased his first bit of land and his first collection of slaves. Four years after this, in 1797, the slaving business going well, he purchased 600 more acres and many more slaves, among which were Sabina, Patience and Venus and Hercules, Apollo and Pompey.

Rabbie Burns, the great Scot poet known for verse like 'A Slave's Lament' and 'A Man's A Man For A' That', would have become a slave driver in Jamaica, too, had his poetry not begun to sell. He would have found a lot of Scotland in Jamaica, with villages and towns called 'Glasgow', 'Inverness' and 'Kilmarnoch' and plantations called 'Hampden', 'Argyle' and 'Dumbarton'.

By the 1800s, the Scots made up a third of Jamaica's white population and they owned nearly a third of all the plantations and slaves there. The Scots were, in some ways, better at the slavery business than were its architects – the English. As slave masters, the Caledonians were without peer. They were brutal and brutish. A slave on a plantation owned or run by one could expect a short, miserable and painful life.

Gillie Heron's great-grandfather, Jamaican-born Alexander Woodburn Heron, the 'Captain' they called him though he never served in any army anywhere, carried on in the 1800s in the ways his Scottish immigrant father had carried on in the 1700s. The father squeezed what he could out of the slave system and the son squeezed what he could out of the semi-slave system that replaced it. Labour was cheap and so was land and so the Captain bought both. He bought so many plantations, he began to run out of names for his plantations. There was 'Wigton', 'Retreat', 'Russell Place', 'Mile Gully', 'Chudleigh', 'Spitzbergen', 'Shooter's Hill', 'Virginia', 'Williamsfield', 'Rest Store', 'Great Valley', 'Cocoa Walk', 'Cane Valley', 'Warwick', 'Asia', 'Bossua' and a host of others, too. Coffee was grown and so was pimento and all sorts of citrus, too. It was lucrative and paid for educations abroad and mansions in Manchester and a Great House in Kingston, and for a top opera singer to be shipped out to Jamaica to amuse the Herons. When not enjoying *Der Freischutz*, Herons were not averse to picking up the gun themselves to maintain the status quo. In 1897, a year of terrible drought in Jamaica, two of the Captain's sons – the blond haired and blue-eyed Walter Vivian Heron and Herbert Hugh Heron – let two of their black countrymen, who were dying of thirst, have it. At Chudleigh plantation, Walter shot one man in the face and shot and "disabled for life" another for drinking from his cattle pond. Not far from there, at the Shooter's Hill plantation, Herbert, who inherited most of the Captain's real and personal estate, shot down another thirsty man. Even the Jamaica *Gleaner*, the planter's paper, could not abide it. "A pity there are men living whose ears are deaf to the cries of their fellow men in distress." These, then, were the Herons of Jamaica, the Herons of Manchester, blond and blue-eyed distant relatives from a distant side of Gillie Heron's Jamaican family.

The Son of No One

"Some ah lawful, some ah bastard, some ah jacket."

Rat Race
Bob Marley

Gillie Heron didn't get any of the coffee or the pimento or the citrus. He was too black for that. He's lucky he got the name. His grandfather, Charles Gilbert Heron, the son of the Captain and a 15-year old seamstress called Josephine, never got nothing, at all. God bless the child that's got his own. God bless the child that's got his own.

Them that's got shall get
Them that's not shall lose

That's what the Bible said and that's how it was in Jamaica. The strong got more, while the weak ones faded, their empty pockets never making the grade. Sometimes in south Manchester rich relations gave a crust of bread and such from which it was okay to help yourself, but not to take too much. The fathers were rich but the sons were poor. Born on the other side of the blanket, Gillie's grandfather got the name and nothing else. In south Manchester, at Shooter's Hill and Retreat and at Chudleigh and Spitzbergen, he was a bastard among bastards, all of them inglorious. They were packsaddles, muleteers, jackets; the misbegot and the misbegotten. They were nullius filius – 'nobody's son' or 'the son of no one.'

Some of these Herons, like their bird namesake, are tall, long necked beasts. Some are not. Some Herons, as any bird watcher knows, are bluish, and have slaty plumage. Others are whitish, and others, still, are dark, nocturnal, crepuscular, their feathered bodies resembling twilight. But a Heron is a Heron no matter whether they bear a likeness to the Great White Heron, a huge, long legged, long necked creature with a yellow bill, yellow legs and white plumage or the Black-Crowned Night Heron, stocky, short necked, short legged with a black bill, a black crown and a black back. The Heron is, as a breed, essentially a communal creature but even such birds have to learn to make it in this world on their own.

Though he was the Captain's first child, because he was born over the blanket, Charles Gilbert Heron, Gillie's grandfather, had to make it in this world on his own. It's hard to make it in this world on your own. A sometimes shopkeeper, Charles' only real skill was spreading sperm – planting it deeply in the rich, black soil of south Manchester, and later Panama.

In this he followed his father, manly man that he was. His father, 'The Captain', fathered dozens of children with the poor, poor black women who tended his land, cleaned his house and raised his blue-eyed, blonde haired 'under the blanket' children. Charles fathered 17 of his own with 6 different women, among them a black woman named Kate, Gillie Heron's grandmother. She raised Gillie's father, Walter Gilbert Heron, to revere Charles though Charles did not deserve it, leaving as he did for the Canal Zone when the little boy was just a little boy. Charles Gilbert Heron never returned, never wrote and never sent money. He spread his sperm in Panama, too, and died there of yellow fever; a yellow-skinned man turned black and blue by mosquitoes. He had been given nothing so he left nothing. Nothing can come of nothing. He had been abandoned and so he abandoned. Charles having done it, it made it easy for Walter to do the same later to Gillie. God bless the child that's got his own. God bless the child that's got his own.

Herons have been flying away, wading away, from their kith and kin from time immemorial. Gillie's cousin Louis Oscar Heron fathered 36 children and provided for none. Gillie's cousin George Egerton Heron fathered a hundred and provided for none of them. When a descendant of George's was asked once who his grandfather was he said, sharply, that he was "some Scotsman who was breeding every woman in south Manchester." Some Heron men have had great difficulty, wrote Richard Mitchell, a great, great grandson of 'Captain' Alexander Woodburn Heron, in 'A Heron Family grew in Manchester', "understanding the concept of monogamy and fidelity, a trait perhaps inherited from Captain Heron."

Pieces of a Man

> "If we can see the present clearly enough, we shall ask the right questions of the past."
>
> ***John Berger***

So they could go on their way without him, his ma and pa decided – Bobbie decided – to send Baby Boy back home, back to the place she had come from; a place he had never been. She had called Jackson, Tennessee home. He would call it home. He had no choice in the matter. His mother's people – the Scotts and the Hamiltons – had called Tennessee, and Alabama, home; in bondage and in freedom.

Scotty's people went down the mines. They took in the crops. They bought a bit of an insurance company. They cut heads. They washed white people's dirty laundry. They had come up from slavery and off the plantation.

The Scotts had some black in them and, I guess, some white in them and the Hamiltons had some black, some white and some Indian in them. They were both from towns where there was no freedom or future around, places where you could not eat or take a drink of water where ever you pleased. They were all chapters and scenes of the places Scotty had been.

Great Scott! - The Scotts

Down there, among the dogwoods and yellow-poplars, is where the Scotts, Scotty's people, are from. They are from Jackson, West Tennessee, which is not to be confused with East Tennessee, where Davy Crockett and Hillbillies are from or even Middle Tennessee, where the Ku Klux Klan got its start.

Jackson was better than a lot of Southern towns but it still had its 'this side' of the town and its 'that side' of the town. Whites mostly kept the North Side for themselves and made blacks live, mostly, on the South Side. Jackson was better than a lot of Southern towns but the police there, like elsewhere, were "Negrophobic" and "promiscuous", a paper said, in their use of blackjacks, billy clubs and gun butts on blacks. It was a damn shame what they did down there to Jesse James Dunlap.

It would have been worse in West Tennessee had it not been for Al Gore's daddy, Albert Senior. And though he did some foolishness, like recommending the US to drop atomic bombs during the Korean War and create a "radiation belt" on the 38th Parallel, Gore Senior did an awful lot of good for black folk in Tennessee. Had it not been for him black folks couldn't have done a lot of the good things they were able to do in West Tennessee, in places like Jackson.

This, then, is where the Scotts came up from slavery and off the plantation. They sang a song full of the faith that the dark past had taught them and sang a song full of the hope that the present had brought them. The Scotts, a song says, were a family that contradicted the concepts. They heard, a song says, the rules but wouldn't accept. That's what a song said.

Scotty's grandfather, Robert William Scott, when he had been himself, had been many things. He'd been president and owner of a branch of the National Benefit Life Insurance Company, and had taken on risk others had shunned. It wasn't easy insuring a Negro in the

South. It was a risky business identifying, assessing and prioritizing risk in a place where, because there was so much hatred, loss was an absolute certainty.

Bob Scott, when he was himself, had also been a sometimes baseball player on his town's team, the Jackson Tennessee Engineers, an all Negro agglomeration. Bob was a fragile man. His body did not produce enough insulin and later he got that disease that sounds like a hissing snake. But he had a strong arm. His arm was so strong, in fact, they called him 'Steel Arm' Scott.

But there was little time for fun and games. After Bob Scott, aged 37, married 25 year old Lillie Hamilton on July 18, 1918 in Jackson, he and his light and damn near white Alabama farm girl from Russellville took themselves a couple of rooms at Charlie and Hattie Moore's house at 242 Tanyard Street in Jackson. In the 1920s, Lillie stayed home and looked after the house while Bob went out and cut hair at the barbershop he'd opened. Folks will always need a haircut. Cutting heads took him from where he was to where he wanted to go.

By the 1930s, Bob and Lillie had moved on up. They had left their rented quarters in Tanyard Street and moved on up to their own house, at 228 Lancaster Street. With them in that house in 1930, was six year old Gloria who, though she went North like everyone else, ended up in the East. There was three year old Bobbie – Scotty's mother and a chief reason for his joy and his pain. There was two year old Sam Ella who, though she lived a short life, enjoyed life the most. In that house at Lancaster Street, too, was lodger Selia Jones, a 38-year old spinster who seemed as though she might never get married. It was a happy house, that house. It should have been. It was, at 3,000 dollars, the most expensive house in the neighbourhood. It was the sort of house someone who was the president of Jackson's branch of the National Benefit Life Insurance Company, would live in. Someday soon perhaps Bob Scott would be like C.C. Spaulding and have 200,000 policyholders and office buildings in three cities and an annual salary of a quarter of a million dollars.

Though the Scotts had moved on up not everyone on Lancaster Street was as lucky. Most of the Scott's neighbours were barbers. Some, like Mr. Williamson next door, were janitors. Some, too, were laundresses who did the wash of others at home. In time, when Bob Scott was no longer himself and things began to fall apart, his wife Lillie, who had hoped for more, became a laundress, too, taking in white people's washing to make ends meet.

Robert William Scott had deep roots in Tennessee. His father, Samuel Scott, Bobbie's grandfather and Scotty's great-grandfather, was born a slave there in September 1856 in a town called Milan in Gibson County, about 30 miles north of Jackson. It's likely Sam was held in slavery by a small farmer in Milan as there were no large plantations in the county, one of the poorest in Tennessee. In 1865, whoever was holding 9 year old Samuel Scott in bondage had to set him free. He was redeemed and regenerated by freedom and by its many and variegated possibilities. Free, Sam returned, for a time, to the weeding. But not, at least, to the overseer's lash.

Marriage was a muddle for Sam. In 1879, aged 23, he moved to Jackson and there married 24 year old Elmira Tyler, a woman from Atlanta, Georgia. Sam liked Georgia women. His mother had been born in the Peach State. Sam and Elmira worked as farm labourers together and had four children together: Emeline, born in 1879; Robert, born in 1881; Dora, born in 1882 and Beulah, born in 1884. But Elmira died young, leaving Sam to raise the children alone till Lucinda Thomas, a Mississippi woman born a slave like Sam, happened along in 1892 with a three year old child of her own, Annabelle, a tragic mulatto forced upon her by a white man back in the Magnolia State.

They were all in need of family and so they became one: no halves; no steps, no-in-betweens; just family. The oldest, Emeline, or Emma, married a Myles, had two kids, and stayed all her life around Jackson. Robert married a Hamilton and stayed around town till they took him, when he was not himself, to the Western State Mental Hospital. Dora married a Williams and moved to Memphis. Beulah, though her name meant 'bride', never married. Annabelle, who always hungered for more, married a McKissack, a poor one, and disappeared into Illinois, dying there, like a lot of good folk from home.

In 1896, 40 year old Sam was a driver of a horse and cart for grocers J.H. Johnston in Jackson. He lived at 119 West College Street with Lucinda, his wife of four years, and their five children. Seventeen year old Bob was employed by the Baptist newspaper The Christian Index as a feeder, someone who keeps the horses fed and watered. His sister, Emeline, worked as a washer woman. The rest of the siblings were too young and were either in school or around the house.

In 1900, 44 year old Sam, 35 year old Lucinda and the five children were living together in Jackson at 205 West Avenue, apartment 4c. Sam was a grocery store porter who could read but admitted he could not write and Lucinda was a washer woman who confessed she could neither read nor write. Bob could both read and write. But he was, like his father, a grocery store porter who fetched and carried for white people. But even this work wasn't guaranteed. Sam lost his job as a porter and had to make do with work as a general labourer. Instead of heading off to Lane or to Fisk, Emeline and Dora had to find work as washerwomen and Bob had to find work as a labourer like his father.

But fetching and carrying wasn't for Robert William Scott. He had spiritual and economic strivings and everyone knew that Tennessee was beyond the veil. By 1908, Bob was cutting heads at the Gem Barber Shop. Sam was working as the driver of a delivery wagon for the grocers

Felsenthal & Tamm, German Jewish immigrants who, like Sam, knew what it was to feel like outsiders. Sam held onto this job and soon there was enough coming in for Lucinda to stop washing white people's dirty clothes. As for the Scott girls, they had all gone their separate ways, taking this one and taking that one's name or, in one case, electing to keep her own.

By 1923, Bob, a married man, is in the insurance game. He is an agent of the Mississippi Beneficial Insurance Company. By 1929, he is the president of the Jackson, Tennessee branch of R.H. Rutherford's National Benefit Life Insurance Company, a black concern with its headquarters in Washington D.C. The Scotts had come a long way up from slavery.

These, then, are the Scotts, Bobbie Scott's father's people, those who had come up from slavery, come up and come off the plantation to sing a song full of the faith that the dark past had taught them, to sing a song full of the hope that the present had brought them.

Grandma's Hands -The Hamiltons

The Hamiltons are another thing, again. Scotty's grandmother, Lillie, was a Hamilton from a place called Russellville in Franklin County in Alabama. The town, if you can call it that, is tucked away in the north-western corner of the state and borders both Tennessee and Mississippi.

Franklin County is not known for much besides producing cotton. Cotton was king there in 'The Heart of Dixie', if Dixie can be said to have a heart. The chief sport there was lynching, which is really no sport, at all. It's no wonder Lillie, who was born there on February 2, 1893, headed North as soon as she could; not to Chicago or New York, but to Jackson and to West Tennessee which is, by the way, 85 miles west of Memphis. Jackson was a railroad town, a hub, which meant there was always likely to be plenty of work available there. Besides,

Lillie had heard that coloured folks, coloured folks like the McKissacks, the Kirkendolls and the Estes, were doing things in Jackson. They had their own coloured college over there – Lane – and they had their own Negro baseball team over there too, the Jackson Tennessee Engineers. Black folk in Tennessee had spiritual strivings and Lillie Hamilton had spiritual strivings, too.

All this is not to say that Lillie Hamilton did not have deep roots in the place she came from. Her family – a little bit of this and a little bit of that – had been in and around Russellville, Alabama for generations and had their hands in all that happened there. The Hamiltons know, for example, that their people came off the plantation. But no one knows which one for sure. It might have been the Forks of Cypress plantation in nearby Florence. But then it might have been the Goode-Hall House plantation in not far away Town Creek. It could even have been the Barton Hall plantation near a place called Cherokee. The Hamiltons know they have African in them. But they also know they have Indian in them, too. They are not sure, though, which one of the Five Civilized Tribes – Cherokee, Choctaw, Chickasaw, Muscogee or Seminole – is to blame for their straightish hair and straightish noses and thinnish lips and lightish skin. It's so hard to know about such things. What is known, for sure, is that Lillie's grandmother, Katherine Hamilton, an African, was born a slave in Alabama in 1842. It's known that in March 1866 her daughter, Ella, a mulatto, was born in Russellville from an encounter Katherine had with a white man, likely against her will. Ella had her first child – Mary – when she was just 13. Many more followed. But only seven survived to adulthood: Mary, Sammie, Morgan, Flynn, Council, Lynch and Lillie, Bobbie's mother and Scotty's grand-mother.

The Hamiltons lived outside the Russellville city limits on a rented farm. They had been slaves and now they were sharecroppers. Ella is illiterate and works the farm with her children. Their house – a cabin really – is built from logs and split into three rooms: one for Ella; one for Lillie and her sisters; one for the boys. Ella had a husband once. But he died so long ago people just stopped talking about him.

In the 1900 census, Ella and family are renters no longer. She is a homeowner. She is 54 years old and has no occupation. Ella describes herself and her kids as 'black.' But by the time of the 1910 census, the Hamiltons – a high yellow people for sure – describe themselves as 'mulatto.' By the time of the 1920 census, the Hamiltons are 'black', again. Race is a topsy-turvy thing in America.

The Hamiltons are peace-loving people, but the boys sign up to go to war in 1917 because they have to and because there is pay in it. It's the military and the monetary. Three of Ella's boys register, as required, for service in the armed forces. But none have to actually fight. So, sadly, they don't get to march in victory down the Champs-Elysees with the "Harlem Hellfighters." Morgan is 27, and married with two children. His draft papers say he is tall, slender and has brown eyes, and black hair. Flynn is 23 and a widower. He is of medium build and height, and has grey eyes and brown hair. Lynch is 18 and unmarried. His draft papers say he is of medium build and height, and has blue eyes and black hair. Morgan has stayed on the family farm in Russellville. Flynn and Lynch have also stayed close to home. Both work as miners near Russellville in the area where ore was first discovered in this part of Alabama. Flynn is an ore miner for the Shook and Fletcher Supply Company, and Lynch is an ore miner for the Sewanee Iron Company. When the work dries up in Alabama, Flynn and Lynch hit the road and end up in Eastern Kentucky in the coal mining encampment of Forked Mouth, in Perry County. Passing for white, they get themselves jobs and lodgings among whites wearing blackface. They dig in the dark, for bituminous coal, three miles down. It is hard to imagine working in the mines, coal dust in your lungs, on your skin and on your mind.

It occurred to them that others don't understand the thoughts of isolation and that there is no sunshine underground and that it is just like working in a graveyard three miles down.

Those, then, are Lillie's people, the Hamiltons, a people with straightish but not straight hair; with straightish noses but not straight noses; with thinnish lips but not thin lips; and with lightish skin but not white skin. Whether it was the farm or the mine, there ain't no place the Hamiltons ain't been down. Which is why, in part, Lillie got married, into colour, and left Russellville, Alabama one day for Jackson, Tennessee.

The bus took her on the Andrew Jackson Highway to the Robert E. Lee Highway through Cherokee and across the border into Mississippi. Then the bus, she situated in the back of course, swung through Bumsville and into Corinth – a place a Negro tarried with caution and care. Then it was on across the border into Tennessee and into Henderson. Finally, it was onwards up South Highland Avenue into South Jackson, the darker side of town, and to Bob Scott.

There were so many other places Lillie could have gone. But she chose Jackson. She could have opted for Huntsville or Decatur. She could have gone to Birmingham or Memphis. But she chose Jackson, a place where black folk were said to be doing things, and where the local whites, by almost unanimous assent, agreed to mostly leave them the hell alone.

They did alright, these black folk when left alone. They began businesses. They went to college; to Fisk to Meharry to Lane. Bobbie Scott, Scotty's mother, went to Lane College, a black institution of higher learning in Jackson that felt newly freed slaves should be able to read, write, and talk right. Bobbie Scott could do all three and sometimes did all three at the same time. In 1946, she was assistant editor-in-chief of the *Lanite*, Lane College's yearbook, and she was vice-president of the Lane College Glee Club, too. She could have majored in music or in English, but she chose, instead, to major in social science, which allowed her to dabble in anthropology, psychology, history, linguistics and international studies. Even then, she was preparing herself to be elsewhere.

Bobbie Scott was a Lane woman through and through; as was her sister Gloria; as was her sister Sam Ella, who was named both for her father Bob's father, Sam, and her mother Lillie's mother, Ella. Bobbie's baby brother, William, was a Lane man, too.

Fair Lane, we love thee, love thee well, It is of thee we love to tell,
Of friendly years of college life,
Of college years with pleasure rife
Of years we could be help employ
Our minds in ecstasy our minds
When soon we would begin this happy tune.

The Scotts were college men and college women and proud of it even though some of these colleges were really Nigger Factories which turned out high-toned, highfaluting Negroes with Bullshit Degrees and Nigger Education who looked up to whites and down on other Negroes. Be that as it may, the Scotts had done well in the dear old Southland. They were not rich. They were something more important. They were respectable, or at least they seemed to be.

But though they had the South in their soul, the Scotts knew if you were of the darker race all you had and all you hoped to have could be taken away upon a white man's whim. So come time for graduation, they had to decide, as did so many others, whether they would take the Southern Railway to New York or the Illinois Central Railroad to Chicago.

Aunt Annabelle McKissack had been part of that Great Migration to what some called the 'City of the Big Shoulders', or 'Paris on the

Prairie' or 'The Big Onion'. They called it this because the more you peeled it back, the more it made you cry.

The Big Onion made Aunt Annabelle, who'd married a McKissack, a poor one, cry sometimes. At first she didn't have to work. The husband, James, a trained lithographer, made just enough as a meatpacker working for Morris & Co. They lived over on East 44th Street in a kitchenette, as did everyone back then. In time, they moved to East 58th Street and to a kitchenette that cost them 15 dollars a week. Annabelle had wished for so much more. She became a seamstress, working from home. He, an aspiring graphic designer, became a chauffeur, like Bigger Thomas, driving Miss Daisy and her relatives around Illinois. It made you want to kill. And though the Big Onion made her cry, Aunt Annabelle still sent lovely letters back to Jackson boasting about sauntering down The Stroll and seeing Basie and Billie at the Regal.

Lillie didn't want her kin to leave but didn't want them to stay, either. She knew they had to go, but hoped change would bring them back, someday. She knew they had to escape from their unhappy homeland to the peace of a distant mountain. So, with Lane degree in hand and the college's Colored Methodist Episcopal perspective in mind, Bobbie, a graduate at only 19 with a weighted 4.9 GPA, left the dogwoods and yellow-poplars for the hog butcher for the world, its tool maker, its stacker of wheat.

The Illinois Central stopped at a lot of places on the way, among them Tugaloo, Duck Hill, Bolivar and Cairo. This was 1946. Styron's Stingo left for a place as strange as Flatbush about that time. Bobbie left for a place as strange as the South Side and for someone as strange, though she did not know it then, as Gilbert St. Elmo Heron.

The First Minute of A New Day

"Your day is done. Night is coming fast upon your day."

Nickleby

Down where he had been left – in Jackson, Tennessee – he learned to make peace with it, to make his house into a home. If he had ever had another home, he could not remember it and if he had ever had other people besides Lillie, this little light skinned lady who always wore a hair net, then he could not remember it.

❧

Nothing interesting ever happened on South Cumberland Street. Sometimes stuff happened on North Cumberland Street. But nothing interesting ever happened on South Cumberland Street. The Scott's house didn't get a phone – Jackson 2-3605 – until Scotty got there. I'm not sure why, but the Scott's house didn't get a TV till 1960. They missed out on an awful lot of *I Love Lucy* and *Father Knows Best*. But at least, before Lillie went, she got to see a little Gunsmoke and a lot of Perry Mason.

He liked TV but he didn't love it. Top Cat and Underdog had a place in his life but it was not a very big place. What he really liked, was reading and writing detective stories. He began writing when he was 10 or 11 and in 5th grade. They were just little two page things. But already, as they say, you could see the developing mind at large in front of you. He'd begun playing, too – banging really – a piano a few years before when he was eight. There had been a funeral parlour down the road that was shutting up shop and throwing everything out, including a beat-up upright piano bought for a few dollars. The Scotts were a musical people. Lillie sang in church and both William and Bobbie had been in the Glee Club at Lane, and Gloria had sung soprano there, too. So it was a surprise the Scotts didn't have a piano in the house. When they got it home, and Scotty got some instruction, figuring out what flatted fourths and ninths were, Lillie had him play 'What a Friend We Have in Jesus', 'Rock of Ages' and 'The Old Rugged Cross' over and over again. He never became better than okay at it and were it not for his words, we might never have heard of him, at all.

Still, though he was what he was on the piano, she showed him off. Lillie showed him off every Thursday in front of her sewing circle. She showed him off at the Berean Baptist Church, where she was missionary advisor to the Young Matrons and where she was secretary of Missionary Circle No. 2. She was also president of the Ladies Missile Club and so she showed him off to them, too. A past president of the Parent-Teachers Association of South Jackson, she enjoyed most of all showing him off to them. But he was never more than average at it, and couldn't, without his words, have made a living at it, but she showed him off, all the same. She even showed him off, as though he were hers and not hers, to Bobbie when she would come down from Chicago full of herself and full of the life up there.

In 1957, she came, ostensibly, to spend two weeks with Scotty. But what was he to make of it when he saw Bobbie had brought with her to the Hog and Hominy state her best friend and landlady, Mrs. William O. Sledge. She had got what she wanted, she said. She was singing alto in a big choir, she said, and working as a librarian downtown in the Loop, she said. Things were good out there in the world, she said. Sammie, Sam Ella, was living in New York, and she had gone, for the summer, she said, to Paris to be with Baby Brother, Airman 1st Class William H. Scott. As for Gloria, she said, she had been working for the state department and had gotten a post teaching at the University of Djokjakarta. Gloria had hoped, Bobbie said, to spend time in Paris with Sam and with William but couldn't and so would have to make do with Bangkok and Singapore this summer, instead. In time they would take him out into the world, too, to Chicago, to New York and even to Puerto Rico. They were something else these Misses, and they expected him to be something else, too.

Aunt Gloria, she who never married and never tarried too long, went everywhere. She went first to Chicago and then, in 1948, to Puerto Rico, to Vega Baja in the north, where she was, for four years, supervisor of three schools. That's how Bobbie came or got to Puerto Rico; Gloria paving the way, as usual. Then, in 1952, when she got that Fulbright Scholarship, Gloria, ever intrepid, set out to study languages in Thailand. But she got sick – the Scotts are fragile – and had to put things off till 1953 and then went, instead, to Egypt to teach English at Cairo's Higher Institute of Education for Women as an employee of the US Information Agency, USIA. Later she made it to Siam and then later, still, to Israel and to Indonesia. She probably bumped into Stanley Ann Dunham and the future president on the road in Indonesia without knowing it. She got around. Scotty remembered that she sent him a camel saddle around the time Nasser nationalised that Suez Canal. Gloria Flynn Scott travelled so much on US government business, in fact, some people speculated, and one newspaper reported, that she was not an educator, or 'public diplomat', employed by the US Information Agency, at all, but a spy employed by the National Clandestine Service.

They were something else these Misses, something else. They were not at the margins. They were at the centre. They were not at the periphery. They were in the world; not at its edges living without hope and expectations. They had come from towns where you got to know what oppression was all about; towns where there was no freedom or future around; towns where you could not eat and take a drink of water wherever you pleased. These were all chapters and scenes of all of the places they'd been.

But on their infrequent trips home to Jackson, Tennessee, even they, the Misses, could see that there was a lot less of the 'yes, suh' and 'no, suh' and 'whatever you say, suh.' You'd have to be deaf, dumb and blind not to know it was the first minute of a new day.

It began, for Jackson, with Lane College students who sat down so they could stand up. They sat down and tried to order a meal at McLellan's and at Woolworth's and sat down in white-only seats on Jackson City Lines buses. This sort of thing, black people sitting down so they could stand up, was going on everywhere in America in 1960 and Jackson people thought it ought to be going on there, too.

When Scotty was growing up there he couldn't swim at the pool off Hollywood Drive the way the white boys did. He couldn't get a shake at the Dairy Queen the way the white boys did, or sit in the circle and watch a movie at the Paramount, or sit in the stall and watch a movie at the State the way the white boys did. He couldn't do anything the way the white boys did. He did everything the way a black boy did. They sat downstairs. He sat upstairs. They sat in front. He, because he was black, sat in the back. It was separate but it was not equal. You could shop, if you wished, in a first class store on the east side of Highland Avenue – Kisbers, Hollands, Montgomery Ward – but all they gave you was second class service. You had, for example, to be certain of your size because you couldn't try anything on. You had to eat on the run because while you could buy something at The Fox restaurant, you could not sit down and eat there. It was all very separate and all very unequal. On the west side of Highland Avenue, over near West Lafayette Street, things were fairer and squarer. Over here, at Nando Jones, is where Scotty got his Buster Browns and Hub-City Drugs is where he got his baby food and diapers and over here, at the Haynes Fish Market, is where he got his catfish; his flat-head catfish; his frogmouth catfish; his hardhead catfish.

It would have been easy back then to believe that because things had always been this way that things would always be this way. Certainly, if you read the Jackson Sun you would have thought things were going to go on and remain exactly as they were. White folks' radio, WDXI and WPLI on the AM, where Wink Martindale worked, kept their heads buried in the sand. They didn't want to know about Brown v. Board of Education or about the Southern Christian Leadership Conference. They only wanted to know that Jerry Lewis had fallen out with Dean Martin or that Marilyn Monroe had married Joe DiMaggio or that The Ballad of Davy Crockett or Mr. Sandman was still high on the charts. If you listened to Jackson's only black radio station, WJAK, which was owned by white men, the Leechs, you were none the wiser, either. Like WDXI and WPLI, WJAK was concerned with keeping things as they were and as they had always been. They didn't tell folks what Rosa Parks did in 1955 in Montgomery, Alabama or what those four college kids who sat down so they could stand up in 1960 in Greensboro, North Carolina, did, either. All you got from WJAK was 'Please Be Patient With Me' when they could have given you 'Don't Let Nobody Turn You Round.' All you got from WJAK was 'Impossible Dream' when they could have given you 'The Best Is Yet to Come.' You got the church news, the pie up in the sky waiting for me when I die news, instead of the real news, the I'd rather be a free man in my grave than living as a puppet or slave news. What could, or should, you expect of a radio station owned by Leechs. Besides, the all black on-air talent – Super Wolfe, Jim Dandy and Little Willie Poe – weren't trying to save the children or start a revolution. They didn't know what time it was and so you couldn't blame them for not knowing it was the first minute of a new day.

It's easy to see why Tennessee people thought things would go on the way things had been going on. It was in Tennessee, after all, that the Klan got its start and that Jim Crow was born and where the first Jim Crow law was passed. The rest of the South quickly followed suit. Lillie had been born in 1893 and so had grown up with Jim Crow – its segregated buses and trains, its segregated restaurants, pools and hospitals. She bought her train ticket at a separate window and sat in a separate waiting room then rode in a separate car. She entered a restaurant by a separate entrance and left by a separate exit. It had been that way when Lillie was coming up and it was that way, a half a century later, when Baby Boy was coming up, too. Both Lillie and he were raised in small towns down South where they got to know what oppression was all about. These were towns where there was no freedom or future around; towns where you could not eat and take a drink of water wherever you pleased.

But when Truman submitted his civil rights plan in 1948 and in 1949 ended segregation in the Armed Forces, things began to look good. When, in 1952, no black people were lynched and four black students were admitted to the University of Tennessee, things looked real good. Everything looked very good, indeed, when, in May 1960, Nashville, Tennessee, became the first major city in the South to desegregate public facilities. Who could have known that nothing would really change? It looked like there was going to be big change. But there was little change. Lillie questioned it – Scotty remembers this. But she didn't challenge it. Maybe it was because there was a 'Stop' sign at the end of her street.

It took out-of-towners to really challenge and change things. Mr. Albert Porter, an out-of-towner who had come to town to take up a job as Lane College's book-keeper, was chosen by students to help change things. Not long after he took on this task, a white man held a gun on him and another white man came, in the heat of the night, to tell him to stop or they would start on his wife and his kids.

The people at the Berean Baptist, who had learned to take things as they were, took to Mr. Porter. Lillie and Scotty took to Mr. Porter, too. He was like her son who had flown away to the Champs-Elysees and she was like his dear mother back in Mississippi. He offered and they accepted a ride to Sunday service and to Wednesday service, too. He took them here and he took them there. Before Mr. Porter and his '56 Ford came to town they had gotten around, for 15 cents, on a Jackson City Lines bus or around in a People's Cab Company cab for 35 cents. Sometimes the Scotts baby-sat for the Porters and sometimes the Porters baby-sat for the Scotts. Lillie opened bank accounts for Al and Portia and Mr. Porter loaned Scotty his Smith-Corona. Though he made his living with numbers, not words, Mr. Porter could see that Scotty had a way with words. Mr. Porter could see, too, that Scotty was really just pieces of a man sliding through completely new beginnings, that he was searching out his every doubt and sometimes winning, that he wanted to be free and that he had no idea why he, we, were struggling here, faced with his, our, every fear just to survive.

Mr. Porter was dangerously close to becoming the father Scotty had never really had. He imagined his own father, Gilbert St. Elmo

Heron, would have been like Mr. Porter. But he had no evidence of this. He had no letters to read over and again. He did have pictures, though. He had pictures that showed him as a baby and his father, a first-time father, fascinated not by family but by the whole business of fathering. There were no photos that showed him growing from stage to stage and his father evolving in his age. But Scotty had a good imagination and what did not exist, he made up. In his dreams, he dreamed he went to his father with many questions on his mind but his father did not want to answer them because he/the world, was so blind. These were the rivers of his father.

But his father, Gilbert St. Elmo Heron, was not a river to his people. He could not boast as Auda Abu Tayi had that he carried 23 great wounds, all got in battle, and that he had killed 75 men with his own hands in battle, and that he had scattered and burned his enemy's tents and taken away their flocks and herds. His father could not boast, as Auda Abu Tayi could, that though the Turks had paid him a golden treasure, still he was poor because he was a river to his people. Gilbert St. Elmo Heron was not, whatever else he may have been, a river to his people, or to his son. Mr. Porter was a river, as ancient as the world and older than the flow of human blood in human veins. His soul had grown deep like the rivers.

When Mr. Porter's soul wasn't growing deep like the rivers or keeping the books for Lane College, he was either trying to start a revolution or taking Lillie and Scotty back and forth to the Berean Baptist. On Sunday it was Sunday school. On Wednesday it was the Wednesday night service. He picked them up and dropped them off, tending and caring for them as if he were the son, and the father. One time he drove them all the way to Decatursville to see a boy who had gone to Merry High with Sam Ella, and whom Lillie would have liked see marry her, marry someone else. Another time, Mr. Porter drove

Lillie and Scotty all the way to Alabama so she could see what was left of her kith and her kin. Lillie's sister, Mary, had been gone these many years. Her sister Sammie had been gone almost as long. Lynch, who had coal dust on his lungs, on his skin and on his mind, checked out while still looking for a lovely day. Flynn, who'd also worked in a graveyard three miles down, went still believing there must be something he could do. Only Morgan, who never travelled far from the family farm, was left. Even he, a simple, sullen sharecropper, was convinced there were better days ahead.

People in Jackson, too, believed there were better days ahead. Mr. Porter believed this, anyway. This is why when some students, Lane College students, asked him if he would, in October 1960, help them stand up he said 'yes.' First, it was the picketing of the buses and trying to sit down and eat at Woolworth's and McLellan's. The buses were easy. The lunch-counters were hard. They poured hot coffee on children and put hot cigarettes out on them. "Get out of here, coons! We don't serve y'all." There wasn't much Southern hospitality in the South. There was, though, a lot of talk about protecting the 'Southern way of life' and how white folks would "fight for it to the bitter end." They didn't, of course, fight to the bitter end in Jackson. Police chief J.R. Gaba and Mayor Quinton Edmonds, who had Lillie to thank for their clean shirts and shorts, knew change was coming and knew they couldn't stop it, only delay it.

It had been a long, a long time coming but everybody could see that a change was gonna come. It had been too hard living for Lillie. But even she would have admitted she was afraid to die. She did not really know what was up there beyond the sky.

Change did come. But Lillie didn't stay around to see it. The change in Jackson began in October 1960 and she was gone in November 1960. She woke up on November 5 not feeling good and called Mr. Porter, her son, to tell him so. But she didn't tell him so. He was on his way to Memphis and she didn't want to burden him. She should have burdened him. He still hasn't gotten over it, Mr. Porter. He'd have been happy to have taken her to Jackson's still segregated hospital and use its still separate entrance and check her into its still separate ward and watch her get separate and unequal care. Mr. Porter wouldn't have minded, if only he had known.

Scotty didn't know much, either. He was up, fixing breakfast as usual – bacon and eggs – and fixing her a wash pan with hot water and washcloth, as usual. He dropped a frying pan but she did not stir. He thought she was waving, but she was drowning. She was much further out than he thought, and not waving but drowning.

She was drowning now, but it had not been that long since they had been swimming, swimming along in Santurce with Bobbie. Instead of flying up to Jackson in the summer of 1960, as she did each year, Bobbie flew them down – Scotty and Lillie – from Florida to San Juan. That was a time that was. Scotty had never been on a plane and Lillie had never been on a plane and had never ever really left the South. They left on Friday 1st July as soon as school got out and were gone the whole summer long till school got back in again. They saw all the historical sites that people see, like the Catedral de San Juan Bautista in San Juan, where the bones of the discoverer of the New World, Ponce de Leon, lay. Down there they bumped into Melvoid Estes Benson and her husband, a military man, in Puerto Rico. Boy, that was a time that was. But times like that don't last. Now, here he was waving and there she was, Lillie, drowning.

Nothing ever happened on South Cumberland Street. But on November 5, 1960, a Saturday I think, something happened at 453

South Cumberland Street. We'd rather it hadn't happened. Especially as she was only in her 69th year. But she got a good send-off. They were all there: Miss Gloria Scott of Bangkok, Thailand; Mrs. Bobbie Heron of Santurce, Puerto Rico; Miss Sam Ella Scott and Mr. William H. Scott of the Bronx, New York, and 11 and a half year old Master Gilbert Scott Heron of Jackson, Tennessee.

We'd rather she hadn't gone, but she had quite a send-off at the Berean Baptist Church on Wednesday 9 November, 1960, the day after John F. Kennedy beat Richard Nixon to become President of the United States. There was music from the choir and a solo rendition from Mrs. Gracie Williamson. There was an invocation by Professor T.R. White. There was a word of scripture from the Reverend C.F. Odom. There were remarks from Mrs. Vivian Bell of the Young Matrons of Berean and a eulogy by the Reverend A.L. Campbell. Mr. Porter, poor Mr. Porter, was a pallbearer. They buried her, Lillie Hamilton Scott, in Elmwood, the coloured cemetery, alongside 'Steel Arm' Scott, who had been waiting on her these twelve long years.

O Lily Scott! We love thy name so dear,
Each day our hearts feel ever close to thee,
We pledge our life and loyalty to thee
We love thy name in all entirety

O Lily Scott! We cherish thee each day
In rain and shine, or on life's chosen way.
O Lily Scott! We pledge our sisterhood,
In life or death, O Lily Scott!

Waiting For The Axe To Fall

"No badda bawl. Him soon come back."

Jamaican Proverb

Gilbert St. Elmo Heron didn't make it to the funeral. He could have made it. He'd been back in the US from his adventures abroad in Europe for quite some time by then.

By then, 1960, he'd been back in the US for six whole years. Yet, not once in those six years and 3 months and 8 days did he send the boy a birthday card; though his birthday fell on the same day each year. Yet, not once did he send the boy a Christmas card; though Christmas fell on the same day each year. He did not send the boy a letter or a postcard. He did not send him a package or parcel. He did not send the boy money. He did not send anything. He didn't send condolences nor did he send congratulations. He didn't send anything. Like his own father, he was not there and so was not there when Scotty sang with the youth choir at Berean or there when Scotty made history at I.B. Tigrett Middle School.

While he, Gilbert St. Elmo Heron, had been away on his adventures in Europe, America, even America, had changed. But he was still himself, his same old selfish self. You know, it kinda serves him right how things turned out for him over there, over there at Celtic, in Scotland, over there in Europe.

Things had looked so good. But they had turned out so bad for Gilbert St. Elmo Heron. In August 1951, he had been on top of the world and was known around the world. "The greatest thing seen at Celtic Park since goalposts" is how one paper described him. But after several up and down again performances he quickly fell from favour and was dropped from the team. Things got so bad that in one game he ended up in the net, but did not score. Rushing towards goal to try and connect with a cross, he missed the ball and slid 15 yards on the wet pitch straight into the back of the net. Newspapers that had been kind to the first black man to play for Celtic, became unkind.

"Little was seen of Heron, who had difficulty working up speed on the slippery turf and too often ran into offside traps" the *Glasgow Herald* said. Glasgow's *Daily Record* was tougher. "Heron's place is in the reserves", wrote Waverley, the *Record's* influential sports columnist. Waverley said he had gone along to the Celtic match for his "first view of the Jamaican, Giles Heron" and had not been impressed. He took exception, Waverley said, with those who said the Jamaican would soon replace Celtic's regular centre forward, the injured John McPhail. "The sooner McPhail is back in the Celtic team, the better for Celtic's prospects", Waverley wrote. Without McPhail, Waverley said, Celtic had lost its "artistry", its "skill, craft, guile." Waverley said Heron was quick but frequently ran offside and ruined many goal-scoring opportunities. "I would say his proper place is in the reserve team, there to pick up the wrinkles and sharpen his wits. I feel he is not whatever he may be in the future ready for the top grade." Waverley cited Gillie's race as a factor. "The coloured boy has something to learn."

Despite poor reviews, he was given another chance to impress against Airdrie, F.C. There was bad news on game day. The *Glasgow Herald* published an article saying the Jamaican had not done as well as hoped because he was delicate and was intimidated by Scotland's harsh weather. "HERON MAY NOT PLAY IN WET WEATHER." According to the *Herald*, Celtic was considering playing Gillie only when it did not rain. As it rained almost every day in Glasgow this would have meant the Jamaican would not have played much, at all.

"If the weather is of the type experienced on Saturday" the *Herald* said, referring to a rain soaked game the week before, "Heron, who probably liked it less than any other player, will not be included." It was the Jamaican's good fortune that it did not rain on game day. He scored an extraordinary goal that day and had a great game. "The crowd applauded an effort which was as fine as has been seen on the ground for many a day." But the good news didn't last. In a game a week later against Morton Football Club, it rained heavily and, predictably, Gillie played poorly and Celtic lost 2-0. Morton's defence, a paper said, "made not one single mistake against the tall Heron." He was replaced by John McPhail and when McPhail was injured again he was replaced not by Gillie but by full back Sean Fallon, a player described, unflatteringly by one paper, as a "great trier" but "no centre forward." When Fallon, too, was injured, Gillie Heron got another chance in a special testimonial, a game intended to honour and reward a well loved Scottish player called Bob Thyne. Though Gillie did well in the testimonial game, he did not return to the Celtic first team for several months. Exiled to the second team, and with a lot of time on his hands, he took good photos and wrote bad poetry.

From the Grampian Mountains in Scotland
Or from Kirkcaldy by the sea
And from Glasgow to the highlands
Or from Ayr to old Dundee.

He had time to contemplate his present and his past. He had time to wonder whether his past actions had anything to do with his current circumstance. He had the chance to wonder if, perchance, he could have done things differently. He decided he had done nothing wrong; nothing he regretted.

Before, when he had left, he let others do his leaving for him. He used borrowed words to say he regretted neither the good that was done to him nor the bad that he did. The memories he had, he said, both the good and the bad, he no longer desired and would fling in a fire. He knew, he said, that way leads to that and if he never came back, he would be telling this with a sigh somewhere, someday.

Gillie languished in the second team, among the reserves. He did well here, among the underachievers. He scored goal after goal; fifteen in all. Celtic took notice of his good form and recalled him to the first team for a big match on December 1, 1951, against cross-town Glasgow rival, Partick Thistle. It was his last chance.

"Gil Heron received tremendous vocal support" a paper reported. But it didn't help. "He tried hard with little luck." Celtic won the game. But it was not thanks to him and so it was back to the second team, and life among the under-achievers. It's not that he had done badly, really. It's that he had not done as well as Celtic would have liked him to do. The first team had won 4 of the 5 games he played and he had scored 2 goals. But still they wanted more. It was not enough, in the end, for a man who had been brought to Scotland and into the Celtic team primarily for the sheer novelty of it. It was not enough for such a man to score and then not to score. If such a man was going to win a regular place on this team he would have to score all the time and every time the ball came near him and even when the ball was not near him.

Though it was clear Celtic had given up on Gillie Heron, Gillie Heron did not give up on Celtic or on himself. He had, at that time, December 1951, 6 months left on his one year contract and so decided that whatever would be would be and that the future was not his to see, que sera, sera.

Out of favour and in the middle of his first Glasgow winter, he looked for ways to rescue and redeem himself. A keen photographer, he turned up in December 1951 with his cameras at a Celtic event that an embittered man, a black man with a chip on his shoulder, would not have attended. There he was, at St Andrew's Hall in Glasgow on December 16, 1951, for the Annual Rally and Concert of the Celtic Supporter's Association. He was in a festive mood and so dressed himself in a Tam O' Shanter and a tartan scarf and looked every bit the black Scotsman he was.

He felt at home in Scotland. But he still longed for home; Jamaica, not Detroit. Besides, there was nothing for him, right then, in Glasgow. He had been dropped from the first team and, on January 2, 1952, got himself sent off for fighting while playing in a second team game against Stirling Albion. He was suspended for seven days and lost a week's wages as further punishment. He longed for home; Jamaica not Detroit. He'd heard on the grapevine that Jamaica's national team had just played Haiti's national team in a four game series and had not delivered the result the Jamaica Football Association, JFA, had been looking for. Jamaica thought itself better than all others in the Caribbean at football, at cricket, at everything. The JFA felt losing or even drawing with small islanders was unacceptable. Gillie Heron heard, again through the grapevine, that Jamaica wanted him, a big-time runner and jumper at Kingston College and a big time footballer at St. George's College, to come home in February 1952 to help Jamaica battle a Caribbean All-Star team featuring players from Trinidad and Tobago, Surinam, Puerto Rico, Guadeloupe, British Guiana and Haiti.

The Jamaica Football Association was determined to win and so decided to bring home from Britain the island's most celebrated footballer. This was Lindy Delapenha, not Gillie Heron. Delapenha was in England playing for Middlesbrough, which wasn't keen on letting its star striker go as the team felt it had a real chance at winning the First Division title that year, 1952. But, Middlesbrough let Lindy go. The JFA decided it would ask Gillie Heron, too, to come back, for awhile, to his island in the sun.

Oh, Island in the Sun

"Though I may sail on many a sea her shores will always be home to me."

Lord Burgess

Lindy Delapenha was the first; the first Jamaican to play professional football in England. To get Lindy, who had won two English First Division titles, to return briefly to his island in the sun in February 1952, the Jamaican Football Association had to agree to insure Lindy's legs for the enormous sum then of 15,000 pounds. The JFA also had to agree to bear the cost of Lindy's flight from London to New York aboard a brand new BOAC Stratocruiser airplane, and then on, in a lesser craft, to Kingston.

To get Gillie Heron to come to Jamaica – a player Celtic did not have a place for on its first team and had suspended from its second team for fighting – the price was much lower than had been incurred by the JFA to get Lindy. Celtic told Jamaica they could have him for as long as they wanted and that he was not to hurry back. He had, after all, been spending most of his time in his rented room at 333 Paisley Road in Glasgow listening to the BBC's Scottish service at 371 mega-hertz. At breakfast he listened at 7.50am to Lift Up Your Hearts and at tea-time he listened, occasionally, to the bagpipe programme. He always listened, of course, to the Football Report at 8.30pm. Not once did it report how not playing was killing him.

When not in his room he was most likely taking pictures of Glasgow's great places. He loved pictures. Yet there was no picture, neither a small one nor a large one, in his room of his once-ago wife or his once-upon-a-time kid. There ought to have been a picture of his kid. And he ought to have sent money so they could hold on to their dreams as he was trying to hold onto his dreams. But it was as if he had never been married and never had a wife named Bobbie and never had a kid named Scotty. He was, as his father Walter had been, a family man without a family acting as though he had never been a family man, at all.

None in Glasgow knew, or cared to know, that there was a Bobbie and a Baby Boy who, in that February of 1952, would have been coming up on three years old and would have been, as all three year olds are, full of the wonder of it all. In his third year, he would already have begun sitting and watching for cues of how he should behave, too, when he, like his dad, was a dad; a 29 year old man coming up on 30 who was really just a boy. "The glory of children" so someone said, "are their fathers."

They're such great actors, these Herons. They act like actors and act like they care. They claim they want to kiss you, but cannot. They claim they want to embrace you, but cannot. They claim they want to have you near them so they can tell you they care, but do not. He didn't care. He knew that no matter the consequences or the fear that gripped his senses, he was going to hold on to his dream. So he went back to his island in the sun.

~

"Heron is coming to prop soccer XI" the Jamaica *Gleaner* newspaper declared on February 12, 1952. Hail the conquering hero.

Heron was coming to prop up the Jamaica All Star XI and would, the newspaper said, "prove as big a draw as Lindy." Gillie Heron looked forward to being big, and being wanted again. After travelling for two days via New York he arrived, finally, at Palisadoes Airport in Kingston, Jamaica, early on Sunday, 16 February. The Jamaica Football Association bigwigs who met him at the airport – Granville DaCosta, Paul Chevannes and Winston Meeks – told him Lindy would not arrive for another six days and that Lindy had expressed surprise when told another Jamaican would be coming out from Britain, too. Delapenha had thought it was he alone, the first Jamaican to play in the English First Division, who had been making history in Britain. He had not realised that Gillie Heron had been making history there, too, in Scotland. This first black thing can be a contentious business.

Gillie knew Lindy was in England. Lindy should have known Gillie was in Scotland. Lindy had known of Gillie Heron when they were schoolboys in Jamaica in the 1930s. But Gillie had not known of Lindy Delapenha back then. Five years younger than Heron, Delapenha had been on the outside back then while Heron had been on the inside. But the tables had turned. Lindy had won two English First Division championships with Portsmouth and was the top striker with Middlesbrough, and was the star now.

Gillie Heron's team told him to go to Jamaica and not to hurry back. Lindy Delapenha's team told him to hurry back as they were not sure they could get on without him. He was to hurry back the Middlesbrough manager told him. He was to hurry back Wilf 'Golden Boy' Mannion, Lindy's teammate at Middlesbrough, told him.

British newspapers called Lindy "the artist", "the dazzler." One said he "danced around" defences and led players on 'the Delapenha waltz.' But those who cheered him one week in England, booed him the next and called him 'nigger' and told him to go back from whence he came.

But Lindy could take it. He was a hail fellow well met sort of a guy and did not lose his head easily. He was the very opposite of a hot-head; a man likely to lose his head and then lose his way. This is, in part, why Lindy did so well in England and perhaps why Gillie did so badly in Scotland. Lindy always kept his head. Gillie always lost his.

"Well, he was a bad tempered boy at school and he used to get into a lot of trouble on the field." This is how Lindy remembers the 14-year old Gillie. "He always wanted to fight and things like that. I suppose it's something that was inborn in Gillie." His parents – Lucille and Walter – would have denied that it was 'inborn' in him as this would have meant it was inborn in them, too. But rage really was in Giillie's DNA. "He was a little bit hot tempered on the field."

He was a bit hot tempered off it, too. Ask anyone who had the privilege of knowing and growing with him. Ask the two women who married him. Ask his offspring. Ask his siblings. Ask his brother, his bigger brother Roy. "Well, he flies off. If you say anything to him, he's ready to hit you or anything like that. He was a bit of a hot-tempered type of person. He didn't take anything."

Not taking anything was part of who he was. He didn't take it from a Wolmer's right back kicking at his shins or a Chicago Swede centre whispering "nigger, nigger" in his ear. But not taking anything is no excuse to strike out at those that love you. He lost his head a lot, and those he loved were always in imminent danger of losing theirs. But, in his defence, he was an athlete, a man asked not to think; only to act. He had other assets, too, besides his head. But there's no question he had a wonderful head. Even when a foot, a right or a left one, would have sufficed to score a goal, Gillie Heron used his head and risked losing it. People made wagers on whether he would be asked to leave the field of play in the first or second half, or whether he would wait until the end of the game to strike out at an opponent. 'What does

Gillie Heron' the joke went, 'have in common with the wives of Henry the Eighth? 'He always loses his head.' It's worth saying that losing your head is what Jamaicans do best. On that island, not to lose one's head at every opportunity or feel a general sense of grievance at the world and everyone in it, would lead people to think you were not trying, not embracing all the possibilities of what it truly means to be a Jamaican.

Before Gillie Heron and Lindy Delapenha arrived in Jamaica in February 1952, soccer officials there began trying to put their house in order. They worried that Lindy and Gillie would find fault with all things Jamaican. "English playing surfaces are much different to ours" a Jamaican paper complained, "and Heron and Delapenha should be given some time to move with our boys, exchange ideas and tricks and build a team spirit in practice." There was something to this; but not much. They had both grown up on such surfaces and had become good, great even, on such surfaces. A more legitimate concern – you want to avoid using the word legitimate in the West Indies if at all possible – was what position would best suit Lindy and Gillie's particular talents. Lindy could be played at just about any position across the forward line. He could do a job for you at inside right, outside right, centre forward, inside left or outside left. You could play 'The Little Dazzler' anywhere. Gillie could play inside right and inside left if he had to. He preferred, of course, to play centre forward. But none of this would matter if the Jamaicans, the locals on the team, didn't pass the ball. When footballers from other places pass the ball, as a rule, Jamaicans will dribble with it. Back in the island from England, Lindy knew he was home when he tried but failed to convince a fellow player to pass him the ball. "The passing and that sort of thing never really came into our minds. Our interests was beating the player, beating the man in front of you, and dribbling. That was our idea of playing. We more or less play for ourselves."

The occasion of this Caribbean All Star football affair would be the first time Gilbert St. Elmo Heron had been back in his island in the sun since leaving, a down on his luck migrant, for the United States in 1939. That was 13 years before. He had been 17 then and a boy. He was almost 30 now; but far from a man. Jamaica was a blur. His family had left Jamaica in the way Jamaicans do: all of a sudden and without explanation. His mother, after walking away from her husband, went first with the oldest, Roy, who was 15 then, in 1935. Then she returned for the girl, Elsie, in 1937. Then it was Gillie's go in 1939. The others – Poley, Gerald and Cecil – took years to get to the US. They did not get through till 1945. Motherless and fatherless, the three had been growing up as Gentles with Grandpa and Grandma Gentles, their maternal grandparents, at 6 Portland Road in Rollington Town, in Kingston.

The Gentles of Rollington Town

Grandpa Thomas Gentles had been many things before he became a babysitter to his daughter Lucille Heron's kids. Born in St Catherine parish, he was known in Kingston as a shopkeeper. But when he had been in Port Maria, in St Mary, he had been in the banana trade and a key figure in the setting up of the St Mary Motor Company. Thomas and Emily had raised a large brood and could easily manage Poley, Gerald and Cecil and, for a time, Gillie, who remembers that his relatives were always away, out on the Big Sea. "Oh, yes we had aunts and uncles that kept getting the boats from Jamaica that would take my aunts and uncles up to America. Oh yes." The Gentles' brood included Charles, a champion cyclist, footballer and boxer, who began his family's fascination with America. Charles, known as 'Doctor' because of his big brains, went to New York in 1916, during the Great War, and was drafted into the US Merchant Marines. But buffeted by racism, this brown man became a keen follower of Marcus Garvey in the US and eventually returned home to Jamaica disillusioned and disgusted by the great land to the north.

Happy to be home, Charles began the Gentles Soap and Oil Factory on West Street in Kingston which, when he died young, caused no end of argument among the Gentles and Gillie's father, Walter Gilbert Heron, who claimed he had sunk all he had into it and had not been properly recompensed or properly recognised. He took Agnes Gentles, Charles' widow, to court, demanding 100 pounds. He lost the case and was ordered to pay 8 pounds and 8 shillings in costs for wasting the court's time with a frivolous lawsuit.

Like him, Charles Gentles' sisters, Alma and Minnie, went to America, too. One settled in New York and the other settled in Cleveland, Ohio, and quickly became a wealthy businesswoman and Negro society maven. A keen horticulturalist when she was in Jamaica, Minnie in 1917 opened a flower shop in Cleveland's Majestic Hotel, then America's finest coloured hostelry. The next year Minnie married Benjamin Harrison Turner, who had studied horticulture at Tuskegee. Once the two were one, they moved The Gentles' Flower Shoppe to Cedar Avenue in East Cleveland where it remained for 60 years. Minnie was canny and knew how to drum up attention for her flower shoppe. In July 1939, she drove up to Canada determined to see King George and his Queen, who were on a royal visit to the dominion, with flowers from the Gentles Flower Shoppe. Minnie, somehow, managed to sneak past the royal security cordon and present Queen Elizabeth with a bouquet of four milk white orchids with a purple throat, among the rarest and most expensive in the orchid family. Minnie's kindness – really her canniness – won her good write-ups in the Canadian, American and British press. "Mrs. Minnie Gentles Turner...recently made headline news when she presented a bouquet of orchids to her Majesty, Queen Elizabeth of Great Britain."

Grandpa Gentles was, rightly, proud of his brood. "If every man had as fine a set of sons and daughters as I have," Maas Tom once told a newspaper, "then their life will be a success."

Another of his brood, Inez, worked for awhile at the General Post Office in Kingston. Later she left Jamaica, like her siblings, for far off fields. Her travelling took her to France, Switzerland, Italy, Spain, and England, where she became a curator at a church in Buckinghamshire. Later, she became a missionary and went to Morocco to save Riffat Berber souls. She had quite a life on the road, did Inez. She skied in the Alps and swam in the Mediterranean.

Gwen Gentles, the youngest of the Gentles' girls, married Aston Benjamin Wilson and moved with him and their five children to Cleveland, where, when Aunt Minnie was ancient, Gwen took over The Gentles Flower Shoppe. Gwen should have stayed at home in Jamaica. Leaving the store one cold Cleveland evening, she was run down and killed by a 'hit and skip' driver, as they called 'hit and run' drivers then.

Randolph Gentles, a cyclist, footballer and all around athlete like his brother Charles, became a mechanic and planned to make do at home. But after he had some trouble in 1921 at the Palace Theatre in Kingston and was fined 10 shillings or seven days imprisonment, Randolph decided he would sail away from Jamaica as a seaman on the Big Sea, like his siblings.

Gillie and Cecil's mother, Lucille, tried the America thing many times. She didn't take to it immediately. She went up in 1916 and went home right after. She went up again in 1919. Still she didn't take to it. She took to Walter Gilbert Heron that year, instead, and married him in a mid-week service at All Saints Church in Kingston on June 4, 1919, in front of Reverend F.A. Bond. Her favourite cleric, Canon Graham, who had taught her the beatitudes when she had been a schoolgirl in St Mary parish, was there, too. The cleric spoke sternly about one flesh, not twain, and that what God had joined together let no man put asunder. But it was put asunder, but not by any other man, nor by any other woman. They did this all by themselves. Walter went up in the hills and Lucille went abroad. It made sense she should go abroad; so many of her siblings had done so and encouraged her to do the same. Besides, her ancestors, her forbears, knew all about the Big Sea. Some had, after all, come against their will on it from the Congo and some had come on the Big Sea of their own accord from Kirkcaldy.

This, then, was Grandpa Thomas Gentles' and Grandma Emily Gentles' brood, another piece of Baby Boy's; Scotty's; Gil's Jamaican family; another piece of the man. These Gentles, were used to saying so long to all of this and so long to all of that and setting sail. They didn't return home often, these Gentles. But they liked a fuss made over them when they did return home.

"MOTHER OF SOCCER STARS IN US HERE TO VISIT RELATIVES" the Jamaica *Gleaner* announced when Lucille Gentles Heron returned home in 1949 for a visit. Lucille's mention in the *Gleane*r was exactly the sort of welcome an expatriate, a humble seller of Forget-Me-Nots and Busy Lizzies in Detroit having a hard time abroad, liked after a long time away. The *Gleaner* said Lucille would be staying on the island for a few weeks and visiting family and friends and would be looking to see what improvements had been made there while she had been away. There had been no improvements at all at 6 Portland Road. It was as it was and Maas Tom and Miss Em were as they were. She asked after Mr. Heron, her erstwhile, once-ago husband. But there had been no improvements there, either. They were no more one flesh, but twain. What God had joined together they, by their own works, had put asunder.

It was Mother Heron's first visit home since she left aboard the *SS Colombia* with 13-year old Elsie in tow, for Cleveland, via New York, on July 27, 1937. She'd gone to start one of those new lives abroad, among the orchids, among the alocasias, in the land of Jim Crow. She stopped first, in Cleveland, at her sister Minnie's flower shoppe at 8920 Cedar Avenue, in the ghetto. She ended up, though, in Detroit among her own orchids and alocasias, in the ghetto. A Black American ghetto is a strange place for a brown Jamaican woman looking for progress to find herself. It was all this talk of progress, this promise of progress abroad, away from her recumbent husband, that made Lucille, who many called 'Rena', leave Walter Gilbert Heron. She knew, too, it was time to leave Jamaica when in 1935 she had to collect Gillie from the Rollington Town Police Station where the 13 year old had been taken after stealing a football. Next thing you know he would end up like Joe Gordon or some other Jamaican badman. It was time to set sail from her island in the sun, the one her people had toiled on since time begun. She knew that she would sail on many a sea but knew that island would always be home to she.

This island in the sun had been home, too, to Cecil Benjamin Gilbert Heron, another footballing Heron. He had been raised, pretty much, by the Gentles and had not wanted to leave for America when his mother finally sent for him. For him, the leaving hardly seemed worth it. He was 16 and enjoying his island. Cecil did not want to go to the US and would not, if he had his druthers, be among those soon heading to the UK, either. He didn't have his druthers. So no sooner had he been forced to move to Detroit than he began plotting how he would get back to his island in the sun.

When Gillie Heron arrived in Jamaica on February 16, 1952, Cecil, his youngest brother, and fellow footballer, was already there, on extended furlough from his regiment in the Royal Canadian Army.

Cecil was good but not as good, everyone said, as Gillie. It irked the younger brother that the older brother got all the headlines. But that's just the way it is when you're a younger brother and you have four brothers above you doing things.

When Gillie, who was the second of the Heron boys, went on to greater things it was usually Cecil who took up his leavings. He had followed behind him like Linus into schoolboy soccer and traipsed behind him into semi pro football in the American Midwest with the Detroit Corinthians after Gillie had gone on to play for the Chicago Maroons. Now, here Cecil was using his furlough to re-acquaint himself with his island and play a few games for his old team in Kingston, Kensington Football Club.

The Heron boys had grown up so close to the Kensington Club, across from Kensington Park, that the strike of cricket bat against cricket ball could be heard from their house on Portland Road. The Herons loved Kensington. But the club complained it had, like the island, been denuded. It had been divested of its people, people like Cecil Heron and his fine, big brothers. Too many, the Kensington complained, had gone abroad to war and not come back. Too many had gone to the 'Mother Country' and were colonising England in reverse. Too many, too, had gone all the way to America and returned only now and then.

Before the denuding and the divesting, the Herons – Lucille and Walter's boys and other Herons too – had helped enrich their island, athletically. There were all sorts of sportsmen among them. There was Donald Heron, a champion weightlifter. There was Leslie Heron, a champion tennis player and there was Mortimer 'Morty' Heron, the champion trainer of race horses. They bestrode the earth, the island, like colossus. The KC's, the JC's, the St. George's, all vied for them; not for their brains but for their brawn. That's how the Herons came to be attending Kingston College in 1934 when 14-year old Roy won the Sack Race at the school's reunion event. In April 1935, at the Interscholastic Sports championship, Gillie, a 12 year old, beat Herb McKenley in the 220 yard dash and was crowned the 'Little Champion.' The newspapers called him "Little Heron" and called him "that wonderful little sprinter." In 1937, he left KC for St. George's and in that same year won the school the Manning Cup and the Olivier Shield, too. They were famed for their brawn these Heron men; not their brains.

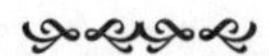

But praises for our past triumphs are, Eldridge says, as feathers to a dead bird. What was past was past. What would be was in front of Gillie Heron when he arrived in February 1952 at Palisadoes from Prestwick to play centre forward for Jamaica in a four game series against the Caribbean All Stars.

"The best players in Caribbean soccer will begin arriving on Saturday night to begin the historic tournament from Feb. 18 to March 1st", reported the Jamaica *Gleaner*. Gillie Heron felt good to know he was numbered among such men; the best. He was a professional. His father, Walter, had been only an amateur. Walter was, as were all Heron men, good at football, good at cricket, good at tennis, good at swimming and happy on a horse. They were awful, though, at being fathers, at being sons. They were awful at family and good at football.

"Heron, Lindy Soccer Giants." Gillie Heron had been used to feeling gigantic, large, magnificent even, and not feeling so in Glasgow had caused him to wonder about his will and his consciousness and his species-being. He'd not had cause to feel large or magnificent for a long time. He enjoyed that the Jamaica papers spoke about him in hyperbole. Hyperbole was the Jamaican way and he loved Jamaica for it. Heron knew, like Woodrow Lafayette Pershing Truesmith, that he was no conquering hero and that he should not be hailed for what he had done abroad in Glasgow. All Heron could hope was that people on his island did not read the Scottish papers or else they would discover that he was not, in fact, a giant in Glasgow, at all.

Many people believed, wrongly, that the 1952 series between Jamaica and the Caribbean All Stars was the beginning of inter-island and inter-colony football. But it wasn't.

The start of the game as it was known in the Caribbean ought really to be traced back to around 1890 and an English cleric who brought his passion for football with him to Jamaica.

The Reverend M.C. Clare, who came to Jamaica to be headmaster at the Church of England Grammar School in Kingston, began a general agitation for the advancement of football in the island. In 1891, Clare, J.W. Toone and Hicks began the Kingston Football Club. Others began the Winchester Football Club and the Clovelly; Public Offices; St Jago and the York Castle football clubs. Kensington and Melbourne's football clubs didn't begin until after the Great War.

By the 1900s, football teams from one part of the Caribbean region had begun playing football against teams in others parts of it. Trinidad and Tobago set up its football association in 1908 and almost immediately began a fierce rivalry with Jamaica. In December 1935, the two competed at Sabina Park in Jamaica for the Inter-Colonial Football title. They are not "better than we are at the grand old winter game" wrote Ken Hill, the Jamaican journalist and activist. But the Jamaicans were beaten by the Trinidadians, who memorialized their 1935 victory in verse.

Trinidad footballers Jamaicans tame,
If they want to learn the game,
Better come to Port-of-Spain.

In 1947, Jamaica was convinced it would get its revenge. But in the final game of the series, Trinidad fought back. It beat Jamaica 6-0 and forced a tie in the series, enabling the twin island nation to hold onto the Inter Colonial Football title. "Ichabod! We Get Worst Beating In Our History" the Jamaica *Gleaner* said. The loss led Jamaican poet Louise Bennett to put pen to paper in exasperation.

Six-three noh good, six-two is bad
Six-one wussara still!
Six-four hooda console me heart
But lawd missis, six nil!

Finally, on Saturday 23 February, 1952, it was time for the games to begin. The stands and seats at Sabina Park were jam-packed for the first game between Jamaica and the Caribbean All Stars. Jamaica was confident. But it was easily beaten, 5-1. It recovered, though, and won the second game 2-1. Heron scored twice. But injured, he did not play in the third game. Without Heron, Jamaica lost 1-0. He had, a paper said, been "sadly missed." With Heron set to play in the final game, Jamaica's only hope was to win the game and tie the series. "HERON returns today for final test at Sabina." It went as Heron hoped; a 1-0 win for Jamaica. The test series was declared a draw. The games, which a record 70,000 came out to see, were a boon for football in the Caribbean. At a reception, the Jamaica Football Association bigwigs thanked all those who'd participated, paying special attention to Lindy Delapenha. Jamaica should create a special post for Delapenha in the Department of Education, the JFA president, said. This way, Granville DaCosta explained, when Lindy was done playing football abroad, he could return home to instruct youngsters how to succeed in sport and most importantly how not to lose one's head. This irked Gillie Heron, who had played in three of the four games and scored four important goals for Jamaica. Yet, it was Lindy who received the special pullover with the JFA's coat of arms on it. Gillie got a trinket.

Gillie Heron had hoped to feel gigantic here on his small island. But he did not. He felt small. It was as it had been in Glasgow; he had done a job for them but no one thanked him for it. The Jamaican papers were not kind to him, either. G. St C. Scotter, the *Gleaner's* sports columnist, praised Lindy for laying the "foundation on which Jamaica improved her playing." By contrast, Scotter had only harsh words for Heron. "Gillie Heron brought down from the Scottish league where he is a pro with Glasgow Celtic did not fulfil the great expectations." The *Gleaner's* readers, too, were mean to him. One reader sent in a list of players he would include in an All-Caribbean football team. He left Gillie off of it. The reader picked Lindy as captain and though he included three other Jamaicans in the side, could not find a place in the team for Gillie Heron. There, in the midst of the cheers, you could see Gillie's tears.

Well, not all the Herons were in tears. Gillie's brother, Cecil, who had been in Jamaica to play amateur football for Kensington Football Club, led his team to victory in the Senior KO crown and helped his team win the 1952 All Island Championships, as well. The *Gleaner* was kind to Cecil, whom it described as "goal hungry Heron." The paper said he had led his team to victory like a "Trojan in attack and defence." The president of the JFA, who had seemed to snub Gillie Heron, paid lavish praise to Cecil Heron. Jamaica would miss Cecil Heron "who will unfortunately be lost to Jamaica soccer as he returns to the United States within another week", Granville DaCosta lamented.

With that, it was time for both Herons to say goodbye to their island in the sun. Cecil was off to rejoin his regiment in Canada and would later go on to Michigan State and make a big name for himself there and later, still, make a name for himself with volleyball in Jamaica and as a tennis pro at the Hilton Hotel in Ocho Rios.

Gillie was off, too, to Glasgow and to Celtic. After all, he still had a few months left on that one year contract the club had given him.

Mother and Child Reunion

"I did you wrong. My heart went out to play. But in the game I lost you. What a price to pay."

Smokey

So, that was that. Lillie Scott, nee Hamilton, of 453 South Cumberland Street, Jackson, Tennessee, was dead and buried and now Scotty would have to go on his way without her. If there was a consolation it was that Bobbie was home to stay. But she was just passing through. She had let Lillie deputise for her for 10 years while she sang alto and fiddled with the Dewey Decimal System and studied Spanish in Santurce. Now she needed a deputy again. William nor Sam Ella had kids – they were a burden to her body – so she deputised them, gave them the job. It's like Scotty always said: "People only ever came and got me when they absolutely had to, when they had no choice."

But Bobbie did have choices – too many choices – and she exercised them all. If she could have she might have left him for another 10 years. But Sam Ella and William, a Phys. Ed. teacher and a white collar worker, had people to see and things to do. So they said they could only do for six weeks what Lillie had done for 10 years. Bobbie needed, she said, to re-organise her life. She needed, she said, to get herself set up for single parenthood. But Scotty was her baby, and her 11 and a half year old boy, and they could not see why he could not be with her in Barranquitas, up in the mountains where the pretty

Puerto Rican people come from, instead of cramping their style at their shared place at 224th Street and White Plains Road in the Bronx.

Bright lights, big city
Gone to my baby's head.

He shouldn't have gone to the Big City, with its bright lights. He should have gone to Barranquitas and she should have taken him. He would have learned more there than he learned in the six weeks he spent at Paul Laurence Dunbar Junior High at 217th Street and Barnes Avenue in the Bronx. He would have discovered, for example, that Clara Lair was born there, Barranquitas, and that it was called the 'Cradle of Great People' for a reason. In the Bronx, he should have learned about Dunbar at Dunbar. But he didn't. It would have helped him to know that Dunbar, like him, wrote poems for the common man and, like him, was precocious and knew how to wear a mask that grins and lies, that hides our cheeks and shades our eyes.

The truth was, even then, aged 11 and a half, New York was killing him. He would be glad when the six weeks were up and he would be back, at 453 South Cumberland Street and at South Jackson Elementary School, with Bobbie who had finally, if reluctantly, come back home. She wasn't happy to be back home. He was. New York had been killing him.

While he had been gone big things had gone on without him. Though change was coming in Jackson it hadn't come quite yet. The buses had been desegregated before he left. But that's as far as things had got. Rather than allow both white and black to eat at their lunch counters, Woolworth's and McLellan's simply shut 'em down. So the sit-ins and economic boycott went on. On November 27, 1960, a week after Scotty left for New York with Sam Ella and William for his six week sojourn in the Bronx, a white man angry at the change going on all around him, was arrested for firing a 12-gauge shotgun into a Lane College dorm and for shooting into the car of a man he thought was black but who turned out to be white. "If I had shot you" the redneck said regretfully, "it was a mistake. I'd been shooting for a Negro."

While Scotty was having a cold old time in New York, black folk were having a hot time in Jackson. Father Christmas decided to skip white folks homes in Jackson that year because they had been naughty and not nice. Despite a two-month long boycott, Montgomery Ward, Kisbers and the other fancy stores on the east side of Lafayette Street still refused to stop discriminating. Unfair and unequal treatment was, they insisted, the Southern way. Black folks promised not to shop there until things changed and whites stopped shopping there because they were fed up of feeling awful for shopping there. When Scotty got back and started up once again at South Jackson Elementary School, change had not come. And when Bobbie got back from Barranquitas, where she'd been perfecting her Spanish and teaching English, change had still not come.

Bobbie Scott-Heron was a mother now, a full time, all the time mother now to Gilbert Scott-Heron. She gave birth to him in 1949, when she was 21, but didn't become his mother, really, until 1961, when she was 34. I guess it's better that it was late than it was never. Had Lillie lived forever, as Scotty hoped she would, Bobbie would have never gotten the chance to be a mother to her son. I can't help but feel that she would have, and could have, gone on her way without him. But she couldn't, as a mother and child reunion was forced upon her.

Whether he liked it or she liked it, he and her, the two of them, were a family now; a small, abbreviated family, but a family all the same. They were, the two of them, despite all, a family: people affiliated by consanguinity, affinity and co-residence. They got on like a family, too; which means sometimes they got on and sometimes they did not get on; which is alright because they were a family. Take, for instance, when, before she'd even packed out the bits and bobs she collected in her 10 years away in Chicago, Santurce and Barranquitas, she decided that though Lillie had done a good job, there was still a job to be done on the boy. He was doing okay, I guess, at South Jackson Elementary, but he ought, she thought, to be doing better. She had done better when she had attended South Jackson and had attended Merry High and Lane College, Bobbie thought. She had graduated magna cum laude from Lane. Gloria, an Alpha Kappa Alpha alum, Sam Ella, and William all graduated with honours, too. The Scotts had a tradition of doing well in Jackson's educational institutions and Bobbie expected this tradition to continue.

Though Scotty began reading at age 3, he didn't place much store in such things. He didn't believe that because a thing had been going on for a long while that it was necessary for it to continue going on. Tradition is a tricky thing. Some things are worth keeping. Other things we can well do without. Scotty thought, for example, semantic inversions and wordplay – which he claimed we brought over with us on the boat – worth keeping, but thought, for example, that whipping kids and cussing kids not worth keeping even though it had been a long-standing tradition.

This boy, Scotty, though he was in December 1960, only 11 and a half years old, was already a ferocious free thinker. If it didn't make sense it didn't make sense. His opinions were formed by science, by logic and by reason and were not influenced by authority, by tradition or by any dogma. The boy had free will. As such, he did not believe – though he sang in the church choir – that an omnipotent divinity asserts its power over individual will and choice. He believed individuals, him and his best friend Glover, who became a preacher, ought to be held morally accountable for their actions. These were big thoughts for a little boy. But this little boy had big brains. Yet it was hard for people, his mother among them, to see that in this fragile frame lived something gigantic. He was perceptive; understood things without explanation. He was well behaved; but he wasn't well disciplined. He was energetic; but he wasn't athletic, really. He did as well as everybody else; but could have done better, much better than them. He would probably have carried on in his under-achieving ways, intimidated by the cold precision of his mother, but happy in himself, his slightly off centre self, had it not been for all that was going on around him.

Gone With The Wind

"There was a land of Cavaliers and Cotton Fields called the Old South."

Margaret Mitchell

He hadn't realised in 1961, eight months after he returned to Jackson from his brief sojourn in the Bronx, that he would be called upon not simply to continue to go through the change, but that he would, actually, be expected to lead the change.

Sometime in the spring of 1961, those who gave a damn decided it was time Jackson started desegregating its schools. Jackson's city buses had been desegregated the year before and by March 1961, black people were able to sit down and eat at the Greyhound Bus terminal's lunch counter in Jackson mostly unmolested. So, it was time to see what could be done about the schools.

Gilbert S. Heron ended up, more by chance than design, in the front line. It so happened that he signed a petition, circulated in his school by the NAACP, saying he would be happy to strike a blow for freedom and transfer from his black elementary school, South Jackson, and attend a white junior high school, I.B. Tigrett Junior High, if given the chance. Dozens of other students from Jackson's three black elementary schools also signed the NAACP petition. They all wanted, like Scotty, to strike a blow against segregation in the South. But when push came to shove people found out exactly what they were made of. Most discovered that when push came to shove they weren't willing.

They had signed the petition, it turned out, just to sign it, just for the hell and for the fun of signing it.

But it wasn't a joke to J. Emmet Ballard, the NAACP's counsel in this part of West Tennessee. He was ready to file suit against the City of Jackson's school board to get it to comply with federal laws to desegregate. Lawyer Ballard ran a profitable practice in Jackson helping folks with the big and the small. A popular figure, Ballard had his hand in everything in Jackson. If there was a graduation, he was there delivering a speech. If someone was needed to offer fine words at a church, he was there enunciating and elocuting. Ballard had done a lot of good in Jackson. Lillie had cause to call upon him when she was around and Bobbie called upon him twice since she got back in town.

Assisting Ballard was the noted civil rights attorney from Nashville, Avon Nyanza Williams, whose first cousin was Thurgood Marshall and whose wife, Joan, was Arna Bontemps' daughter. Scotty would have liked Arna had he met him. He and the Renaissance Man had many things in common. Perhaps they would have talked of reaping or why you can't pet a possum or talked about W.C. Handy, who the old man loved and the young man would come to love. One loved Langston already and the other would come, in time, to love him and both of them really loved their maternal grandmothers a lot. Both of them, too, had an uncle important to them named Buddy. The old man of letters would have told the young man, had he met him, to seek the city he sought; to hold fast to his dreams and always believe that we have tomorrow.

It was hard to believe in tomorrow and hold on to your dreams if you were black and in the dear old Southland. Not believing in tomorrow made dozens of Scotty's classmates, who had earlier signed the petition saying they would be happy to transfer from their run-down, overcrowded black school to a white school with state of the art facilities, recant. Some persisted, though.

On August 24, 1961, C.J. Huckaba, superintendent of the City of Jackson school system, desperately trying to hold back the inevitable, sent a letter to Bobbie Scott Heron saying her request for her son, Gilbert Scott Heron, to be transferred from South Jackson Elementary School, an all black school, to Tigrett Junior High School, an all white school, had been "considered" but "not approved." Similar letters had been sent to Mr. and Mrs. Gillard Glover, the parents of 12 year old Gillard Sylvanus Glover, Scotty's best friend, who attended South Jackson Elementary with him, and to Mr. and Mrs. Frank Walker, parents of 13 year old Madeleine Carol Walker, a student at all black Lincoln Elementary who had attended school with Scotty at the all black Catholic school St Joseph's when they were infants. The fight wasn't over, though. It was just beginning. Their transfer denied, all three families appealed the decision. They were encouraged by Lawyer Ballard and Lawyer Williams, both of whom threatened to raise hell and high water down in Jackson and bring the SCLC and all kinds of out of town black folks, Jews, and the Yankee media in there. By September, white folks were waving the white flag of surrender. On September 8, 1961, Scotty, Gillard and Madeleine were all sent letters from Commissioner of Education R.L. 'Buddy' Patey saying their appeal would be heard by the Board of Commissioners on October 2 in the Assembly Room at City Hall. Whether what would be would be, or whether it wouldn't, was all the talk that Christmas of 1961 in South Jackson. On January 24, 1962, Bobbie and the other parents got the good news. "Mrs. Heron: Your appeal regarding the transfer assignment of your child has been considered by the Board of Education and by unanimous decision of said Board he is hereby granted transfer to Tigrett Junior High School." It was historic. Black children and white children would for the first time go to school together in Jackson, Tennessee.

"Tigrett School Enrolls Three Negro Students" read a headline in the *Jackson Sun* newspaper on January 25, 1962. The newspaper never ever featured black people in its pages and had done a good job ignoring the civil rights movement going on all around it. The paper didn't send reporters to cover the bus boycott nor the marches nor the sit-ins at the lunch counters, nor the boycott of downtown businesses that discriminated against black folk. This Tigrett School story, though, was one even the *Jackson Sun*, and white folks round about there, could simply not ignore.

Scotty, Gillard, Madeleine and their parents all arrived, as they had been told to, on January 25, 1962 at 8.45am at Tigrett, 15 minutes after school had let in.

Scotty had a head full of hair. Had he known he would end up in the paper – up on the front page – he would have had a cut. He had on his Sunday Best: that beige, patterned jumper; his best trousers; his best shoes; and that top coat with the big black fur collar. He had a scowl on his face. But Bobbie had a smile. She was dressed to the nines. She had on those fin-like witchy glasses that were all the rage then; a double set of large pearls; a big black bell coat and black pumps. You'd have thought she was off to the opera; not to face down rednecks who wanted to do harm to her one and only.

But they were not met by an angry white mob. No one spat at them or threw rocks at them or called them 'nigger' or told them to go back to where they came from. The naysayers didn't get a chance. The newcomers, to whom the final goings-on were revealed only the night before, arrived after classes began so as to ensure a mob would not mill around and fix for a fight. Tigrett teachers didn't get much notice, either. They were told minutes before classes began that Scotty and the others were on their way and that they were to be treated as well or as badly as other students were treated. School principal William Algea in his regular morning announcements on the school PA system let Tigrett's 661 white students know that their lily-white world in West Tennessee had gone with the wind.

R.J. Huckaba, Jackson's superintendent of schools, was not happy. He predicted no good would come of integration. White kids were smart, he said, and black kids were dumb; that was, Huckaba said, just the way it was and the way it would always be. This apparent difference in intellect was, Huckaba insisted, not because black kids attended schools that had inferior facilities but because they were simply an inferior people. But Madeleine Carol Walker, Frank Walker's kid, confounded Huckaba and his kind. Tested on her first day of class at Tigrett, she did very well, indeed. She beat out most of the class in a big science test and was revealed to be, much to the amazement of her white teachers and white classmates, 'unusually gifted.' Madeleine had no choice but to do well. Her father, Frank, a fierce advocate for equality, ended up losing his job as a drapery installer at Holland's department store in Jackson because he had refused to let anybody turn him, or his daughter, around.

And she didn't get turned around. Madeleine thought about Fisk but settled on Memphis State and stayed happily at home in Tennessee where she became a dietician. Gillard went off to law school in Boston and sold insurance and became a preacher in Florida. We all know, of course, what happened to Scotty. He didn't get turned around, either, not for a long time, anyway. But truth is, if you ask any one of them they'll tell you they did get turned around a little by being put in the front line at Tigrett. But this is the price that has to be paid when you want your folk to continue that straight and steady march up from slavery and off the plantation. Scotty and Gillard missed South Jackson Elementary and Madeleine missed Lincoln Elementary, even though a very nice white girl sometimes sat and ate with her in the lunchroom at Tigrett in a singular act of solidarity. "All three of us were complex; Gillard, Scotty and me. I'm not sure if we went in complex or came out of there complex."

But when you are Frank Walker's daughter you do not always do what is best for you but what is best. But Madeleine doesn't want to talk about that, that father and daughter stuff that goes down through the years. She wants to talk about how Scotty, who gave her a poem she has now lost, was then and not as he is now. "He is brilliant. He was always brilliant. He was ahead of his time. Remember to say that. Make sure to say that."

A couple of weeks after making history at Tigrett, someone from *The Crisis* – Dr. DuBois' journal – called. They were, the photo editor said, sending a photographer along to take some pictures of the history makers and desegregators. So they all met up – the Scott-Herons, the Glovers, and the Walkers – once more for the sake of history. The parents squeezed into a settee and the three kids stood behind it. Given fair warning this time, Scotty got a hair cut; a clean cut. What with his dark suit and white bow tie, the boy looked like he was one of them Fruits of Islam, a bean pie and bow tie brother.

After that, things went back to normal. Bobbie Scott Heron settled down to a job at her alma mater, Lane College, working as a secretary in the Health and Physical Education department part of the time and working as a Spanish instructor at the college the rest of the time. Bobbie was doing about as well as a black person could hope to do down there, Down South and maybe even Up North. Yet she felt sorry for herself. She'd thought she'd seen the last of the dogwoods and the yellow poplars and wasn't happy, at all, to be at home; if you could call down there home. When you've been, as you had always wished, a librarian in The Loop and a graduate student in Santurce and a teacher of English in Barranquitas, it's hard to be content with Down Home. Still, she spoke not too much of this and got on with things. She got busy at the Berean Baptist and liked that they asked her to solo and said they loved her alto. She got busy on campus, too, and sang at events put on by the Theta Iota and Kappa Sigma chapters of the Omega Psi Phi fraternity.

She and Scotty were like Julia and Corey. She was a single mother and he was a precocious pre-adolescent. Julia's husband, a fighter-pilot, had been shot down and killed in Vietnam. Bobbie's husband, a footballer, wasn't dead, but he was dead to her. Like Corey Baker, Scotty had barely known his father before his tragic and untimely death. Bobbie and Scotty's life was like a sit-com. There were Kodak moments and there were moments when it was best to go straight to a commercial. At least they were not alone. Andy Griffiths kept Opie busy so he didn't brood and become forlorn over his dead or missing parent. Ben Cartwright made sure his 3 sons, by 3 different women, didn't dwell on the strangeness of their circumstances too much. In Family Affair, Uncle Bill does his best by his dead brother's children. Strange how one of them ends up, in real life, dead of an overdose, anyway. Families do fuck you up; but they don't have to.

The truth is Bobbie and Scotty were lost in space. They each lived on a planet that remained undiscovered by the other. She had her sorority and her singing and he had his paper route, his piano practice, his detective stories and all the other good, and bad things a 13 year old boy has. Occasionally, there were intersections; very occasionally. She sang. He tried to sing. She wrote. He tried to write. There was too much of him in him and not enough of her. He was too much the athlete and not enough the artist; the serious artist. His teachers at Tigrett concurred. It didn't matter. He was planning on going back to black and going to Merry High School when he got done with Tigrett, anyway. But she was already making plans to leave again; this time with him and not without him. He would have preferred to stay. But she just had to go.

When word of their leaving got around, Mr and Mrs J.A. Cooke decided to throw Bobbie and Scotty a going away party. Bobbie had worked for awhile as a secretary for Cooke, who was a professor of Health and Physical Education at Lane. There was a full house at the Cooke place that Saturday July 16, 1962. The Shaws were there, as were the Brooks and many others to boot. It was a very polite send off from Jackson's very polite set. They snacked on fancy hors d'oeuvres and munched on mince clam and on assorted crackers, too. There was meaning in everything at the event, even the poinsettias and dahlias on the dining table. There were white dahlias, which symbolised 'dignity', 'good taste' and 'gratitude to parents' and summer poinsettias, which symbolised 'good cheer' and 'success.' Bobbie said she hoped she and Scotty would have all of the above up North. "So, where are you going? New York?" asked someone who already knew. "No" Scotty said. "We are going to the Bronx, to the Bronx Zoo."

Walter Gilbert Heron, father of Gillie,
Jamaica, 1914, aged 30 years

'Captain' Alexander Woodburn Heron,
Gil Scott-Heron's great great grandfather,
circa 1890

Gillie Heron (2nd from left in back row) with mother, Lucille, and
brothers and sisters, Jamaica, circa 1934

Gillie seated on ground far right, with St. George's football team, Jamaica, 1938

Gillie Heron, Canadian Armed Services, Jamaica Division, 1943

Gillie Heron playing in the North American Professional Soccer League for the Detroit Wolverines against the Pittsburgh Strassers, 1946

Gillie Heron on his debut for Celtic Football Club on August 18, 1951

Gillie Heron, back row, 3rd from left,with Celtic team-mates, 1951

Brian Jackson, aged 3, with his father Clarence, Brooklyn, 1955

Scotty - Bobbie behind him - on their way to integrate Tigrett School, Jackson, Tennessee, January 25, 1962

Scotty in the back row, left, Bobbie in glasses, celebrating desegregation of Tigrett School with the Glover and Walker families, April 1962

Brian, aged 16, with his mother Elsie in their Brooklyn apartment, 1968

Denis Heron and Gil on the road, circa 1978

Gil and Bobbie in her East Harlem apartment, 1999
(photo by Monique de Latour)

Gil and Gillie, backstage after Detroit concert, 1993

Gil Scott-Heron in performance, Paris, 1998 *(photo by Monique de Latour)*

Gil Scott-Heron, New York, 1997
(photo Monique de Latour)

Brian and Gil, Johannesburg, 1998
(photo by Monique de Latour)

Gil Scott-Heron
(by Nate Creekmore)

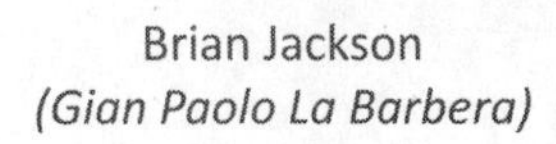

Brian Jackson
(Gian Paolo La Barbera)

Gillie Heron and daughter Gayle, Detroit, 2006

THE BLACK ARROW BOWS OUT

HISTORY MAN: Striker Gil Heron in action for Celtic in the early 1950s

Celtic's Jamaican hero dies

By John Ferguson

CELTIC hero Gil Heron – the first black footballer to play for the club – has died aged 87.

STYLISH: Heron playing pool in

Gillie Heron obituary, Scottish newspaper, Glasgow, 2008

The Sense of an Ending

"The thrill is gone."

B.B. King

When Scotty and Bobbie left Jackson, Tennessee for New York, New York in July 1962, Gillie 'Black Flash' Heron, his star dimmed, had been back in Detroit from his Great Adventure in Glasgow, which had not been so great, after all, for ten years and more. He had come back to Detroit a forlorn figure, to the factory and the foundry, the factory and the foundry.

Not once in his years back – 12 of them – did he come to see his baby boy nor did he ask his once-ago wife to send the boy Up North for a vacation visit or something.

Gillie had been a family man without a family but now had a new family, which included his Margaret, his Gayle and his Denis, but not yet his Kenny.

In between the factory and the foundry and his new family, Gillie wondered not about his old family but about football and what should have been but in the end was not. He wondered about going out from Glasgow to Jamaica, at the behest of the national team in 1952, to feel gigantic and coming back to Scotland feeling small. He wondered about what could have been in Glasgow, and at Celtic, but in the end was not.

He returned to Glasgow and to Britain in March 1952 from his six week sojourn in Jamaica to find that Celtic had slipped down the league table and was teetering on relegation. He had helped Jamaica eke out a draw in the test series against the Caribbean All Stars and felt, if given the chance, he could help Celtic, as well.

It seemed such a long time since the newspaper, the *People* had said, "The Black Flash has promising debut" and said "Celtic had found a player who would grace any team in the country." It had been such a long time since the *Daily Express* said "New Celtic Star- He's From Jamaica!" Since then, his day had turned to night. "Black Spot For Gil!" a newspaper said.

It had been so long since the press had said something good about him. He remembered how a Chicago newspaper had said after he joined Celtic that he had a "world of speed" and can "shoot them hard and low." The paper said his "ball control was good and he could dribble the length of the field when he felt the occasion called for a one-man effort." But the Chicago paper had also said, and this is what was troubling him now, that he had a bad temper. He wondered if his temper had held him back in Scotland as the paper claimed it had in America.

"Heron's soccer career in the United States was always in the limelight, and his critics were many, both good and bad" the paper said. "He learned his soccer in Jamaica, studied the rules religiously and even had some referee assignments there. It may have been this training that made him feel he knew the rules better than the referees in these parts. He continually had verbal run-ins with officials throughout the country which resulted in numerous suspensions. His inability to curb his tongue was the one obstacle which stood in his path of being labelled a great credit to the sport."

It's true; Gillie Heron had a temper. He was sent off for fighting with a Stirling Albion player in a reserve game and was suspended for a week. Fighting was added to a laundry list of complaints about the man. The Jamaican was weak and wan and not tough enough for the game was one. The Jamaican wasn't serious about the game, and didn't practice enough was another. The main charge, though, was he liked to drink, dance and party too much.

"We're talking about practice. We're talking about practice, man.
We're not talking about the game. We're talking about practice."

Charlie Tully, a teammate and sometimes friend and sometimes foe of Gillie's, complained that the Jamaican liked nothing so much as going on the town in Glasgow in "a pair of yalla shoes." This was rich coming from Tully. After all, Tully – known as the 'Cheeky Chappie' because he took whatever liberties he could – was no choirboy himself. Tully owned a bar – Tully's Bar – and was known to like a drink. John McPhail, the centre forward whose injury gave Heron a chance to play centre forward for Celtic also owned a bar. Patsy Gallacher, a Celtic legend who played for the team in the 1920s, also liked a good drink and a nice fight. He got so angry at a referee one time he waylaid the official after the game and beat him so badly the ref had to be rushed to hospital. Patsy was a bad boy but the good people of Glasgow loved him for it, anyway. Gillie wasn't loved for it. That's just the way it is when you are a black man in a white man's world. What is viewed a virtue in another man is viewed in you a vice. Minds are made up about you when they should be un-made, should still be open. It didn't take long, for example, for Sean Fallon, a teammate of Gillie Heron's who had taken him on the town when he had first arrived in Glasgow, to make up his mind about him. "He liked the dancing. He was one of those lads into music. He was more into music than football. I don't think he took the game too serious."

It's true that Gillie Heron liked the nightlife and he liked to boogie in the town. He liked to go where the people danced. He wanted some action. He wanted to live. But he didn't like the nightlife more than he liked the football. He liked nothing so much as the football. Gillie Heron liked the night life as much as the next man back then who had seen the world at war and who could not believe he had, somehow, survived it all.

"Look," Gillie said in a newspaper interview shortly after arriving in Scotland in 1951, "I don't want to stick my neck out, but why don't you guys enjoy yourselves a bit more? Here is a city about the size of Detroit, and it drops dead at 9pm. Why, over there (Detroit) that's just late afternoon; you start out to enjoy yourself about then."

Another charge against Gillie was he was not as tough as a man a shade over six foot tall and around 180 pounds ought to have been. "To be fair" said Sean Fallon, who was replaced by Heron at one point in the Celtic forward line, "he wasn't as fit as he should have been."

Newspapers complained that for a man who was accomplished at football, basketball, cricket, hockey, swimming and sprinting, Gillie Heron lacked "resource when challenged." One newspaper claimed the Jamaican, a former boxer, was "unable to transfer his pugilistic tenacity" to the football field.

It was also Gillie Heron's bad luck that he was not liked by a powerful group of his teammates: John McPhail, Sean Fallon, Charlie Tully and Jock Weir, all men who feared the Jamaican might overshadow them and perhaps take their place on the team. Gillie's teammates did not feed him the ball when they should have. They preferred instead to pass it around among themselves. "He just didn't get any support. And he was the sort of player who needed support" said writer Tom Campbell, who saw Heron play. We all need support. Just ask Gillie's wife and kid, left behind long ago as though they had not existed. He had rendered them invisible and he had now been rendered invisible, too.

Celtic should have loved him, as many times as he put the ball in the back of the net for the club. In the five games he played for Celtic – three League Cup matches; one Division 'A' league match and one Testimonial – the Jamaican scored three times; which by anybody's reckoning is a good rate of return. How many might he have scored had they let him play more often. He scored 15 goals in just 15 matches for the reserves, a remarkable scoring record. Had he been anyone else he would have won quick return to the first team with such statistics. But he was not anyone else; he was a black man in a white man's world and what was in another man a virtue, was in him a vice. He said as much in one of his poems.

Tell me sir,
Oh tell me true
Is there another just like you
A man who's skin is not so fair
A man who's persecuted here.

When he had first arrived at Celtic in 1951 Gillie Heron had been called a "broth of a boy" and a "golden boy" and hailed by a newspaper as "the greatest thing seen at Celtic Park since goalposts." But by May 1952 he could see his end at Celtic. "I may go home" he told a newspaper. "I wouldn't get the same thrill from another club."

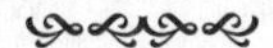

Beyond a Boundary

It had been a thrill being at Celtic. But that was over now. He had considered going home to Detroit, to Kenilworth Street and to the room in Lucille's rooming house, he, a big man, shared with this or that sibling. But he didn't go back where he had come from; well not immediately, anyway. He'd had to get gone from Celtic. He was released on May 27, 1952. He had to get gone from there; but didn't have to get gone from Glasgow. So he stayed around a while. Celtic had given Gillie a free transfer, which meant they didn't want anything from him nor anything for him. He was a free man, a free agent; but not in a good way. He didn't have to go home, but he couldn't stay there. He tried, in a poem, to say how much he cared.

And as my unpredictable world collapses
My dreams continue to be unanswered...
And so another day passes and I am alone
Thinking the things I always do
Wishing my only wish comes true.

He gave football a rest. It was the end of the season, anyway. He found refuge in a bat and ball on the other side of Glasgow at Poloc Cricket Club. Poloc had heard Heron was in town and could play cricket as well as he played football. He did well at Poloc as he had done, at cricket, for St. George's Old Boys in Jamaica and as he had done in the US for the Michigan Cricket Club of Detroit, an all West Indian agglomeration that included those that fetched and cleaned and those that were crisp and clean. There was a PhD; three auto workers; and a dog food tester. There was a professional whistler; a wrinkle chaser; there was a student of scatology and there was a student sent by an island government who was a student of nothing, at all. Sometimes the MCC batted a ball with other West Indians in Chicago and sometimes it went up to Canada to bat a ball with whites. It was a brief relief from their colour-coded American existence.

When Gillie arrived at Poloc in June 1952, already there was Laurie Fidee, another Jamaican who traced some of himself to yon bonnie, bonnie banks of Loch Lomond. It was Fidee, who had played for Jamaica and for Lucas Cricket Club in Kingston, who had encouraged Poloc to sign his countryman. Heron had been the only West Indian playing football in Scotland in 1951. But in cricket he was not a 'first' or an 'only.' He was one among many. There were so many Jamaicans playing cricket in Scotland, in fact, that a newspaper called it the "Jamaican invasion of the Highlands." Among them was R.L. 'Dickie' Fuller; Aston Powe; Irving Iffla; Donald Aitcheson and Laurie Fidee. They were the best batsmen on their Scottish teams. One ran up 1200 runs in a handful of games. They were the best bowlers, too. One took 47 wickets in a handful of games. "West Indians Outstanding In English, Scottish Leagues" a newspaper said. With people of his colour and from islands in the sun like his highly regarded in the game, Gillie Heron felt at home playing cricket in Scotland in a way he had never felt quite at home playing football in Scotland. There was no barracking from the terraces every time a shot went wide or every time a header went awry. There he had been the 'Black Flash' and the 'Black Arrow,' a poppyshow and a plaything. Who knows what would have happened if there had been a Laurie Fidee to help him feel at home at Celtic the way a Laurie Fidee had been there to make him feel at home at Poloc.

Gillie and Laurie formed quite a partnership at Poloc. Heron and Fidee ran up the runs and took the wickets in game after game against the likes of Drumpelier, Greenock and Ferguslie. The thrill had returned. "Footballer Gil Forces A Cricket Draw" read a headline. He'd suffered winter in Scotland, a time when the vultures circle beneath the dark clouds. But this was summer, and seeing the old sun shining through made him think that he could make it, too. He figured problems come and go but that sunshine seems to stay. He looked around and realized he'd found a lovely day.

He had been the only one when he had played at Celtic. Now he was one among many; a world of black men dressed in cricket whites. But it was not, in the end, his world. He was okay at it; at cricket. But he was no Worrell; no Walcott; no Weekes. He wasn't even, really, a Fuller or a Fidee, those who earned their living all the way away in Scotland because there was no living for them and their everyday talents in among the wickets and bails in England.

But though he liked cricket, where he was clapped politely by a few hundred, Gillie longed for football where thousands shrieked and bayed. Football longed for him, too. While he was away playing cricket for Poloc, the offers began pouring in from clubs that wanted him with them for the new 1952-53 season.

"Unfortunately, the trial promise was not fulfilled" wrote a paper of Gillie's unfulfilled promise at Celtic. "Perhaps the climate and the heavy grounds were to blame. But still several clubs – English, Irish and Scottish – were interested in him." An Irish club offered him 150 pounds to sign for them and offered him 9 pounds a week plus bonuses and other sundry pleasures as part of the package. An offer came, too, from Bradford City Football, an English club in the lowly Third Division. Bradford's manager, Ivor Powell, was very keen on Gillie Heron and promised to get the best out of him. Nicknamed 'Mr. No Nonsense', Powell was a harsh taskmaster who players said operated a 'rule of fear.' Maybe he could have been the father figure to Gillie that Walter Gilbert Heron had failed to be. But Ivor never got the chance. Gillie told a paper he "wanted to stay in Scotland" and would, in the 1952-53 season, play football at Cathkin Park in Glasgow for Third Lanark A.C., a club that, like him, had enjoyed early success but had been on the outs for awhile now.

It was not just the football that kept Gillie Heron in Glasgow. A girl kept him there, too. If you are a boy, it is always about a girl. If you are a girl, it is always about a boy. For Gillie Heron it was about football and about a girl, a girl he wrote a lot of poetry about.

The first time that I saw her
my heart did skip a beat
And boldly I approached her,
this girl I had to meet

Sometimes he told her that when his heart got lonely he wished for her and that when he was in need of love he wished for her and whenever he had a problem he wished for her. He wished for her. He wished for a smoke, too. And when he wished for a girl and for a smoke he went to the corner shop and there they both were: Rothman's; Player's; Benson and Hedges and Margaret. He liked to smoke and it was her job, 23 year old Margaret Frize, to sell him his smokes. Everyone in Glasgow knew already what Gillie liked in a girl. He'd outlined it in the newspapers for all to see.

"And the girls – Gilbert gets warmed up – the girls here are just as pretty as any place else. If they let you notice it. But, no! They dress up to please their grandmothers and nobody else."

Margaret Frize – one of five girls and a boy – did not dress up to please her grandmother. She dressed to please Gilbert. Neither was concerned that noted newspapers had warned that Cardiff, Bristol, Liverpool and Glasgow had become home to a 'Half Caste Problem' or that noted biologists had written papers on 'The Long Term Implications of Genetic Mixtures' or that he already had a wife and a kid back home; neither cared. He wasn't there. He was here where he was wanted by a girl and wanted by a team at Cathkin Park, on the other side of Glasgow from Celtic.

Third Lanark Athletic Club had, like Gillie Heron, enjoyed early success but had been on the outs for awhile now. He played his first game for his new team on August 9, 1952. "Hi-Hi-Hi For Heron" read a headline. He scored two goals and was declared "an instant hit" and praised for "scoring a dandy double." He won his second game, too, and was declared 'Man of the Match.' He attracted the attention of two big English clubs, Manchester City and Hull City. They offered to buy him from Third Lanark. But both were rebuffed by Thirds, who said Gillie Heron had a bright future at their club. But this bright future, as it usually did for him, soon turned dark. It wasn't long before he could not find the back of the net and wasn't long before Thirds' manager, Alex Ritchie, let Heron know he was no longer welcome at Cathkin Park and told him he'd have to hang his football boots elsewhere.

Gillie Heron had thought he'd done with the coming and the going. But here he was coming and going again. Celtic had, at least, let him stay there a year. Here he was now being told by lowly Third Lanark A.C., the season barely two months old and with everything to play for, that he should get gone from there. It was one thing being let go by one such as Celtic, but now even one such as Thirds was letting him go, to go where he was not exactly sure. The moment moved him to write bad verse.

What is there that's left for me
There's nothing left at all.
When my dreams all fade away
There's nothing to look forward to
But the closing of each day.
What is there that's left for me
A life that seemed so grand.

It looked again as if he would have to go home to America and perhaps to Bobbie and to his Baby Boy. But he didn't. He hung around Glasgow instead with his Margaret, waiting for the 1953 cricket season of silly mid-offs and silly mid-ons to arrive. He signed for Ferguslie Cricket Club and was confident that after the cricket season was over a football team would come in for him.

But no team of note did come in for him. Two English Third Division clubs – Torquay United and Workington – asked him to sign with them. But he declined and signed, instead, with a non league side, Kidderminster Harriers. It was a strange decision, governed entirely by the dollars and the cents.

Kidderminster, a Midlands town of around 20,000 then, was excited a big time player from Jamaica would be coming to their tiny hamlet. The local paper applauded the Harriers' executive Ted Gamson for convincing a player of Gillie Heron's stature to come play for them. "Mr. Gamson appears to have accomplished a good stroke of business."

Gillie didn't score in his first game, but he did score "two brilliant headers" in his second game. He scored, a paper said, "a goal worthy of inclusion in any FA text book." The way he controlled the ball, the paper said, was "masterly." Gillie Heron "went up like a panther to nod home a corner", the paper said. He scored a second goal which was equally impressive. "Heron jumped higher than the goalkeeper's out-stretched arms to steer home a perfect cross."

Gillie stayed at Kidderminster about as long as he stayed anywhere. He stayed a full football season, from August 1953 to May 1954. But like all his other stays, his time here was filled with unfulfilled promise. He rarely played. But when he did he usually scored. Yet, for all this, he was left off the Kidderminster squad more often than he was included in it. He ended up in the reserve team. It was a strange way to treat one of the team's top goal scorers. He knew his days were numbered there as they had been numbered at Third Lanark and before that at Celtic.

"Heron On Transfer List" the *Kidderminster Times* reported on March 12, 1954. "A surprise announcement by Kidderminster Harriers' secretary, Mr. E. Gamson, on Thursday, was that the club's Jamaican centre forward Gil Heron, has been placed on the open-to-transfer list." It was hardly the thanks he expected after helping the Harriers win a share of the Herefordshire Senior Cup and being Kidderminster's second top goal scorer. Nonetheless, Kidderminster Harriers announced at the end of the season that it would do away with most of its high priced imported players like Gillie Heron and depend, instead, on local lads who would cost the club nothing, really.

So that was that. Gilbert St. Elmo Heron's Great European Adventure was over. It was time to return home to America now. On July 18, 1954, as soon as the football season came to a close, he boarded the *SS Neptunia* at Southampton bound for New York. Heron had heard there had been a lot of change in America. He'd heard that in 1952 there had not been a single lynching anywhere in the United States. Wow! It seemed the country had grown up a lot while he had been away; which was nice to know seeing as he planned on, at some point, bringing back from over there, his Margaret.

Man-child in the Promised Land

"Our wrongs remain unrectified and our souls won't be exhumed."

Muse

It could have been anywhere; but it was the Bronx, Hampden Place in University Heights in the Bronx to be precise, that they were heading to. It sounded pretty enough. The 'Hampden' made one think of Hampden Park, the Scottish stadium Scotty's father had occasion to visit with Celtic. The 'Place' made one think of somewhere posh. It wasn't just a 'road' or a 'street' or an 'avenue'; it was a 'place.' But Hampden Place was not posh, nor was it pastoral. It was a cul-de-sac, dark and a dead end in more ways than one. There was only one way in and one way out. It was difficult, if not impossible, to get out of a place like Hampden Place, and University Heights, and the South Bronx, once you'd gotten in.

When Scotty had come to the Big Apple two years before, in 1960, after Lillie died and Bobbie had to get back to Barranquitas, his Uncle William, a public sector worker, and his aunt Sam Ella, a P.E. teacher, had brought their nephew with them from Jackson to the tiny place at 224th Street and White Plains Road they shared. Now, 2 years later, William was living on his lonesome on the 2nd floor of a University Heights 3-bedroom in a cul de sac called Hampden Place, a stone's throw from the Major Deegan and a stone's throw from the 207th Street Bridge which lay across the Harlem River and linked Manhattan to The Bronx.

University Heights, which got its name because New York University had been there before thinking better of it and moving off to Manhattan, liked to think of itself as in the West Bronx, wherever that was. But it was in the South Bronx, with all that came with that. There were twice as many school dropouts there; out of wedlock births; suicides; and addicts there than anywhere else in New York City. Half the people there lived on AFDC; on Home Relief; on Supplemental Security Income, on Medicaid.

The place had always been poor. It was poor when the Houlihans and the Rosenbergs were there. It was poor when the Odoms and the Jeters got there. It was poor when the Rodriguez and Gonzalez went there, too. The place had always been poor no matter who lived there. All sorts of people had called this place home over the years. Now it was the turn of the Scotts – William Scott; Bobbie Scott and Gil Scott-Heron – to call this place home. They weren't welcome nor unwelcome there. They were just there. They were nowhere, like everyone of every colour there.

If a person had come to Hampden Place looking for a better life it would probably have been best if they turn around and go back immediately from whence they had come. If, however, you had come because you had been given no choice in it then of course you had to stay, come what may. Scotty was such a person. Besides, he had already started becoming what he was going to be. For one such as this, one who had begun playing with words and playing with ideas, there is no better place in all the contiguous United States for them to be. The area had all that one such as he could desire to inspire and set his pallet afire. There were plenty of sistas who sure was fine before they started drinking wine in the bottle. There were gents in wrinkled suits that had done damn near blown their cool in the bottle. The place had the fire to inspire.

No one, so it seemed, could have come to University Heights on purpose. It had to be that they had taken a wrong turn, as people sometimes do. How Uncle William, who had been vice-president of his freshman class at Lane in 1948 and president of the sophomore class in 1949 and who had sashayed down the Champs-Elysees in the 50s with his white girl, and who had a tie and shirt job, found himself in University Heights in the 60s, is a puzzle. It was a puzzle, too, why Bobbie chose to join William there.

But the truth is anyone who'd been looking could see she had been desperate to get away from there to somewhere, anywhere. Jackson had no horizons. But this place had no horizons, either. It was one thing to leave Jackson. It was another thing to leave it for this. She'd had more than most folks down there. She'd had use of a house, long bought and paid for. She'd had a job at the college and a place in her church. She was somewhere. She left this to go to somewhere which was nowhere. But, I guess, she had to move on. She had to see tomorrow. She had to move on. She had to get ahead. She couldn't look back because there was nothing there but sorrow. She had to move on to get ahead, I guess.

As for him, him who had no choice in it, he wondered who now had his paper route and who was playing his piano and who was sneaking down his back hall at 453 S. Cumberland and if anyone was shelling peas on the veranda as Lillie liked to. Which one of the three bears, he wondered, was sleeping in his bed.

In some things, up here was like down there. Old people sat outdoors in the summers to catch some cool and kids played in the street and on the sidewalk. Up here the boys played stickball and punchball and the girls jumped rope and played potsy. Down there you had the Klan. Up here you had the gangs; gangs you sometimes had to run from like the Fordham Baldies or the Golden Guineas or the Ducky Boys.

Down there he'd had South Jackson Elementary and Tigrett Junior High. Up here he had Creston Junior High, up on 181st Street between Jerome and the Grand Concourse.

Creston

Creston, like University Heights, had all sorts: blacks and whites and other things in-between. Scotty had been a big deal as a 13-year old at Tigrett and his name and his likeness had appeared in the *Jackson Sun*, in *Jet* magazine, in *The Crisis* magazine. Up here he was the Invisible Man.

Before he'd had a chance to prove he could or he could not, minds were made up about him and his Tennessee drawl and his country 'bama clothes. Before you could say 'hey presto!', he was assigned to 9-5, the lowest academic grouping in the 9th grade and dumped into remedial reading. He dwelled there, in this sphere, our Black Bob Dylan, our Godfather of Rap, dabbling in amateur dramatics and making a little name for himself with a ball. In time he moved up from 9-5 to 9-2. It wasn't far up, but it was up.

He didn't know if he could have faced this new life, and put aside his old life, if it had not been for Sam Ella. Aunt Sammie was his most favourite Scott. The penultimate Scott; she was two years older than William and two years younger than Bobbie and four years younger than Gloria. She was the last of the Scotts, but one. Bespectacled and big footed, she was Big Bird before there was a Big Bird. It was Sam Ella, who was named for her father's father, Sam, and for her mother's mother, Ella, who took him to Yankee Stadium and took him to see Ebbets Field. She took him, though his mother would not have approved, to the racetrack, to her all-night rent parties and also let him see her speed on her motor bike. Sam Ella was his favourite Scott and though Up There wasn't Down Here, Sam Ella made it bearable.

DeWitt

After junior high school in The Bronx, it was time for high school in The Bronx. After Creston it was time for DeWitt. Had he been back home in Jackson he'd have gone to Merry High as his mother and his aunts and his uncle had. If he had gone to Merry he would, being him, have had a band of merry men following him around while he robbed from the rich and gave to the poor. But he wasn't back home. He was in The Bronx. So he went, as you did if you were a man-child in this particular Promised Land, to DeWitt.

Named after some big shit in the Big Apple, DeWitt Clinton High School had once been in Manhattan but was in The Bronx by the time Scotty came along. Back before when someone would have had to cross the Harlem River and go down onto Central Park to get to it. It was a big old school then and it was a big old school now. Back then it had 12,000 students, and was the biggest such school in the world. It never got small. When Scotty went there it was still big. Then, 4,000 boys looking to become men, attended DeWitt.

Scotty wasn't the only sensitive soul to be schooled there over the years. Bob Kane came up, kinda, with Batman there. Romare Bearden, kinda, came up with collaging there. Bud Powell came up, kinda, with bebop there and Sugar Ray Robinson came up, kinda, with boxing as a beautiful thing, there. Jimmy Baldwin had been to DeWitt, too. Both were lucky enough to have a teacher take an interest in their artistic expression when they were young. But Scotty was luckier. He, unlike Baldwin, was lucky his single parent knew he was a sensitive soul and so did not get him an insensitive stepfather, one determined to smack the sensitive out of him.

In time, they – he and Bobbie – moved on from Hampden Place and University Heights. Uncle William had already moved on and they were unable to afford the rent there. So Bobbie and Scotty – the

Mother and Child Reunion – moved onto Manhattan and their West Side Story.

They had come North from Jackson and were now going South from The Bronx to Chelsea, a place that had been known for its piers, its factories, its warehouses, its lumberyards, its rooming houses. It was a land, once, of Irish teamsters and Irish longshoreman. But by the time Scotty and Bobbie arrived there it was known for its Robert Fulton Houses and its Puerto Ricans. 'Little Ireland' became 'Little San Juan.'

Home had been Hampden Place. Now it was the Robert Fulton Houses, a mighty 6-acre public housing complex which stretched from 13th Street to 19th Street and stretched from 9th Avenue to 10th Avenue. Nine hundred and forty five apartments were spread throughout the complex's 11 buildings. Three of the buildings were 25 floors high and almost touched the sky. Bobbie and Scotty lived in one of these, in a 2-bedroom on the unlucky floor. And though it was Jose Feliciano's neighbourhood, Chelsea made a little room, too, for Scotty and for H. Rap Brown, who lived over on 18th Street and for Julius Lester, who lived over on 23rd Street and for Edwin Birdsong and for Richie Havens who lived in the neighbourhood, too.

It was over here on 17th Street, that he began writing about junkies, junkies walking through the twilight on their way home, junkies who left three days ago but whom no one seemed to know they were gone. It had already occurred to him back then that home was where the hatred is and that home is filled with pain and that it might not be a bad idea if he never went home again.

Miss Leaf, Miss Nettie Leaf, his English teacher at DeWitt, liked what he was writing and what he had to say. An educator of uncommon empathy, she took him on the way a good teacher takes on those who need to be taken on.. She arranged for him to be shipped out of

DeWitt, or 'Dumb-Wit', as some called it, with a scholarship, to Fieldston, up on the hill in the swanky part of The Bronx.

Fieldston

He, Leaf and Dr. Heller, the man behind the Fieldston scholarship offer, met at a Howard Johnson and mapped out the artiste's future. He would leave DeWitt and join Dr. Heller up on the hill at Fieldston.

Dr. Heller thought the young Heron was an excellent type for Fieldston which declared as its purpose the development of "individuals who will be competent to change their environment to greater conformity with moral ideals."

Scotty didn't know about all that, nor did Bobbie. What they did know was that this was the first genuinely good thing that had happened to them since they'd been in the Big Apple.

He was one among a handful at Fieldston. He counted five like himself there. He got an expensive education for free and Fieldston broadened its mission beyond educating bourgeois brats in The Bronx. He wasn't unhappy about it. He'd been happy to leave DeWitt and was happy to be at Fieldston. He was often late, but rarely absent and his quips made him a hoot and his small gifts on the basketball court made him a great sport. He was so popular, in fact, if his prep had had one, he would have been its Homecoming King. He worked on weekends doing what he would end up doing forever: playing music to amuse himself and playing music to earn some money to help out around the house.

The students loved him but the educators apart, of course, from Dr. Heller and the gym teacher, were not among his fans. His January 1967 Home Report shows this. His English teacher, Mrs Katherine Eastman, gave him a C+ and said he had ability but was ill-disciplined. "Gil, when treating a subject that interests him, writes with considerable vigour and pungency. This is particularly true of creative assignments. However, his range of interests should be extended, and he needs to accept the discipline of logical expository writing."

His History teacher, Mr Earl Clemens, who was black, tried to teach him about the past but he was more interested, Clemens complained, in playing the fool and amusing the white boys. Clemens warned Scotty that popularity, alone, would not take him very far in life. "Gil is tremendously popular with his classmates. But no amount of popularity can, for me, compensate for his not working up to capacity more often. His attention span is much too short – even at this grade level – and there has simply been too much frivolity."

Scotty's Sociology teacher gave him a C+ and said while he appeared interested in the study of society and how sociology could lead to social change, he was a poor test taker. "In class Gil sometimes seems to be an active participant, but on tests which require an organized presentation of the material we have studied, he has not done well." Gil, the broad conclusion was, does not do near his best.

He didn't do what could be called his best later at Lincoln, either. His mother and his uncle certainly didn't think so, anyway. In May 1967, it was over for him at Fieldston. But it was just about to begin for him, that September 1967, at Lincoln University in Pennsylvania, the US' oldest black college. He wanted to go there because he'd heard Thurgood Marshall, and Oscar Brown Jnr, and the first president of Ghana, Kwame Nkrumah, and the first president of Nigeria, Nnamdi Azikiwe, had all gone there too. He wanted to go there because Melvin Tolson, he of Hideho Heights, had gone there, and because Larry Neal, who lost himself in a jet stream of mad words, acts, bits of love-memory the summer after Malcolm, had gone there too. But he wanted to go there, most of all, because Langston Hughes, who had written about a dream deferred in the 1930s and was writing about

The Panther and the Lash in the 1960s, had gone there. He, like Langston, played it cool. He dug all jive. This was the reason, living as he did in rough, tough Chelsea, he stayed alive. His motto, as Langston's, was as he lived and learned, to dig and be dug in return.

And, though Langston did not seem angry enough for his generation, Scotty adored him all the same. He went looking for Langston when he was at Fieldston, to write a paper on him. He found him, in 1967, in Harlem. The old man was gracious to the young man and the young man asked the old man how it was he had come to master so many different art forms: writing poetry, writing songs, writing columns. The young man told the old man that when he had been a boy in Jackson he had looked forward each week to reading the old man's column in the *Defender*. The young man didn't tell the old man, though, that he, like him, had a strange relationship with his father or that home was where the hatred was.

Back then, Scotty was glad to go any place that got him away from home. It was becoming a place where the hatred was. For Bobbie, it was a burden working at the City of New York Housing Authority, which didn't pay much, and it was a burden paying the 73 dollars each month the City wanted for 13H, her 2-bedroom place on the 13th floor at 419 W 17TH Street in the Robert Fulton Houses. Her diabetes, which had only recently been diagnosed and had put her in a coma while Scotty had been out interviewing for a place at Fieldston, was a big burden, too. Scotty was her biggest burden, though.

A big bother for Bobbie was the way Scotty played, played with words. It was, frankly, frustrating for someone who had been well-schooled in the South and was stringent about syntax, about the Simple Present, about the Simple Past and who was picky about Past Participles. He was a budding black poet but she wasn't having it. After all, she was a kind of an artiste, herself. She'd sung some with a big city choir in the City of the Big Shoulders back in the day and had begun singing now with a big city choir in the Big Apple. She'd sung spirituals with Dorothy Maynard up at 145th Street and sung Handel at the Oratorio Society on Broadway. Oh, she wished she could be a full time alto and artiste. But all she was, really, was a part time and unpaid alto, and a full time, and poorly paid, pencil-pusher in the public sector.

But all this was her fault; not his. Any mis-steps she'd made were her mis-steps; not his. Any mistakes she'd made were her mistakes; not his. New York was nowhere, and she should have seen that. Besides, no one had stopped her being young and foolish when she had married that Jamaican and later gone off to Barranquitas and to Santurce. So why shouldn't he get his chance to be young and foolish, too?

Lincoln

There was no finer place for a young, gifted, and black man like Scotty to be young and foolish in 1967 than Lincoln University, which is around 100 miles south of the Robert Fulton Houses, 125 miles north of Washington D.C. and 15 miles from Philadelphia.

Everyone at Lincoln – almost everyone anyway – was as young and as appropriately foolish as their age and condition required they be in 1967. The world needed changing and they, Scotty and Brian – more about him later – were going to change it, demolish it and make it anew.

Scotty – he became 'Gil' at Lincoln – made himself anew, made himself as he wanted to there. Before this, at St Joe's; at South Jackson; at Dunbar; at South Jackson; at Tigrett; at Creston; at DeWitt; at Fieldston, he had been mostly known as 'Scotty' and sometimes known as 'Gil.' On official documents he, of course, had always, from state to state, been known as either 'Gilbert S. Heron or 'Gilbert Heron.' The Scott, the better part of him, had been, on paper, almost invisible. Before he began making the world anew he had to make his name anew. He made the 'Scott', which had always been relegated to a simple 'S', equal with the 'Heron.' He decided that as the Scotts were really his "primary family connect" and so this should be reflected in his name. "I have signed things since 1967 or '68 as 'gil scott-heron'". "I was identified and respected in Jackson as a Scott: 'Bob Scott's boy'. I was identified as though The Herons did not exist."

It wasn't long before Gil, who was elected president of the freshman class, was a legend in his own time at Lincoln. In between shooting hoops, writing poetry, playing pinochle in the Student Union building and attending the occasional class, he chased girls and led demos protesting the shooting of students at Jackson State College in Mississippi by National Guardsmen. He led protests, too, against Lincoln University's slow-walking, slow-talking Stepin Fetchit school administration: the honourable so and so's and honourable this and that's with B.A.'s from Morehouse, M.A.'s from Fisk and PhD's from Howard who were holding back the time, and, in fact, really didn't know what time it was, at all. Gil knew what time it was. That's why he, in his capacity as president of Lincoln's freshman class, invited The Last Poets, a young, gifted and black ensemble who'd been telling niggers to wake up and telling niggers they were scared of revolution, to perform at Lincoln in 1969.

He'd loved Lincoln but came to hate it. He loved that Saunders Redding was teaching him Negro Lit and that his Psychology prof was wild and into student power. He loved that he'd won the lead in a play and that his novel Coup D'état was going okay. He'd loved Lincoln but came to hate it because though the material was cool, a lot of the teachers weren't. He'd loved Lincoln but came to hate it, and other hifalutin black colleges like the one his hifalutin folk had attended, it was just a Nigger Factory that turned out self-hating, self-loathing

Negroes who held things back rather than pushed them forward. He had blood in his eye. He was a Soul on Ice. He was ready to Seize the Time. He was willing to commit Revolutionary Suicide. He was a guerrilla; not a gorilla. So he was at war with Lincoln as he had been at war – hot water and cold war – with just about every place he'd been. It had been a war to get him into Tigrett. It had been like a war over at Creston. DeWitt seemed always on a war-footing and at Fieldston he'd been in a war, a phony war, some educators claimed, with himself, his recently Get Out of The Ghetto gorilla self.

He was a guerrilla, he said, not a gorilla. So a guerrilla, naturally enough he was at war with Lincoln and with the Know Nothings who ran it. He believed brothers had been holding back too long and if they weren't blind they would see that it was time they ought to be coming on strong. He thought he understood the riddles of the ages, thought he understood the universal mind. He was ready, he felt, to place his footprints on the everlasting sands of time. He didn't believe, as Lillie had devoutly and Bobbie did diligently, in a Superman. There ain't no such thing as a Superman. There was, however, a Spider-Man. He was Spider-Man.

He was called 'Spider-Man' at Lincoln because he squeezed his skinny frame, night after night, through a barred college window so the Black and Blues band could sneak into the music department's rehearsal rooms and play music like in 'The Harder They Come'. Black and Blues, a band started by Victor Brown that he and Brian – more about him later – were members of, needed a place to practice so they could become more so than just musicians, bluesicians. Tired of clashing with the administration and satisfied his work had been done, and well done at that, he resigned his position as president of the freshman class, a post those who wanted to go into politics later, coveted. He wasn't interested in conventional politics or being president of the freshman class or even the United States. He was interested in poetry and music and interested in the red, 'bout the black and 'bout the green and singing 'bout the red, black and green.

The Life of Brian

Brian, too, was interested in the red, black and green. So, they decided to sing about the red, the black and the green, and other things, too, together, though they didn't necessarily see things, all things, the same.

For instance, Gil was a 'B' Movie and a We Beg Your Pardon, America kinda guy, a Paint It Black kinda guy, while Brian was A Prayer For Everybody To Be Free kinda guy, and It's Your World kinda guy. Brian believed, for example, that the ground beneath our feet was made for us, all of us, and that there was no one place that we belonged. He believed, too, that our spirit is free and that life is made for us to be what we want it to be. He believed you don't have to be lonely because in your world you are truly free and that the thoughts that fill your mind are a very special kind and that they are home to you and that we all have a home inside that was meant for us to be what we want to be and that this home does not, necessarily, have to be filled with hatred. Still, despite the differences, they both, Brian and Gil, believed the music of life filled their souls and that love made them feel whole.

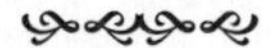

Gil was 20 and Brian, 'Stickman', 'Stick', was 18 when they met at Lincoln in 1969. One was a junior and the other a freshman. "We were best friends. We were actually brothers. I really was his brother" says Brian. They got each other and they didn't need a dictionary or a thesaurus. Brian says Gil and he were at their weakest, though, when it came to their families; in particular their fathers.

"He's an only child and I'm an only child. We talked about that a lot. We kind of felt that was a bond. We were both looking for father figures because at some point in our lives we had been missing father figures. It was important to us. It shaped our views of ourselves."

Both had attended funerals for their hearts. Both had eyes veiled by salty wetness and both had stood arm in arm with loneliness. Both, too, were convinced their epitaphs would read: "Love Forgot You."

Brian knew where Gil was coming from. He'd been there. His story was not so different. One day his father, Clarence Robert Jackson Jnr., walked away, too, from him and from his mother, Elsie Louise Jackson nee Bouie.

Their fathers having walked away, Gil and Brian knew all about walking away, too. They had great teachers. Both ended up walking away from Lincoln without ever graduating. Their fathers hadn't taught them much, but they'd taught them, at least, how to walk away, how to take leaves of absences, how to take incompletes; how to walk away. Gil walked away from Lincoln first. He wanted to take a break from Lincoln and write a novel, a novel about a bird, a vulture. The Dean of Men said he was crazy, crazy for feeling so blue, crazy for wanting to leave Lincoln for somebody new. He left, anyway, but not before seeing the school psychiatrist, who said maybe he was wasn't so crazy, so crazy. He left on a leave of absence and came back and then left again for good. Stick walked away, too. Having both walked away, they decided they would walk on the way of life together as more so than musicians, bluesicians.

Blood Is Thicker Than Mud

"Good fathers make good sons."

Anon.

Gayle Margaret Heron is a big girl now. But Gayle will always be her daddy's little girl. So, of course, she remembers the good he did and not the bad he did. She remembers when he was a hero and not when he was a zero. She remembers this one time when her daddy – when he was a young man on the streets of Detroit – stood up for someone he didn't even know and got beat down for his trouble. She says he was a good son, a good neighbour, a good husband and, most of all, she says he was a good father and that her father was not a stone, though his voice could sometimes be like gravel and his lips granite-white. He had, after all, been there, or at least been around, at her play-dates and her PTA meetings. She says he was always there. People who study these things say if he hadn't been there, she, Denis, and Kenny would have been smokers, would have gotten into trouble with the law, would have struggled at school, would have made poor choices in the people they took into their lives. They would have suffered all this had he not been there.

All Gayle knows is he took care of her. So she took care of him when his cerebral cortex was all but eaten away. She doesn't call it Alzheimer's or dementia but she knew her daddy was sick and that he was dying. "He is within his own memory." He took care of her so she took care of him. He smoked. She smoked. They smoked together. She knows, and he remembered, he used to be big in football and that he once out-ran Herb McKenley. "There are so many things he used to do." She wonders about the money he made or could have made. She never saw any of it. If there was any, it was gone by the time she, Denis, and Kenny came along. "We wouldn't be sitting here. We'd be somewhere else." All of this is speculation. They are here where they have always been, at Washburn, at Six Mile, in Detroit.

She never saw him play. But she did see him referee. She watched him tell white people what they could and could not do. "I remember the Arabs and white people always hollering 'get that nigger!' because daddy and his colour were not supposed to be out there ruling them, telling them, or blowing a whistle at them."

He was a hero, her hero, not a zero. She remembers he used to be a security guard and that one time he worked at the Jervis B. Webb factory and that he worked on the assembly line at Ford, where she worked too, and that he used to earn some change taking wedding and christening photos, too. People couldn't afford colour pics so he took them in black and white and he and his Margaret coloured them in with oil paints and paintbrush. Gayle remembers this. This Gayle remembers. She has good recall does Gayle. She does not remember or does not recall, though, hearing, early on, about a baby boy or a Bobbie. Nothing was said. If something was said it was not said to her. She didn't know, for example, she says, that her daddy had promised someone else, long before he met her mother, his Margaret, that he would have her and hold her from this day forward. She was in her memory, Gayle, but these things, somehow, were not in her memory.

Thank God for Gayle, though. If not for Gayle – in her family full of men – this man and that man might never have met, might never have deigned to meet each other, at all. It took a woman because they were men and men are mountains: impassable, unreachable. They met for her, not for them, not for themselves. That is what they told themselves. They didn't need to meet. They could have continued on this way forever without meeting. It was for her they met, they said, not because they needed to meet.

Gayle says she met him in 1969 when he was 20 and she was 15. But she is not in her memory. She actually met him in 1975 when she was 21 and he was 26. He was there, in Detroit at the Fort Shelby Hotel, to sing about the first minute of the new day.

It really was for him, back then, the first minute of a new day. He had signed in 1975 with Arista Records, a big new label run by Clive Davis. Davis had once been big in the recording business and wanted to be big in the recording business once again. Clive wanted to be big and wanted Gil to sell some records and be big, too. *Billboard* magazine believed he was going to be big and said Gil and his buddy Brian were making "exciting music" that would, *Billboard* predicted, make them superstars in 1975. It was the first minute of a new day and this is how he happened to be in Detroit, and happened to be performing there at the Fort Shelby Hotel, and happened to meet his sister, his half sister Gayle.

"His mother never told him about us. His mother never told him that his father had re-married and had another family. She told him he was an only child." This is not true. His mother did tell him about them. His mother did tell him his father had re-married. His mother did tell him his father had another family. She told him, her son, that he was the son of Gilbert St. Elmo Heron, who was the son of Walter Gilbert Heron, who was the son of Charles Gilbert Heron, who was the son of Alexander Woodburn 'The Captain' Heron, who was the son of Alexander Heron, who was the son of William Heron. She told him all this and more. She tried not to tell him, though, that not once did the father send the son a birthday card though his birthday fell on the same day each year. Not once did he send the boy a Christmas card though Christmas fell on the same day each year. He did not send the boy money. He did not send anything. He neither sent condolences nor did he send congratulations. He just didn't send.

But Bobbie made sure to send, though. She found an address, in the divorce papers, and sent, hot off the press, a copy of her son's volume of poetry, Small Talk at 125th and Lenox, and a copy of his novel, The Vulture, both of which were published in October 1970 when he was just 21 years old. When the Flying Dutchman company released a recording of Small Talk at 125th and Lenox, Bobbie made sure to send a copy of that, too. She was generous like that. She sent the Nat Hentoff review that appeared in *Jazz & Pop* magazine and which described her son as a "protean phenomenon." She sent St. Elmo the review from *Billboard* magazine which said her son – this one good thing they had done together – was "astonishing" and the 21-year old poet, novelist and songwriter, who also plays the piano and sings, has an imagination that is "sophisticated, literary, and formally compact." She sent the review from the *Chicago Tribune* which said her son's book, The Vulture, was a "pretty good book" and the author is a young man who "bears watching" because he "knows how to write a novel." She sent the Leonard Feather piece, too, from the *Los Angeles Times* which described her son as a "brilliant young poet-novelist." She sent him, too, the *Ebony* review from February 1972 which said of her son: "He is a genius and he is beautiful." She made sure, of course, to send a copy of the 1971 US Senate report on equal opportunity in education that mentioned "Whitey on the Moon", a poem written by her son and which she came up with the punch line for. "I think I'll sen' these doctor bills, Airmail special (to Whitey on the moon)." It made sense she came up with the punch line. She usually had the last word. Here, she had the last line. She didn't get a writer's credit. But anyone who knows her, and him, knows she should get some credit for his sardonic, sceptical sense of humour and that very singular way he has of seeing and saying things.

Anyway, the mother made sure to send the father, his new wife, and their kids, a copy of the 239 page Senate Select Committee hearing which cited her son and the poem he and she had written together. Bobbie could have had her own post office, she sent so many things. She didn't send, though, the *Washington Post's* stinging review of her son's book of verse which said his work dealt mostly with the seedy side of black life and is "not so much verse as a series of street raps" which, it said, had "short-lived power and intensity." She didn't send this one. She didn't like it but if she was honest, she agreed with the *Washington Post*. She did not believe their son's writing would last much beyond this angry moment in history. She knew things had to change. But she wasn't keen on a radical re-ordering of the Western cultural aesthetic and didn't accept that a Western aesthetic that had produced Handel and his Messiah, Debussy and his Nocturnes and Mendelssohn and his Elijah had run its course. She didn't know what Black Dada Nihilismus was and didn't agree that poems are bull shit unless they are teeth or lemons piled on a step. She was keen, though, to know how we judge a man. She had, after all, loved from her need to love; not because she had found someone deserving. She had, after all, come to understand that it was best to judge a man by his dreams, not alone his deeds and she had, after all, come to understand that it was best to judge a man by his intent, not alone his shortcomings. She, too, had sifted through ashes and found an unburnt picture.

There wasn't much that she liked about these new black poets and their new black poetry. She liked her son, of course, but did not like what her son had to say. There was just too much of the street;

too much Stackolee and Jimmy Reed in it and not enough Longfellow, not enough Poe. Bobbie believed, like Whitney Young, that Bach was more important than Bebop and that a poem was no place for cornbread and black eyed peas and watermelon and mustard greens. You'd never have thought the son had gone to Tigrett and been drilled to elocute and enunciate and been expected to go to Tuskegee or maybe to Meharry. She, like the *Washington Post* reviewer, felt his awareness/consciousness poems that screamed of pain and the origins of pain and death had blanketed his tablets.

She was selective, Bobbie was, in her sending. She sent St. Elmo only what put her son/their son, and the Scott's raising of him, in a positive light. She sent so much, in fact, that it began to wear on Gillie's wife, his new, white wife, Margaret, who, having come from Glasgow, was always up for a good fight.

"Hope Scottie's hair doesn't grow too tall" Margaret wrote in a letter to Bobbie. "Gil abhors the Afro Look." She wasn't lying. Gillie did abhor the Afro look. He didn't like the name and how it sounded so African and didn't like that Heron hair had the African kink rather than the European straight and thus would bush up and puff out. He had always tried to beat down and brush out and bash down his own rebellious and intractable kinks, this red man who thought he was a white man but was, in fact, a black man.

Bobbie had thought she knew St. Elmo. She hadn't. Twenty seven months is no time, at all, to know a man. Margaret knew him, and told Bobbie so when she asked if a copy of the 1947 *Ebony* magazine which featured the footballer after he became the first black person to play the game professionally in the United States, could be sent to her son.

"NO. We do not have the *Ebony* magazine you wanted him to bring you" Margaret replied. "He is opposed to Negro culture as a rule. His family is the same."

It's true. St. Elmo was never comfortable being called 'black' nor with the whole 'black thing.' It's true, his family, the Herons, were the same. They had a weakness for the white, for those void of hue and greyness. They, the Herons, appreciated the purity and the cleanness of whiteness. Leopold Walter Gilbert Heron married a white woman; Gerald Winston Gilbert Heron married a white woman; Cecil Benjamin Gilbert Heron married a white woman; Roy Trevor Gilbert Heron married a white woman and of course, after an early misstep, Gilbert St. Elmo married a white woman, too. They were only following orders, after all. Lucille Heron had made it clear that nothing black – I guess including her – could ever be any good. This Jamaica of theirs had given them an inner logic that had no outer sense. You were not simply 'black' there. You could be golden apple (peaches and cream); apple blossom (fair white); pomegranate (swarthy white); lotus (pure Chinese); jasmine (part Chinese); sandalwood (pure East Indian); all-spice (partly East Indian); satinwood (coffee and milk); mahogany (cocoa brown) and ebony (black). Out of many, these Jamaicans were certainly not one people. Theirs was a schizoid state of existence: inaudible, invisible and nameless. It was the psychopathology of colonisation.

It was complicated in Jamaica. In America it was simple. If you weren't white you were black. In America he was a black man in a black ghetto with a white wife and a white mask. He played a white sport. But he was black. He had a white wife. But he was black. They were nowhere. They had been somewhere when they were over there. But over here, they were nowhere. Who knows why he, St. Elmo and his Margaret, bothered to come back at all from over there to a place where their love was illegal in 29 states. But that's what he did when the football was over, over there. He came back over here. But why come back, at all? It wasn't long before he wished he hadn't and she wished she hadn't, too.

He came first, on July 18, 1954, aboard the *SS Neptunia,* from Southampton to New York.

She, still a 'Miss' because he was still a married man, came later. They would have to get used to this flying by night, this hiding in plain sight. They had to be careful. In Detroit, where they intended on living, living there, too, were 35,000 fully paid up members of the Invisible Empire, The Knights of the Ku Klux Klan. The KKK didn't like it but Michigan was one of the few states where miscegenation was permissible. Their love was not allowed, though, across the state border in Indiana nor in Idaho; neither in North Dakota nor in South Dakota nor in South Carolina; not in Nebraska nor Nevada nor North Carolina or in Alabama, Arizona, Arkansas, Utah or Oklahoma. Their love wasn't wanted in Wyoming or West Virginia nor in Mississippi, Missouri or Maryland or in Tennessee or Texas. Their love wasn't wanted in Colorado, Delaware, Georgia, Kentucky, Louisiana, Florida, or in Virginia. In more than a half of the states of the United States, their love was not only illicit, it was illegal. If, for example, he and she went for a drive south from Detroit to Indiana they could have been arrested and imprisoned for 10 years for their crime of passion and crime against God and nature. That's how it was over there, which is different from how it was where they had been. It makes you wonder why he came back, at all. President Harry Truman was to blame. In 1948, he ended segregation in the armed services and guaranteed fair employment in the civil service. In 1950, he helped begin the slow dismantling of 'separate but equal' and when the Supreme Court said, on May 17, 1954, that little black children and little white children could, and should, go to school together, St. Elmo decided, two months later, it was time to leave over there and come back over here. But while Harry S. Truman had a part in all this, he didn't want no part in race mixing, himself, no matter how cute the couple. "I don't believe in it.

Would you want your daughter to marry a Negro? Well, she won't love someone who isn't her colour."

This was what they were up against, our Gillie and his Margaret. When he had been a 5 year old boy in Jamaica, the American eugenicist Charles Benedict Davenport had come to research for a book called Race Crossing in Jamaica. In it Davenport hoped to prove that biological and cultural degradation had taken place in Jamaica because of miscegenation. Davenport, a student of craniofacial anthropometry, would have been intrigued by Gillie Heron's head. It would have appalled him, showing as it would evidence of both the Caucasoid and the Negroid. His head was of a doliochocephalic shape and, too, of mesocephalic shape. It had, too, a narrow nasal aperture and a wide nasal aperture and receded zygomas and a large brow ridge. Heron's head was like this because, as you know by now, he had a bit of the Scot and a lot of the African in him.

Who was black and should get back and who was brown and should stick around and who was white and so was alright, and who was the first love and who was the only love, was what went back and forth between Bobbie Scott Heron and Margaret Frize Heron. She and Bobbie, who would not let decree nisi become decree absolute, feuded and fought and squabbled and sniped.

"When I met Gilbert Heron in Scotland he was asked if he was married" reads a letter from the second wife to the first wife. "To the soccer officials and me he considered himself a single man. Therefore I didn't consider I was doing anything wrong by befriending him." Nothing was off limits in this correspondence. The second wife told the first wife that the day Gillie married her was "the darkest day of his life." The child, Scotty, was not off limits, either. "I'm sure by now you should realize Gil never visited you before to feed or clothe your boy...He denied the boy both to his family and me. He made the biggest mistake of his life when he married you." This is how it went on between the second wife, angry about illegitimacy, and a first wife, who had loved and lost and who would not, easily, let the man out of the marriage. She gave up on the man, eventually, but would not give up his name, and never married again.

But despite the fussing and the fighting, the bitching and the back-biting, Scotty – the child of the party of the first part – and Gayle, Denis, and Kenny, the children of the party of the second part – were glad to know one another. For them it was a family affair and, as you know, family is in the blood and blood is thicker than mud.

Gil had known of them, kinda, and they had known of him too, kinda. They knew he had lived for a time in New York and knew he had lived for a time in D.C. and was on the radio and on the TV and was famous for being young, gifted and black. He knew they lived in Detroit and knew they lived on Washburn and were almost white but not quite. Though blood is thicker than mud, it's just as well when he was in the Motor City for a show in 1975 that Gayle came a-calling because had she not he never would have, blood or no blood.

"I went to the show and told his manager that I was his sister."

"So you're his sister, huh?" the manager asked.

'Yeah, but he don't know about me. He's never met me before."

"So how are you his sister?"

"Because his daddy is the same person I have as a father."

The show over, she got up to leave. The manager said, "Wait a minute, I thought you said you were his sister."

"Yeah, I am."

"Then how come you don't go speak to him."

"I told you he doesn't know me. And I don't know how he's going to react to this."

"Just go over there and tell him."

"Gil", she said.

"Yes", he said.

"I hear that we're related."

"Ok. How are we related?"

"Through Gil Heron."

"Yeah. Ok. Now, how are you related to him?'

"I'm his daughter."

He fell back against the table and said, "What? That means that..."

"Yeah. I'm your sister." He grabbed her and hugged her and took her up on stage to meet Brian and the band. He told everyone "This is my sister. This is my sister."

"So I came home and I told my mother and she said, 'It's time he met his father.'"

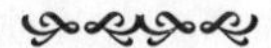

Gil thought he had done as Nietzsche had instructed: "Face life as you find it – defiantly and unafraid." He thought he had done, as Nietzsche had instructed: "Waste no energy yearning for the moon." He thought he had done, as Nietzsche had insisted: "Crush out all sentiment." He thought he had crushed out all sentiment, and remembrance of things past.

But then when Gayle took him, the long lost son to meet the lost-found father, her father, his father, he realized he had not crushed out all sentiment.

"Gil Scott-Heron, this is Gilbert St. Elmo Heron." The two had not seen one another since the one was one and the other was 28, in 1950.

Gayle came and got the son at the Fort Shelby Hotel and took him, driving through the light snow, to Washburn Street to meet the father. The son thought the father would be there to greet him. But he wasn't there to meet him. He was at work and was not going to take a day off no matter who was coming, even a long lost son. He arrived after dinner was done.

He was as he had imagined him: tall, caramel-coloured, cool and aloof. They talked but there were not a lot of words. There were a lot of 'hellos' and 'how ya doings.' There was no hugging and tugging; no holding back the tears that had been holding back the years. They were not, are not, warm and fuzzy these Herons. He was cool and he was cool. It was cool, just cool.

"It was like he met him but he didn't know him" the daughter of the one man and the sister, half sister, of the other man said. It had been too long. Too many years had passed. The essence of a black life had been lost in the hour-glass. "Here was a man" the half sister said, "who raised another family, but didn't raise him. He met him because of who he was, and that was that."

That wasn't that, not really. There was some back and forth over the years; not much, but some. But considering it consumed him, it was a surprise there was so little of it in his work, his writing, his songs.

He met his old man in 1975. His first chance to make mention of it in song would have been, I guess, a year later, in 1976, on *It's Your World*. But the only song about an old man on there is a song about the

105-year old Florida man Ed 'Possum Slim' Meyers, whose "righteous anger" drove him to kill and wound two people who robbed him. There was nothing, though, about *his* old man. Maybe it was there and I couldn't see it. He talked, instead, about being manhandled by media overkill, goosed by aspiring vice presidents and violated by commercial corporations.

It took years – two years after he met his old man on that Sunday in Detroit – for him to say something about it in song. "It was on a Sunday that I met my old man. I was twenty-six years old, Naw, but it was much too late to speculate, Hello Sunday, Hello Road." It wasn't a lot. But it was something. He said a lot more in *We Almost Lost Detroit*. The song's title is from the book of the same name by John G. Fuller which looks at the partial fuel meltdown at the Enrico Fermi Nuclear Power Generating Station near Detroit in 1966. Had there been a full meltdown, millions in and around Detroit, including the Heron family, would have been killed. *We Almost Lost Detroit* reflects, Gil said, his "concern for loved ones: My father, two brothers, sister and stepmother all live in Detroit." The nuclear plant stood out on a highway "like a creature from another time. It inspires the babies' questions, 'What's that?' for their mothers as they ride. But no one stopped to think about the babies or how they would survive, and we almost lost Detroit this time. How would we ever get over losing our minds?"

His half sister Gayle was 11 when the partial meltdown occurred and his half brother Denis was just 10. The youngest, Kenny, had been conceived but had not yet been born. He'd have lost them, and his lost-found father, had there been a full meltdown. He was hot about that.

Though he wrote about his new found family and his lost-found father in song, the father stayed cool, cool about him, and his former life and former wife. If the son had expected the father would give him a call, he didn't. If he had expected he would fly out to the house at

1927 Marthas Road where he and some of the Midnight Band bedded down in Hybla Valley, Virginia, he didn't. He just went on getting up at 4am and leaving the house at 5am and arriving on the assembly line by 6am. This was his life and he kept on living it as he had lived it all along.

Oh, they shared some things. He told him about growing up down South with Lillie, moving up North with Bobbie and how, even though he wasn't a big-time athlete or anything, he had played a little ball at South Jackson Elementary and at Fieldston, too. Then he, in turn, told him about his time in with the Detroit Wolverines, about his time with the Chicago Maroons, and about his time with Chicago Sparta. He told him, too, about his time in Glasgow, at Celtic. He told him about Charlie Tully and Bobby Evans and how he played against Rangers' Willie Woodburn and Willie Waddell. "It was something my father always wanted to do. He wanted to play against the best. That's what the people who are the best want to do. They want to compete against the best. So he went."

St. Elmo told Scotty about Jamaica and about Wigton and how his great, great, great-grandfather was a Scotsman and how this Scotsman had owned 600 slaves, among them Sabina, Apollo and Hercules. He told him he, like him, wrote poetry and that though Bobbie, his mother, had studied literature and taught literature and loved literature and he didn't read so much, it was likely he and not she he had got his writing bug from. He had been, he told him, a writer long before he had been a thought and an afterthought. He was not one of those rapping poets, going on about black this and black that and shooting lines and cuss words all over the place. He was, he said, an iambic pentameter man, a rhyme and reason man. He wrote about love and life and loss; not about the CIA, the FBI and COINTELPRO.

"When I first met him it was like I was meeting him as a footballer because that's what I'd heard about and that's what he was best known for. But he went upstairs and brought down some poems. I was very impressed." He shouldn't have been impressed and wouldn't have been impressed had the verse been by anyone but his old man. "It's great to be an American/And live in the land of the free,/And have the rights and freedom/That's meant for you and me." He was deadly serious. Any irony was unintended. "It's great to be an American/ And see the stars and stripes/take a walk along Fifth Avenue/See Broadway all in lights." There were more poems; none for his first wife. Almost all were for the second wife. "It's been a very long time/Since you and I were wed,/It's been many sweet and loving years/Since our final vows were said./I've lived a rich and fruitful life/And I'm happy as can be,/ I have a sweet and lovely wife/ Who's so in love with me."

He wrote a lot of poems; but none about Scotty. He wrote poems about the Olympics, about great Scottish footballers, about Desert Storm; but none about Scotty. He wrote poems about Christmas, about Pope John Paul, about King Arthur's knights; but none about Scotty. He wrote about anything and everything, really; but none about his first born. Roethke wrote about his son, The Lost Son. Silkin wrote about his son, Death of a Son. DuBois wrote about his son, The Passing of the First-Born. But he wrote nothing about Scotty, his first born. He wrote a poem, though, for his parents, whose disagreements were dragged through the streets of Kingston and whose eventual divorce made it into the pages of the *Daily Gleaner*. "Having been driven away and deserted by my wife Lucille Isabelle for over three years, I do not hold myself responsible for her or any debts she may contract. It is my intention to marry at an early date, signed Walter Gilbert Heron, Hartlands, P.O." Why these people, Lucille, who ran roughshod over him, and Walter, who abandoned him, deserved verse is anybody's guess. "I sometimes often wonder/How my life would really be,/Without the good and beautiful things/My parents gave to me." Scotty could not say for sure what his parents had given to him. Wherever it was he had gotten his way with the word, it was not from his father, from the Heron side of him. "So for future generations/ The one thing I'd love to see,/Is the attention and love from parents/ As my parents did for me." But this was not true. His parents had not done anything for him and he, in turn, had not done anything for Scotty. His poems had no wisdom about them, except one, The Mouths of Babes. "It seems from early childhood/They love and even hate,/These tiny little children/Whom the Master did create./Out of the mouths of babes/Who try to show the way,/Of brotherhood and fellowship/ We'll learn from them some day."

The father learned nothing, really, from the son. He did learn, though, that if he put the name 'Gil' and the name 'Heron' on a book of verse someone would want to publish it and maybe someone would want to buy it. No one knows if anyone did buy any of the books but Aaron Peal, a small publishing house in Detroit, published I SHALL WISH FOR YOU all the same. "INTIMATE! ANGRY! PROVOCATIVE!" it says on the cover. "An anthology of Expression; Intimate and Revolutionary." The son might have been a revolutionary, but the father was certainly not. The truth is he abhorred the Afro and was opposed to Negro culture as a rule. His family was the same. Yet, the back cover of the book says the father "expresses outward antagonism of most of society's norms." There was nothing normal here. The child was father to the man. And though the father had not written any poems for the son, the father found use for him in his book. "Not unlike his son, world famous poet/activist Gil Scott Heron, the anger in both works, both poetic and oratory, motivates either disdain or acceptance, or both." He hoped a book with the name 'Gil' and the name 'Heron' on it would motivate acceptance or, if it didn't, at least it might make him some money or win him some of that fame his big son took for granted. Like his son, he was a performance poet. He put his voice and his verse on a cassette to what his publisher called a "pulsating Island' beat." The father never had much use for the son. But at least he had found a way to make some use of him.

The son, once he had met the father and spent some time with him, did not have much use for the father, either. He did, though, make use of his father, or the father figure, in his early work. In those poems and songs, the father often appears as a victim, a person put upon by prejudice who cannot, through no fault of his own, fulfil his responsibilities to his family. "Told my old man to leave me when times got hard (so hard)" he says in *Who'll Pay Reparations On My Soul?* "Told my mother she got to carry me all by herself. And now that I want to be a man (be a man) who can I depend on, no one else." Abandoned by his father, he is in solemn and searching mood, too, in *The Prisoner*. "I need somebody, Lord knows, to listen to me, I'm a stranger to my son who wonders why his daddy runs." Gilbert St. Elmo Heron was a great runner, as footballer and as father. The father having run off, the boy has to make it, in the poem *The Middle of the Day*, on his own. "There is no one here to guide you, you've got to do it by yourself. Go and tell your daddy he was right in what he said, cause the laws of independence don't apply until you are dead, though you like him here to push you cause you feel a need for him." He needed him and so, in *The Needle's Eye,* went to see him. "They seem to carry all their feelings, crushed and crumbled up inside, inside, inside, inside, so I went to see my father, many questions on my mind, but he didn't want to answer me, God, the whole world must be blind. Him who don't fit through the Needle's Eye, him may someday go insane, insane, insane, insane." He didn't quite go insane but his yearning remained the same. "And though it's been too long and, too many years have passed, and though the time has gone, the memories still hold fast. Yes as strange as it seems, we still live in the past, the essence of a black life lost in the hour-glass." What he really wanted was an unbroken family and someone to sing him a lullaby as in *Your Daddy Loves You.* "Now sweet lil ol' brown eyed girl, hey, now, Now that you're sleepin', I've got a confession to make, Of secrets that I've been keepin', Me and your mama had some problems, A whole lotta things on our minds, But lately, girl, we've been thinkin' that we were wastin' time, Nearly all the time, and, Your daddy loves you, Your daddy loves his girl." This is the way he would have liked it to have worked out: an argument, a disagreement and reconciliation. But it was, instead, abandonment, separation, and divorce.

Scotty could write, and so he should have written more about what ailed him, what nagged and ate away at him. He wrote some things. But he never said enough. He never told the whole truth and nothing but. He should have said more. Isn't that what poets do? Some do. Billy Bragg, 'The Bard of Barking', has that lovely song for his father, Tank Park Salute, in which his dad kisses him goodnight after he says his prayers and leaves the light on at the top of the stairs. Horace Silver, of course, wrote that song for his father and Luther Vandross wanted simply to dance with his father again. These are okay, in their way. But it's the songs about the bad dads that are the best. Take, for example, Randy Newman, who wanted his dad to hurt like he did. "I ran out on my children, And I ran out on my wife, Gonna run out on you too baby, I done it all my life, Everybody cried the night I left, Well almost everybody did, My little boy just hung his head, And I put my arm around his little shoulder, And this is what I said:, 'Sonny, I just want you to hurt like I do, I just want you to hurt like I do, I just want you to hurt like I do, Honest I do, honest I do, honest I do.'"

It's not that he said nothing. He did say something. In the poem, *Coming from a Broken Home* he talks about his grandmother and his mother – but not his father. He says his "life has been guided by women" and "because of them", he says, "I am a man." He says, "womenfolk raised me and I was full grown before I knew I came from a broken home." He was sent down South, he says, to live with Lillie, who was not a "typecast Black grandmother", until "this was patched and 'til that was patched" in his newly single mother's life. "I HAD NO STRONG MALE FIGURE! RIGHT?" he declares defiantly. He does admit, though, that "too many homes have a missing woman or man" and that "maybe there are homes that hurt." He hurt but could not, would not, say so. His tribute to those raised in broken homes is a defensive tribute, at best; a thumb of the nose to "all the ologists, hypothetical theoretical, analytical hypocritical." Yet, elsewhere he says "taking babies from their mamas and leaving grief beyond compare." He is a running man. "My life is one of movement, I've been running as fast as I can, I've inherited trial and error directly from my old man. But I'm committed to the consequences, whether I stand or fall...My life's been one of running away, just as fast as I can, but I've been no more successful at getting away, than was my old man." He could not outpace his demons. "The thing I fear cannot be escaped, eluded, avoided, hidden from, protected from, gotten away from, Not without showing the fear as I see it now, Because closer, clearer, no sir, nearer, Because of you and because of that nice, That you quietly, quickly be causing, And because you're going to see me run soon and because you're going to know why I'm running then, You'll know then, Because I'm not going to tell you now." In *The Other Side*, which he said was not about him, he calls on his father to save him. "I'm saying, I don't want to call him, I don't want to know him, I don't want to need him, I don't want to know, I don't want to know but I know." He knows he is a Heron, a son of Gilbert St. Elmo Heron. "I was and am a Scott-Heron. I am also the son of Gil Heron. No doubt. Placing me along the lines of those who preceded me was easy enough, but tracing the facets of who and what was responsible for which of my assets and debits were inherited from which direction was more difficult. Because the subjects were not available to testify and be observed and the witnesses at hand were all prejudiced either for or against. So, as a spindly-legged youngster I made my faults and factors all mine." He tried to make his faults and factors all his. Some were his. Some weren't.

"My mother and my father had problems, but I didn't have any problems with either one of them. So I admired her and what she was trying to do. I admired what he had done and how well he did it. I think the best is all you can do. That's all anyone should be able to ask of you."

So that's how it was with Gil and Gillie. They were strangers in the night exchanging glances. One earned his money on the assembly line and liked corny, processed-headed Arthur Prysock singing Your Body Makes Eyes at Me, and could not see why black was beautiful. The other was known as the 'Black Bob Dylan', rented Roberta Flack's old house outside D.C., loved Jimmy Reed singing Bright Lights, Big City and wanted to paint it black. One sported an Afro. The other abhorred them. One loved Black culture. The other could not abide it. One was an alienated black man and the other a dis-alienated one. Both were pieces of a man. They shared a name; nothing else. Both promised to keep in touch, but never did. Once in awhile he called to speak to his sister or to his brothers; but never to speak to his father. Once upon a time there had been so much he had wanted to say to the man. Now that he had met him, there was nothing for him to do but put it in a song.

"It was on a Sunday I met my old man.
I was 26 years old.
Naw, but it was much too late to speculate.
Say, hello Sunday, hello road."

Me and Baby Brother

"Me and baby brother used to run together."

War

It was Gayle who found him. But it was Baby Brother, Denis Walter Heron, who was 19 when he was 26, who he felt most at home with. It was Baby Brother who was most like family to him and who really got to know him, for awhile at least.

Like all Herons, Denis is watchful. Like a Heron he has a natural suspicion of those of us who are not Herons and even of those who are Herons. Where others hug and tug, Herons stare each other down like gunslingers. In this, their bird namesake would not recognise them. The heron is, as a breed, essentially a communal, social creature who builds strong bonds of trust with one another. Unlike herons, Herons are inclined to disperse after breeding. They usually migrate, leave, at night, so as to avoid the drama and the disappointment. In this, their bird namesake would not recognize the Herons. By contrast, herons are monogamous creatures who often mate for life. Walter and Lucille called it quits. Gil and Bobbie called it quits. Gil and Brenda called it quits. That's a lot of calling it quits. It's clear these Herons don't know how herons are supposed to behave.

They might not have known how herons are supposed to behave – you know, be communal and be social and be together forever, but the Herons sure looked like herons. Baby Brother, who was 19, was a tall, long necked beast like his father. Denis is, of course, the Great White Heron: yellow legs and white plumage and Gil would be the Black-Crowned Night Heron because he is darker. Gayle is the Night Heron. She is stocky, short necked, and short legged. But, be they light or dark, be they tall or short, they are all Herons.

Gil and Denis

They got along instantly; well, not instantly but almost immediately. Actually, it took quite a time for them to warm up to one another. To avoid talking about what they should have been talking about, they talked sports and talked music, instead. They talked about the Mets and the Tigers and the Jets and the Lions. Eventually, they got around to talking about having the same father but different mothers. It's not easy talking about that stuff. They discovered – him 26 and him 19 – that they didn't mind being around one another. It was cool. So cool in fact that Gil asked Baby Brother to be his Moriarty and come out on the road with him, where he would experience what it meant to be a man among men and what it meant to be young and American at a time when so many people who were young and American were asking what it meant to be young and American. Bliss was it in that dawn to be alive, But to be young was very Heaven!

He didn't see himself at Ford and longed to get away from his father, Ford, the assembly line and the stale, meagre, and forbidding ways of custom, law, and statute. America was a country in romance! He took him not to favoured spots alone, but through the whole Earth.

"You can't be far enough away from Detroit, dude! We're talking about Detroit. I knew people in Detroit who said they had gone to Holland and saw all these tulips and people who had gone to China and seen the Great Wall. I sat in awe of all those places. I wanted to go to all these places, and smell them, and see them."

It was what the father feared would happen: his boy had been stolen from him by his boy. Denis had found in his father only the facsimile. In Gil, he had found the actual thing.

"I don't see you at Ford."

"I don't see me at Ford, either! The thing was that Gayle and Dad were there for a long time. I worked on the morning shift with my dad. He would get up every morning at 4; go downstairs and make coffee and at 5'o clock he would come into my room and say 'are you going today' and that meant I had fifteen minutes to scramble around, bump into doors, and get myself together and get into the car because he wasn't going to be late. This was the life."

This wasn't the life St. Elmo had sketched out for himself. There was a time when Detroit was actually the place to be. It had solid jobs and solid benefits. They made things there, American things. But he was stubborn. Even when Americans didn't want to buy the things made in America, in Detroit, anymore he wouldn't move, wouldn't hear of it, wouldn't concede that perhaps he had to make a few corrections in his directions. Even when Twelfth Street and Clairmount went up in flames in July 1967 - 'It was a Black Day in July'- he wouldn't move. So it was a relief when one day Gil called Denis and said: "I got a spot on my road crew if you want to come and hang out. This might be worth your while." It was worth his while. It lasted from *Secrets* to *Moving Target*. His father had regaled him about all of the places he'd been, but he didn't go to the places they went to. If this was intended as revenge, it was the best revenge. It was insidious and undermining, it was in the bone and it ate away at them.

"I think he was somewhat resentful of it because this was a part of his life that he'd kept us away from. And they were surprised that I took to Gil so well. They kept telling me: 'You can come home if things aren't comfortable.' I said it was cool and had more fun than any 24 year old should have. It was insane. It was insane."

He came aboard the 'MB 13', the Midnight band bus, a few weeks after Gil, Brian and the band had been on national TV as the special guest on Saturday Night Live of Richard Pryor. It had been a good show. All in the Heron household on Washburn, and the Scott household at 106th Street and 2nd Avenue, stayed up till 11.30pm to see him sing something political, Johannesburg, and something personal, A Lovely Day.

It's strange how he ended up on there. Gil knew Richard's work but didn't know Richard. Richard didn't know Gil's work but had heard he was the big, black poet who had turned down a chance to appear on the Johnny Carson Show and told the late night host, who rumour had it had disowned his own black grand-daughter and disinherited his son, to go fuck himself. What had really happened was Roberta Flack, a friend of Gil's, had told him she was scheduled to guest host the Carson Show and wanted him to perform. But when Roberta didn't get her promised chance to guest host, Gil told the show's bookers that he wasn't interested in appearing on the show without Roberta. This impressed the shit out of Richard, who'd heard about it on the entertainment grapevine. He called Gil up. "Are you the man who didn't go on the Johnny Carson Show because Johnny was gonna *be there*?" Gil said: "I hadn't really looked at it like that." Richard dropped the phone, screaming with laughter. "Look, this is Richard Pryor," he said. "When I heard you weren't going to go on because Johnny was going to *be there* I thought it was the funniest thing I ever heard." He told Gil he would soon be appearing on the new late night comedy sketch show Saturday Night Live, and would like very much for him to appear on the show with him. When Richard said he planned on dedicating the show to the history of black people in America, Gil said: "Well, if you're gonna be there I'll do it."

Big Brother and Baby Brother

He liked having a brother. He called Bilal 'brother' and called Barnett 'brother' and, of course, he called Brian 'brother.' He called everyone 'brother.' But Denis was actually his brother – a half brother; but a brother all the same. He liked the word 'brother' and never neglected to use it in a song, a poem or some prose. He used it 45 times in Small Talk at 125th and Lenox; 76 times in The Vulture and 124 times in The Nigger Factory.

This thing he had with Baby Brother was his first real unvarnished chance to know his old man and all that his old man was about. Denis told him some things. Other things he didn't get into. He could see no profit in it. All that had happened in the now years and the maybe years in the Windy City in 1948, 1949 and 1950 between a country girl in country-girl college clothes from the Hog and Hominy state and an island guy in yellow shoes from Jamaica, by way of the Motor City, was from his father's other life. His father's life had really begun, as far as Denis was concerned, in 1951 when he was in Glasgow and when he met his mother, Margaret, who sold him his smokes. Bobbie was behind him then, and so was Gil, too.

When Gil wasn't singing, writing or reading and Baby Brother, who was first a member of the road crew then the band's road manager, wasn't putting up this or taking down that, they talked. Baby Brother told him how he had been, for his family, his father, their father, the great hope. He told him how, because he was Gil's son, he did everything: soccer, track, baseball, and basketball from 8 years old to 15.

St. Elmo had done all those things and so he, his son, had to do all those things, too. Gil wondered if he would have measured up. He was a three sport athlete at South Jackson. But that was only Elementary. His father, their father, was, he found out, a rough tough taskmaster. It was good to hear this. It was good to hear his father wasn't the father from the Cosby Show or the father from the Brady Bunch or the father from Father Knows Best. It was good to hear he was more Fred Sanford than Cliff Huxtable; that he was more like Frank Gallagher than Mike Brady. It was good to hear Baby Brother had not had a warm and fuzzy childhood and that his father, their father, had not been a warm and fuzzy father.

"I tried to constantly tell him he was a rough taskmaster; that it was not a fun childhood. When we would have those moments, he used to quiz me and say that I'd lucked out and got to grow up with Gil and stuff like that. He felt as though I got something that he didn't. What he didn't understand, which I tried to explain to him, was that it was a challenge and a difficulty. It wasn't a bed of roses." He tried to tell him that though he'd not had his dad, he did have his mother. "I think he lucked out in that his mom was brilliant, her articulation, her eloquence. She was smart, well-read and had an approach to things. I tried to tell him that." Bobbie was always good – generous and loving even – to Baby Brother when he came by her place in New York and Margaret was just as good to Gil when he came by her and Gillie's place in Detroit.

The Big Brother liked that his Baby Brother thought of Bobbie like that. It was nice to hear that stuff about his Mom. But he would still have liked to have found out whether his father was warm and fuzzy for himself; by growing up with the man. He would have liked, no matter what Baby Brother told him, to have played ball with the man; played catch with the man; flown a kite with the man. You know, all that corny father and son shit you see on American TV. But that's how it gets started. You are out together, just flying a kite for fun, kicking a ball for fun and somehow, somewhere, things get dark, primal and competitive. You didn't kick the ball hard enough. You didn't throw the ball straight enough. One time, Baby Brother ran the 60 yard dash for the City of Detroit at the Youth Games when he was a 10-year old. "I got second and thought it was pretty good. My dad said what happened? Did you have a bad start? I said 'Dude, I'm the second fastest kid in the fucking country!' It was a rough and tumble childhood and many times the father certainly did not know best. There was that other time Baby Brother got kicked out of Little League when he was 10 or 11 because St. Elmo punched out an umpire. "It wasn't pretty."

Sometimes you learn more from the bad than from the good. Baby Brother learned a lot and now he nurtures, not criticizes his own. He has made sure not to yell, speak harshly or get into any of that extracurricular stuff.

"That segment and intensity of my life is not going to carry over. There are certain things you take from your parents and you carry on and you think these are good and positive things. There are other things that you are going to just stop. This will not be a tradition in my family. The intensity of anger and literal hostility and violence, I don't see that. It's taken me all this time to control my temper."

This is not how Gil imagined it. He was glad now that his mother and grandmother and aunts and uncle hadn't answered him when he had asked them about his father, his Pops, over and over again. It was better that this kind of thing come from a Heron and not from a Scott.

Sometimes it's best we do not know, do not know who we are, really are, and where we come from, really come from. Sometimes the best thing you can do is do better. Gil did not do better. As a father himself, he ran as fast as he could and claimed the reason for this is he inherited trial and error directly from his old man. "I'm committed to the consequences, whether I stand or fall."

Those who loved him, and this includes his kids, cared whether he stood or fell. There's Rumal; there's Gia; there's Nia; there's Chegianna. They cared. There's his ex-wife, his ex-fiancé, his ex-girlfriends. They cared. His ex-wife Brenda, who starred in *Mandingo* with Ken Norton and with Jim Brown in *Black Gunn* and married a black banker after the black revolutionary, cared. His onetime fiancée Lurma, who was born the same year as him and the same month as him and worked as press secretary to Marion Barry and defended the mayor almost as fiercely as she defended Gil, cared, too. His ex-girlfriend Monique cared. She designed the covers of some of his books and tried to intervene and did so much more. She cared, too. She wanted him to get help when it could have helped and told him he'd had lots of opportunities to be better but didn't seem to care to be better.

Though he didn't always understand it, or think he deserved it, people cared about him. Not caring for him is not why Baby Brother, Denis, his road manager, left Gil, left the road. He left because of how he was as a man, an imperfect man, who really didn't give a damn. He'd always had a problem with discipline; that's in part how he made his name, as a rebel against established authority and outmoded mores. Getting to a place on time, when you said you would, and doing what you promised you would, is not an outmoded more. He'd always been tardy and unreliable. But after Stick left and after his thing with Brenda went west and after his thing with Arista began going South, he lost all sense of caring, of giving a damn. He started not turning up for shows, for interviews, for anything. The road manager, Baby Brother, just couldn't manage. "I started looking for an out and after too much of this, in 1983, I packed up and moved back home to Detroit and then later settled in New York." There was a time when he and Baby Brother couldn't stop talking. Then, one day they stopped talking altogether.

Me and baby brother
Used to run together

Come back, baby brother
Come back, baby brother

Brian's Song

"You got everything; and so much of it."

Peggy Olson

They were brothers before he really knew he had a brother, Brian and him. They weren't a comedy act, but if you knew them you could see a certain humour, and tension, was derived from their uneven relationship. Most people thought 'Stick' - Gil had called him that as a tribute because he had stuck to him like no one ever had – was the straight man. But Gil was the straight man. He was the funny man, too. He was greedy like that.

Sometimes they seemed like Hope and Crosby or Morecambe and Wise or Abercrombie and Fitch; inseparable. But they were really Martin and Lewis, and would end up angry and alienated from one another like Martin and Lewis. They were like Burton and Taylor, and would end up angry and divorced from one another like Burton and Taylor. What they were, really, was Piccolo and Sayers. Stick was Brian Piccolo to Gil's Gale Sayers; except Gil was the one who ended up sick and dying. The way Stick sees it, he is Roebuck and Gil is Sears. The way Stick sees it he is Pippen and Gil is Jordan: both made a contribution, but only one got the credit. The way Stick sees it while Gil is acclaimed the 'Black Bob Dylan' and the 'Godfather of Rap' he has not been acclaimed, at all. The way Stick sees it; he is Watson to his Holmes. He is Engels to his Marx. And, you know, he's not wrong. Both made a contribution. But only one got the fame.

It's true. There has been a tendency to give it all to Gil. But some have known better. "Scott-Heron's work presaged not only conscious rap and poetry slams, but also acid jazz, particularly during his rewarding collaboration with composer-keyboardist-flutist Brian Jackson in the mid and late '70s", The *Washington Post* said. *The Observer*, too, has given credit where credit is due. "Together throughout the 1970s, Scott-Heron and Jackson made music that reflected the turbulence, uncertainty and increasing pessimism of the times, merging the soul and jazz traditions and drawing on an oral poetry tradition that reached back to the blues and forward to hip-hop. The music sounded by turns angry, defiant and regretful." Just like the two men, themselves.

At first they were complementary like amoeba and paramecium or like cytosine and thymine. Later they were like, like-charges that repelled not unlike-charges that attracted. As anyone knows, all particles are surrounded by other particles that are shadow versions of themselves. All these particles will, eventually, collide and create a kind of pressure that drives the ordinary particles apart. We'll get back later to how they were driven apart and why Gil felt the need to call Stick a "motherfucker" and told some scribe that someone should have "pushed the mute button on him a long time ago."

"Now, more than ever, all the family must be together
Every brother, everywhere, feels the time is in the air
Common blood flows through common veins and the
common eyes all see the same
Now, more than ever, all the family must be together."

Anyone who paid attention to the stars in the sky, would have seen it coming. Gil, who paid a lot of attention to such things, was a fire sign, Aries, the sign of the self, and was thus supposed to be hard headed, impulsive and egotistical. Stick was an air sign, Libra, the sign of partnership, and was thus supposed to be a peace maker prone to indecisiveness. It was in the stars. They were polar opposites, six suns apart in the zodiac. Still, they were convinced opposites attract and that together they could turn weaknesses into strengths and minuses into pluses and deficits into surpluses. They were great artistes but poor economists. It was in the stars.

Still, though the two had their bad times – long, awful bad times – the two had their good times, too. He was 20 and he was 18 when they first met at Lincoln in 1969.

"We spent so much of our time hanging and talking about what was going on: about life; about being a young black man; about growing up; about love; about everything. We talked about everything and it came out in our music."

And it is "their" music and not just "his" music. The thing was collaborative. It's as Malcolm Cecil, the record producer and synthesizer master, said: "Gil is primarily a poet, secondarily a vocalist, thirdly a composer and fourthly a musician." Stick was the opposite. He was primarily a composer, secondly a musician and thirdly a vocalist. For the most part, Gil brought the lyrics and Stick brought the music. Brian would usually have some chords, some notes ready. Gil would ask him, 'what's the feeling, what were you feeling when you wrote that song, or what is it that you're trying to say?' When they worked on *Free Will* he asked him 'what is freedom? How do you get it and what does it really mean?' Stick says Gil was brilliant in that he could take a feeling and elaborate on it with words and build it into something that was amazing. It was the same with *Or Down You Fall*. "This was about having to show different faces and what kind of masks do you have to wear in order to survive. I think one of the most telling lines in that is, 'go away, I can't stand to see your face because you've seen the weakest me.'" Stick says Gil and he were at their weakest when it came to their families; in particular their fathers.

"He's an only child and I'm an only child. We talked about that a lot. We kind of felt that was a bond. We were both looking for father figures because at some point in our lives we had been missing father figures. It was important to us. It shaped our views of ourselves. We considered ourselves loners, on the outside of society. We liked that. I liked it. I liked the idea of being an observer more than a complete participant. You get to be very comfortable being alone. So much so that when you're around other people you enjoy being alone."

So it was a shock when they – Brian, Gil, and The Midnight Band – were in Detroit in the winter of 1975 to perform at The Fort Shelby Hotel and the father Gil knew he had, but had not seen in 25 years, turned up.

"Gil was very excited because his half sister got in touch with him and asked if he would like to meet his father. He was 26 years old. He was very ambivalent about it. He was scared to death. He was angry that his father had gone on and started a whole other family. He was angry he never contacted him. He was angry it took 25 years to meet his father and he was only a few hundred miles away, basically in Detroit."

Stick's father, Clarence Robert Jackson Jnr., had walked away, too, from him and from Elsie Louise Jackson nee Bouie, so he knew where Gil was coming from.

"It wasn't that different. My father and mother divorced when I was five. I remember the thing he said to me as he walked out the door. He knelt down and said, 'take care of your mother.' I remember this. 'Take care of your mother.' I knew, I knew he wasn't coming back.

The way he said it, there was such an air of finality. The only thing I wasn't sure about was whether I'd ever see him again."

He did see him again and it didn't take 25 years. He saw him every other week or so. His father moved to Harlem, to 127th and Broadway. The boy, Brian, as is the custom among us, was raised by women; by Elsie and by her mother Annie Elsie Bouie nee Black. Annie's husband, Freddie Thaddeus Bouie had, like her daughter's husband, Clarence, gone away, too. No, not out for sugar but to his grave, in 1938, the same year Joe Louis knocked out Max Schmeling in the first round of their rematch, the same year Hitler was chosen by Time magazine as its 'Man of the Year', and the same year an aurora borealis, which some claimed looked like a "a curtain of fire" and others said looked like a "huge blood-red beam of light", appeared in the skies across Europe. That was the year, 1938, that Freddie Thaddeus Bouie died, so, the quacks said, of 'arthritis.' This is how Stick, or Brian to his folks, came to be raised by women, as is our way, because the men had gone away, somehow, somewhere.

So the women gathered and they took Stick and made a nice home for themselves at 2308 Beverley Road in Flatbush across the street from, wouldn't you know, the Sears & Roebuck. Clarence had agreed to pay 27 dollars a month for his boy's upkeep and for his boy's lodgings. He did and he didn't. Unable to afford Flatbush, the boy and his mother moved to Crown Heights, to 985 Park Place, just down the block from Freddie Hubbard and Louis Hayes, and around the corner from Olu Dara, Nas' old man. Every other weekend or so, his father would make the journey across the Brooklyn Bridge.

"He would just sit there and read his paper. I felt like an obligation to him. He'd come around 10ish and if the weather wasn't good, he'd sit in my room. And I'd tell him what was going on and he'd kind of grunt and read his paper." It wasn't always like this. There was fishing sometimes and they played ball sometimes. They did all the stuff, in fact, fathers and sons do when they are trying to be fathers and sons. Sometimes they got in the car and headed upstate. Sometimes they went out and had a munch for lunch. Some of the time there were good times. But good times can't be all the times.

Clarence Jackson was better as a friend than he was as a father. As a friend and a man-about-town, he was top notch. "He was the guy that would crack everybody up at a party. 'Jack', they called him. He was a hoot. Around me he wasn't a talker. At a party, you couldn't shut the guy up. I'd hear him sometimes around his buddies cracking everybody up, laughing. I didn't really get too much of that. I didn't see much of that."

They had their moments, though, the father and son. Sometimes, during home visitations, as they call these court prescribed events, his father – a parole officer – would let him play with the gun he carried to protect himself against parolees with a grudge. "I used to think that was so cool. A couple of times he used to empty the chamber and let me try to shoot it. I didn't have the strength to pull the trigger. It wouldn't click." It was cool, too, the time when his father picked him up by his heels and held him upside down. "One day I swallowed a pin and my dad's first reaction was to pick me up by the ankles and shake me upside down to try and get it out. My mother said, 'what the hell are you doing?' There was some panic, some caring there."

Clarence Robert Jackson Jnr. wasn't much better, really, than Gil's dad. But at least Stick's dad was there. His uncle, Ralph, a cop, wasn't much better, either. Uncle Reggie was the only salvation. The black sheep of a family that favoured jobs in law enforcement, Uncle Reggie had a lot of fancy ideas about freedom, actual and artistic. He was to the Family Jackson, a flake; a flake who loved jazz and had gone abroad to Denmark, of all places, and had, of all things, brought back a Danish wife, a sweet, sticky thing. "My family was weird and maudlin and morose." Some of the Jacksons – no not those Jacksons – were afraid of art and artistes; didn't trust it, didn't trust them. Stick's grandfather, Clarence Robert Jackson Senior, who worked as a cab driver for 65 years, never trusted it and told him so.

"Me and Gil were at the height of our popularity and had just played at Carnegie Hall. He said, 'that's really great, that's really great. But when are you going to get a job?' I said, 'Pop, I just played at Carnegie Hall. I always get paid.' He said, 'Yeah, you're getting paid now. But what about 15 years from now?'"

Stick's dad wasn't like this. He loved art and artistes. When he wasn't carrying a gun and watching over parolees, he was carrying a paint-brush and a palette and putting Pollock to shame. The cat was hip; very hip. It was at his father's home in Harlem that Stick was, in a way, introduced to music. Ben Riley, who was playing drums for Thelonious Monk at the time and was a good friend of Uncle Reggie's, used to stop by to talk jazz. One day he gave Stick a set of drumsticks and a practice pad. But Stick's mother wasn't having it. She wasn't having the trumpet, either. "The damn thing was just too loud for the land-lord. We settled on the piano."

Gil and his father had poetry in common. Stick and his father had music. The boy learned music and the father liked music, Charles Lloyd's music. They had the music, but Clarence still didn't visit as often as he had agreed to nor did he always come up with the 27 dollars a month he had agreed to, either. These led to ups and downs. But at least his father was around. Gil's was off somewhere, heavens knew where.

"I told him my father was not around either and he said at least you knew him. When I would complain about my mother he wouldn't say too much. I could see he was thinking, 'you had two adults there that were taking care of you. What more do you want?'"

Gil would have been happy, he thinks, with what Stick had, a sometimes and sometimey father. But it's not like he didn't have Bobbie. But Bobbie, as a mother, was not all that she could have been. Mothers are supposed to be sugar and spice and all that's nice. But Bobbie sometimes had frogs and snails and puppy-dog tails in her.

"I can't actually say Bobbie was a sweet person. She wasn't sweet. There was something about Gil that kind of made sense to me when I met his mother. She was very acerbic. Her humour was extremely sarcastic. She seemed to make fun of Gil a lot. She twisted words around a lot." She was a Black Dorothy Parker; full of bon mots and caustic witticisms. She was the kind of person who might have said, as Dorothy did, "if you want to see what God thinks of money, just look at all the people he gave it to."

He hadn't given it to her. She couldn't afford the place she had shared with her brother at Hampden Place. She had to move to the first place the city got and allotted her in 'Little San Juan', at 419 West 17th Street at 9th Avenue, on the 13th floor. Next was 'Spanish Harlem', the Franklin Plaza Apartments at 315 East 106th Street at 2nd Avenue, apartment 19A. She didn't live where she would have liked and was not doing what she would have liked, either. She would have preferred to have been a librarian, interacting with intellectuals or earning acclaim as an acclaimed alto. She earned her money, instead, pushing a pencil for the New York City Housing Authority. She so wanted to be an artiste, a bona fide one. But she was not one; not like her son, the one whose art she did not think was art. All this conspired to make her sometimes acid-tongued and sometimes cruelly critical, in a way that often hurt her one and only son.

She had a way with words, but hated the way her son used words, played with words, made up words, like in his poem, Comment #1. "the i-ro-knee uv it all uvcourse/iz when a pale-face sds muthafuckuh dares look/hurt when I don't call him brother& tell him 2/go find hiz own goddamn revolution." There was just too much of the street, too much watermelon and mustard greens in it.

"It would have been a constant effort on my part to try to please her, to show her that I was worth something, that I was really going to do something. I saw that in Gil when he was around her. He needed to prove to her that he was really somebody, doing something out there that was real." Stick sometimes had the same struggle with some of his people. Still, though they had nothing, or at least not the something they wanted, they knew he would end up to be a something. Our folks are funny like that. They might not always believe in themselves – how could they? - and though they don't and won't always tell you, deep down and in there, they believe in you.

"To be honest, my mother dug at me, too." She believed her baby could do so much better than Gil. "I thought Bobbie kind of took it a little too far sometimes. I used to feel for him. I really did. But he had a thick skin."

Actually, he didn't have a thick skin. It was wafer thin; transparent even. He never forgot a slight and always endeavoured to settle a wrong. He had a shit list upon which everyone who ever hurt him was included. His father was on the list. His mother wasn't. She should be, says Stick.

"Bobbie really kind of left him. He never talked about that. But she did. She went to Puerto Rico and left him with his grandmother. I guess she thought she was going to have a life. So not only was he left by his father, but he was also left by his mother. She only came back because his grandmother died. And I think she was pissed about it. She resented him, in a way. I think he knew it."

He did know it, and like New York, it was killing him. He wanted to be her 'sun', the thing that lit up her life. But he knew he wasn't. He wanted her, though she was a diabetic who been in and out of comas and lost an eye, to save him from himself. "Hey, I need to go home/Yes Mama could change it,/ and Daddy could help me/ Yes I could go home/Yeah mama don't need to see me this way/Touch me this way/Love me this way/Find me this way/Hey I can't go home." It began to creep into his work. But if you asked him if this concerned him in anyway, if it was autobiographical, at all, he would parry and then counter-riposte.

"It was so easy for him to throw a quip out there and deflect and redirect any sentiment and any feeling. The cat was an escapist. He would rather die than deal with himself, and deal with his emotions."

But in *Winter in America* – the first big, special thing Gil and Stick did together – the two did nothing but deal with their emotions.

"A lot of the material on *Winter in America* was a result of how close we were. It was us against the music business. All the themes on there were to do with alienation and wishing for a past that really didn't exist. Listen to 'Back Home' or listen to 'A Very Precious Time.' None of these things had happened. It was things we wished had happened."

The album was recorded on the Strata-East label after they'd said bye bye to the Flying Dutchman label and to Bob Thiele, who'd produced recordings for everyone from Coltrane and Mingus to John Lee Hooker and B.B. King. They'd had a three album contract with him and they'd delivered their three albums: *Small Talk at 125th and Lenox*; *Pieces of a Man* and *Free Will*. They could perhaps have stayed but Gil had demanded that Stick get equal credit and billing on their albums. But Thiele refused. Whatever the case, they were glad to be free of Flying Dutchman, but were not sure what the future held. With no offers on the table, they signed with Strata-East, a tiny jazz label run like a people's co-op by trumpeter Charles Tolliver and pianist Stanley Cowell.

After recording *Winter in America* at D&B Studios in Silver Springs, Maryland in September and October of 1973, Stick and Gil delivered it to Strata-East in New York for release in May 1974. It was a very precious record and a very precious time. Even now, Stick delights in talking about how *Winter in America* came about and how it came to be produced not just the once, but the twice.

The first time around, Stick says, there was just Gil and him. Stick played piano and a fender bass and Gil handled the vocals. There were a couple of flute things in there and some crazy narratives, too. 'Now more than ever all the family must be together, every brother everywhere feels that the time is in the air, common blood flows through common veins and the common eyes all see the same, now more than ever all the family must be together.'

"When you get to the end of the album you realize it's about a guy who had come back from the war and who had lost his mind. The narratives were actually excerpts from his sessions with his analyst. That was the punch line. Gil liked to deliver a good punch line. So you had to get to the end of the album to figure out this guy is in a nuthouse. But, you know, we listened to it over and over again and said this is too maudlin man, way too morose. We couldn't do it." So they backed off. It was too austere, they decided, too demanding, too difficult.

"So we took out a handful of the songs. We had a song on there called 'White Horse Nightmare' because the guy in the story was always strung out on smack. The song was really bizarre." It was too out there. So, they recorded it again, dropping some things and including some things. "We wanted to make it a little more upbeat. So we took out the whole thing about the story line. "Rivers of my Father" was included and so was "Back Home" and "The Bottle" was in there, too. We put in *H_2O Watergate Blues* and one or two other pieces. We did a reprise of "Peace Go With You," "My Brother" and called the recording *Winter in America*. It was a vanity album, really. People called me and said I just heard *The Bottle* on the Frankie Crocker

Show. I'd walk down 116th Street and hear it. The highlight of that year was when my grandmother came up to me and said I just heard it on the street. And I said what did you do, she said she went up to them and said that's my grandson. It was all for real. Apparently at that point that's what we were going to be doing."

That was what they were going to be doing. But there was more to music than making music. No one knew you had made the music unless someone wrote about it. Neither liked the press, people who, as Frank Zappa had complained, can't write, interviewing people who can't talk, for people who can't read. As Stick was even less likely to suffer fools than was Gil, Gil was drafted into service with the press corps. It was just as well he did the press as when he didn't the journalists just asked Stick questions about him, anyway.

In 1975, he was included in that *New York Times* article about 'Superstars of Tomorrow' and credited by the *Washington Post* with creating 'a new black music.' In 1976, he was called by the *Atlanta Daily World*, "today's most articulate spokesman for social change" and by The Guardian, "one of the most interesting new leaders of the black cause in America today." In 1977, the *Washington Post* said he was part of a "street wise intelligentsia that made a folk art of putting down Uncle Sam in public." In 1978, the *Associated Press* called him "among the last of the balladeering social critics." The stuff about him being the 'Godfather of Rap' didn't come till later, till Jon Pareles said it in 1984 in the *New York Times*. "Mr. Scott-Heron can claim to be a godfather of the rap movement."

Though the press was mostly kind to him, he remained wary of it and its overanalysing and over-defining. "We overanalyze. We let others define, a thousand precious feelings from our past. When we express love and tenderness...Is that Jazz? Is that Jazz? Is that Jazz?"

His first major interview appeared in the *Washington Post* in August 1974, right after he and Stick had completed *Winter in America*.

In it, Gil said what he always said. He told the newspaper his mother was a librarian, though she had only worked briefly as one in Chicago in the 1950s. She was actually employed, for most of her life, as a liaison for the New York City Housing Authority. He told the newspaper his father was a Jamaican soccer player who had played in Scotland and not that he was an assembly line worker who worked the early shift at the Ford factory in Detroit. He said he had attended Lincoln University in Pennsylvania – the same one Langston Hughes attended. He never said he hadn't graduated and that this left his mother forlorn and his Uncle William, who had graduated with honours from Lane as had all the Scotts, furious. To cover his tracks, he always said he got his Master's at Johns Hopkins and that he was an associate professor of creative writing at Federal City College in DC. He sometimes mentioned that his alma mater invited him back when he became big as a guest member of faculty. He wasn't an urban guerrilla. He was an urbane guerrilla. He did not like people to know what he did not like people to know. He didn't like, either, that the *Washington Post* reporter, Angela Terrell, had said he kept his life "deliberately misty" and had quoted unnamed friends as saying he was "nice but a little hard to know." He didn't like this and he didn't like that it had been revealed he owned two cars. One was a "shaggy" down at the mouth 1964 Pontiac Tempest, like the one mentioned in *My Cousin Vinny* (1992). The other was a 1967 Mercedes 4-door sedan that he said fit his long legs and was used for frequent road trips. It was the same with Bob Marley. He bought a BMW, he said, only because the 'BMW' stood for 'Bob Marley and The Wailers.' There were things Gil liked about the *Washington Post* article and things he didn't. He didn't like the title: GIL SCOTT-HERON: A JAZZY BLEND. But he was glad the paper had remembered his hyphen. He was happy, also, that it had revealed he had once worked as a gardener, a dishwasher and in a dry cleaners' shop, where he had also lived for a time. It made him sound real; like a man of the people and not of the bourgeoisie. He didn't mind, either, that it had been revealed he had once been elected freshman class president at college, but that he had resigned "dramatically" after the administration blocked his attempts to shake the old school up. He had angered the administration by inviting to campus, in 1969, The Last Poets, the angry ensemble whom he and Stick would forever be mistaken for. According to Last Poet Abiodun, after the gig Gil came backstage and said, "Listen, can I start a group like you guys?"

The thing he liked best about the *Washington Post* article was the bit that revealed he had been known as 'Spider-Man' at Lincoln because he had squeezed his skinny frame through a barred college window. This and putting on that Last Poets show, showed he'd been standing up for things long before he got into show business and got paid for standing up for things. Besides, he was a lot like Spider-Man. He had genius level intellect and had pre-cognitive powers which alerted him when something bad was about to happen.

His 'Spidey Sense' hadn't warned him, though, that his ma and pa were going to split and he was going to end up an orphan living not with Aunt May and Uncle Ben in Forest Hills but with Lillie in Jackson. His precognitive powers hadn't warned him that on November 5, 1960, Lillie was not going to wake for breakfast and that he would have to go North. What's the point of having precognitive powers when they can't tell you this? He didn't have super strength but he did have agility and could cling to things. He was self obsessed, filled with rejection, filled with inadequacy and filled with loneliness. In this he was like Peter Parker, not Spider-Man. Spider-Man didn't have an adult mentor. But he did. He had Mr. Porter, a black superhero who was able to leap racism with a mighty bound, and also be a father to his children. It was Mr. Porter who had let him know that with great power there must also come great responsibility.

"Gil's whole thing is to support those around him", a friend quoted in the *Washington Post* article. He liked this. But he didn't like what the unnamed friend had to say next. "Brian Jackson could have been pushed aside while Gil became the superstar. But he went out of his way to make sure Brian got due recognition. Gil always resented attempts to push him into a star mold."

Clive Davis knew how to make stars and in 1974 he was looking for a star to sign to his new label, a black star, one that knew what time it was and didn't need a weatherman to tell him which way the wind was blowing. In 1973, Davis was fired from his job as president of Columbia Records, a post that had made him, in the 1960s and 70s, some said, the most powerful man in the recording industry. Davis was looking for talent for his new record company, Arista Records, a company partly owned by Davis and bankrolled by Columbia Records that he launched in 1975. Arista would be a "broad, diversified label" and would be a "ready alternative for major artists as well as discoveries", the company said. In no time Davis had turned Arista into one of the most profitable record companies in the world. Davis signed Barry Manilow, Patti Smith, Lou Reed, the Kinks, and Hall & Oates. But his first signing, though, was Gil Scott-Heron.

Me and the Devil

Clive had liked *Winter in America*, and in particular "The Bottle," when he had first heard it in 1974. He had just begun Arista Records and liked what he had seen of Gil, too. "Gil Scott-Heron was an original — is an original," he said. Only thing was; he didn't want Stick, didn't want Brian. For Davis, it was a case of what sold. Chris Blackwell did this to Bob and Peter and Clive Davis did this to Gil and Stick.

"Clive Davis thought basically this was all Gil. He thought I was a tag-along. He asked who wrote The Bottle and Gil said he did. Clive said I only want to sign Gil. I don't want to sign the two of them. Gil said forget about it. So I said wait. You and I know what we do. Why don't you sign, make the money and I get half of whatever we do together. Fifty-fifty. It doesn't matter what this guy says because we have our agreement." They set up a joint bank account, at the Virginia National Bank. Gil put his money in it and Stick put his money in it. They set up a publishing company, Brouhaha Music, and instructed ASCAP that all royalties should be paid to the company. It was fifty-fifty. It was brother to brother.

"I don't know what Clive Davis had against me. He'd listen to our recordings and say 'I like it, I like it. But I don't hear a hit.' We would both sit there stone-faced waiting for him to say whether he was going to accept it or not. He would say: 'Can you do something like 'The Bottle?' I need a hit.' We'd say, 'Maybe you have to change your concept of what a hit is. Maybe if you learn how to sell what we do to our audience you'd have a hit. Why don't you advertise our music in *Jet* magazine or in *Ebony*?' His response would be, 'That's small potatoes. That's not the market. That's not where the money is.' Clive enjoyed the kudos of having a Gil Scott-Heron on his label, but wanted to sell more than 100,000 or 200,000 copies. "We always had this conflict with him. He always looked at me as 'the jazz guy' with all those fancy chords who was keeping Gil from doing another 'Bottle.' One time he wanted to hook Gil up with this pop guy from Chairman of the Board. Are you kidding me? We laughed in his face." Stick saw Clive Davis this way. But Gil didn't; not at first.

"I've never sat down with the Arista people and had them say they wished I'd sell less albums. But I've never had any overt pressure from them to make my music more commercial. I don't think anyone feels it is their place to pressure me since I've been with the Arista label longer than just about anyone besides Clive Davis." Gil prided himself on knowing a wolf in sheep's clothing. "Clive is very sensitive to what artistes are about and what kinds of conditions they need to work in. Arista offered me a freedom that was unavailable from any other large label."

Gil couldn't be convinced. So it was only a matter of time before Stick went one way and he went the other way. They both worked on their excuses. Stick said Gil was a writer stuck in a band of musicians, musicians that wanted to stretch out and do more than just play "The Bottle" every night. Gil said he was just a "simple blues guy" who wanted to play 'simple stuff.' Stick had been the musical director. But Gil decided anything Brian could do, he could do better. "It became a power play between the two of us. I said you're the leader. You're the spokesperson for the band and I was the guy behind the scenes who was taking care of the music. I told him you don't seem to be happy with the way I'm doing that. So, I resigned."

That's not the way Gil saw it. He believed, Stick had been itching to leave for a long while. He first noticed it with *Bridges* in 1977. He only contributed one song to that – Vildgolia. The next year, 1978, he only contributed one song to Secrets – A Prayer for Everybody. The year after that, 1979, it was clear he was on his way out when he offered up Corners for the *1980* album. To Gil, the composition had the sense of an ending. He supplied the lyrics, but the music begged for what he gave it.

"The turning of the decade is meant to separate; ten years left to history, ten years left to fate. The turning of the decade like corners in your life; turning only to the future instead of left or right. And if we see where we've been somehow more clearly than before. And if we see where we are going somehow, like the opening of a door, They're not there to stop you flowing; to somehow freeze you in the past/ Signposts are meant to shape your growing, There's nothing there to hold you back."

Gil said Stick was feeling held back, held back from becoming a great composer and a great arranger in a great band. He didn't want to hold him back, he said, so he let him go. Besides, Clive had warned him that Stick had been recording some off-the-book stuff of his own to take with him as a calling card when he left. That's not the way Stick recalls it. The two had talked, he says, and agreed that he could use the reserves from their recording budget to cut some tracks of his own. Still, if this was part of the leaving, he would be sorry to lose him, he said, because Stick's music made his lyrics elegant and powerful. He reminded people that he had predicted "greatness" for Stick when he had first met him in 1969 at Lincoln and they had been in Victor Brown's Black and Blues band. He reminded people that he had predicted greatness for him then and was not going to stand in the way now of Stick and his greatness.

They were like the Fabulous Baker Boys; the Fabulous Baker Boys after Michelle Pfeiffer went on her way. They were brothers, too; brothers from another mother, and another father. But just because they had been brothers, neither was going to allow that to freeze them in the past. Nothing was going to hold them back. So, when they got back home after a long time on the road, they had it all out. Stick said, "'Hey man, I think we need to write again and the other thing we need to do is take a break.'" They didn't write again. But they did take a break; a long break that has lasted from here to eternity.

Stick and Gil – the one had described the other as "the best composer I know" and the other had described the one as "one of the greatest writers of the 20th century" – ended there, kind of.

In 1980, Brouhaha, Stick and Gil's publishing company, was dissolved by decree, without any brouhaha. "Trusting him, fifty-fifty, you're my brother, I'm your brother, came back and bit me in the ass!"

Five years after Stick got bit in the ass; Gil got bit in the ass, too. Clive Davis owned a piece of Arista, but not all of it. In 1979, it was sold to the German company BMG and in 1983 BMG sold 50 per cent of Arista to RCA.

RCA wanted to make Gil a hit maker in its hit factory. After the success in 1981 of B-Movie, the company pressed him to work with a hip hop producer they felt could double his sales and make him popular with a whole new demographic. But though he liked words, he didn't like rap and didn't like being called its father or its godfather. He liked it about as much as his mother liked his early poems and songs.

"I don't think it is fair to describe me as the 'father of rap.' I think there may be a difference between poetry and rap. The beat in rap seems to be more important that the words. That's not the case in my music."

But, still, RCA pressed him though he refused, to work with a rap producer. "Why should I listen to some son of a bitch on West 57th Street tell me what to play for black people?" Why, indeed.

"I'm all for getting a new audience, as long as you do not lose the old one. Maybe Arista just got too big. Now they're bringing kids who were at school when I was making music to tell me how to do it." Clive used to say, 'leave this off' and 'put this on.' We'd discuss it and somehow always find a hit." They did have some hits: Johannesburg had been a hit in 1976; Angel Dust in 1978 and B-Movie was a hit in 1981. But they could have had more hits and sold more product if Clive had released a bunch of other songs Stick and Gil said could be hits. Hits! Hits! Hits. They wanted him to sell 55 million units, like Whitney.

Asked whether he believed he would ever find a major record company that would allow him to make music as he pleased he said: "I don't know if it is possible. I hadn't found one till then and haven't found one since."

Gil was used to having things his own way and doing things his own way. The way he saw things was what made Clive want to sign him in 1975 and what made him get rid of him in 1985. Gil had always been inordinately proud of being the outsider who'd managed, somehow, to operate in the commercial mainstream. He was the spook who sat by the door. He was the man who spoke up for the little man yet had a deal with the big guys. He hadn't compromised. He was as he was when he had been challenging segregation at Tigrett and confounding his teachers at Fieldston and defying the Dean of Men at Lincoln. Defying authority had won him a book deal when he was just 19 and won him a record deal when he was just 20. Defying authority had made him what he was: independent and individual. He hadn't sold out. He hadn't compromised. Though some had made a few corrections in their directions, he believed he hadn't. The Midnight Band had made a few corrections in their directions. They had become The Nine-to-Five Band. Sure, Bilal, the mighty saxophone man, was still an urban guerrilla who'd, somehow, got himself caught up in that Brink's armoured car robbery case. But Adenola – I mean Eddie Knowles – went to the ivory tower and became a vice-president for Student Life at Rensselaer Polytechnic Institute and Barnett – 'The Doctor' – Williams had become a nine to fiver, filling out time sheets and dealing with personnel issues as a regional supervisor for the School Age Child Care Program in Fairfax, Virginia. Bob Adams was an optician, grinding eyeglasses for a living. And, of course, Stick had lately been tapping the keyboard of a Dell computer for the City of New York more than he had been tapping an 88 key Fender Rhodes electric piano. We all make corrections in our directions.

"I see success as still being independent, and an individual, 11 years after my recording career started" he told the *Los Angeles Times* in 1981. The paper had asked him if it troubled him, at all, that he had not become the superstar it had been predicted he would become. "Even though I may not be as big as a lot of folks who've shown up in the last 11 months, I will probably still be here when they're gone." But it was him that was going, going, gone. In 1985, Clive Davis, with RCA's blessing, cancelled the contract of the first artiste he'd signed when he launched Arista Records a decade before.

With no record label, and money hard to come by, the man who had warned against the advertising industry used his beautiful baritone to sell soft drinks and tyres for Madison Avenue. That was his voice on the 'You Know When You've Been Tango'd!' commercial and his big baritone in that commercial for that big tyre company. "Make it all commercial, there ain't nothin' folks won't buy. New fuel to fire up the monsters of Free Enterprise and Gizmos and gadgets, batteries to make them run. Just give your check up at the first of every month." Hungry for a cheque, in 1995, he let Nike use his Revolution Will Not Be Televised in a TV commercial selling basketball sneakers. "The revolution will be led by Jason Kidd, Jimmy Jackson, Eddie Jones, Joe Smith and Kevin Garnett...The revolution is about basketball, and basketball is the truth." A lot of people were not happy. But Gil didn't care. "I thought it was well done. A lot of people criticized, but a lot of people criticized Jesus."

Cocaine Is A Hell Of A Drug!

It was around the time of the end of Stick and the end of Arista and the end of his marriage to Brenda and the end of everything, that what had been merely recreational usage became full-time abusage. Crack caught hold of him, in his down and distressed condition, and wouldn't let go. Down on his luck and spending too much time in the dead end streets of drug addiction where there is no turning back, he had become a character from Home Is Where The Hatred Is:"You keep saying, kick it, quit it, kick it, quit it, God, but did you ever try, to turn your sick soul inside out, so that the world, so that the world, can watch you die." He had become a character from "Angel Dust": "He was groovin', and that was when he coulda sworn, the room was movin', But that was only in his mind, He was sailin', he never really seemed to notice, vision failin', 'cause that was all part of the high, Sweat was pourin', he couldn't take it, The room was exploding, he might not make it, Angel Dust, Please, children would you listen. Angel Dust, Just ain't where it's at, Angel Dust, You won't remember what you're, missin', but down some dead end streets, there ain't no turnin' back."

His crusade against Angel Dust had led him, in 1979, to record a public service message for radio which won an advertising award: "This is Gil Scott-Heron with an important message for everyone. Angel Dust is bad news. It's a powerful drug and a proven killer. Even trying it could be the mistake of a lifetime. Don't be a fool. Don't play with your life." Anti drug groups applauded. But a church group, which misunderstood the song and thought it was encouraging drug use, tried to have Angel Dust banned from the radio and taken out of record stores.

All this was back when he mattered, when he was better, truer and purer than the rest of us. He always knew better; better than us. He lived the right way; a pure, righteous way, and berated us to live the right way, too. Each new album, from *Small Talk at 125th and Lenox* to *Moving Target*, was like a clarifying, purifying, ablutionary ritual. Perhaps this is why some who, perhaps have fallen short, fallen on the bumpy road of life, have, if they were to admit it, had been happy to see that one such as him could fall short, too. He addressed this in his song Don't Give Up.

"I never really thought of myself as a complex man, Or as some-one who was really that hard to understand. But it would hardly take a genius to realize, That I've always been a lot too arrogant and a little too fuckin' wise, That was a combination that made folks feel duty bound, To do whatever they could to try and shoot me down. To head off some of the things I might possibly say, And see if they couldn't take some of my pride away. To bring me disappointment and teach me to fear it, Obviously these are folks that just didn't have no spirit."

He said he didn't use dope, but we knew he did. He said he didn't use anything, but we knew he did. It's not that he used, it's that he couldn't stop using. Maybe it's because so many of his heroes used. Lady and John Coltrane used. "Ever feel kinda of down and out you don't know just what to do?, Livin' all of your days in darkness, let the sun shine through, Ever feel that somehow, somewhere you lost your way?, And if you don't get help quick you won't make it through the day, Could you could call on Lady Day?, Could you could call on John Coltrane?, They'll wash your troubles, your troubles away, your troubles, your troubles away." Billie used. It killed her. Her husband helped to keep her high and as she lay in the hospital dying she was arrested on drug possession charges. Coltrane used. He had his wife and his mother lock him in a room, allowing him only bread and water, to help him get the gorilla off his back. Miles used. He had to go home, to his father's house in St Louis, to kick and finally quit it. Gil needed to go home.

He had been writing songs about home, about hatred and about individuals with habits for years. Since he was a fresh-faced teenager, he had smoked the occasional joint and taken the occasional swig of wine, but could not be said to be abusing any substance or being abused by a substance in return. He wrote Home Is Where The Hatred Is, for example, when he was 21 in 1971. It was praised by critics, and made those who had been addicts and had quit uncomfortable. It was a dead-on accurate depiction of the life of a heroin addict. Included on the *Pieces of a Man* album in 1971, it caught the attention of James

Brown sideman and arranger Pee Wee Ellis, who was selecting songs for a 1972 album he was working on for Esther 'Little Esther' Philips. He had heard Gil's song and recommended it to Esther, who had been a stone-cold heroin addict on and off for 20 years. 'No, thanks' Philips told Pee Wee. She did not, she complained, want to sing a song that had obviously been written by a junkie. She didn't want nothing to do with junkies now that she was no longer a junkie herself and was clean. But the songwriter wasn't a junkie, Pee Wee Ellis protested to Philips. He was just a kid, a kid who lived in the projects down in 'Little San Juan' and spent all his time playing ball at the courts on 13th Street. Philips said the only way she would record the song was if she met the songwriter first. If he was, as she suspected, a junkie hiding his habit as she had for years, she would not record the song. A meeting between Little Esther and Gil was arranged at her record company's offices at Rockefeller Centre in Manhattan. Gil had been playing basketball and walked into the meeting in shorts and a stringy undershirt that exposed his arms and legs. "When I came in the joint where she is, she looks at me and says `Damn, I lost the bet.' She could look at me and see I wasn't on dope, but she had bet her husband that I was, because I knew things that she figured I couldn't know unless I was a junkie. That's when you know you've done your job. That's when you've been blessed, when you are able to translate an experience you've never had so thoroughly." Esther Philips turned "Home Is Where The Hatred Is" into a big hit. It became her signature song. Most people thought she had written it, so close were the details of the song to her own life of addiction. "A lot of people think I'm on dope now, because they hear this song. I don't do dope no matter what they think, I just did a good job." The album "Home Is Where The Hatred Is" was featured on, *From a Whisper to a Scream,* was nominated for a Grammy. Little Esther's winning streak didn't last, however. Twelve years later, in 1984, she died of liver and kidney failure, caused by prolonged drug use. A junkie walking through the twilight, she was on her way home.

༄༅༄༅

The way Stick sees it Gil got his comeuppance. For a long time he had wanted him to hurt like he had. Gil suffered a world of hurt. He was dropped by Arista and was not picked up by another big label, as he thought he would be. Later, he found himself in the company of Freddy Cousaert and Castle Communications and TVT and Steve Gottlieb and Peak Top Records and Intersound Records and Phantom Sound & Vision Records and Delta Music and Pickwick Records and Acadia/Evangeline Records and most recently Richard Russell and XL Recordings. There ain't no place he ain't been down. While he has been down these roads, the music he is the godfather of, rap, was on its way up while he has been on his way down. He didn't have a label, really. But he could still tour. He toured non-stop, at home and abroad. But as it was hard to feed his habit abroad without getting caught up in the law. He confined himself, mostly, to performing, when he was up to it, close to home. In August 1990, in California to perform at the Long Beach Jazz Festival and at the Watts Summer festival, he told the *Los Angeles Sentinel* newspaper he had been on a 2 year long sabbatical from the music business so as to care for his ailing, diabetic mother, who'd suffered several comas and lost her left eye to the disease.

"She's fine now and I'm back into my music. Sometimes, it is not so much breaks in your career, as it is things that happen in your life. My mother and her health pertains primarily to my life." This was only partly true. He loved and worried for his mother of course. But he'd been living with Bobbie at her East Harlem apartment because his habit had become costly and had eaten up what he had and left him without a home of his own.

A few months before, in May 1990, he had been arrested in London at Heathrow Airport with 18 grams of cocaine. In 2000, he was arrested in Harlem with 1.2 grams of powder cocaine and two crack pipes. After breaking his plea deal, in which he'd agreed to attend a rehab clinic for a period of two years, he was sentenced to 1 to 3 years and told by New York State Supreme court judge Carol Shenkman, "You've had all these opportunities to help yourself, and you just don't seem to care."

In 2002, when he was released from prison on parole, Stick and he tried to reconcile, put all the shit behind them. Megan, the 3rd of Stick's 3 wives – his ups and downs had made him hard to live with – thought something good might come out of it for him. They'd tried before, but it had never held. In 1998, Gil invited Stick to come tour South Africa with him. Afterwards, they went their ways again for another 5 years, until October 2003. He was playing SOBS, Sounds of Brazil, in New York and had invited Stick up onstage – Stick on flute and Gil on electric piano – to perform 'Your Daddy Loves You.' That was a Kodak moment.

"I was reluctant. I had seen him before this and he didn't look like he was prepared to do anything like that. Still, it was cool to hang with him anyway." It was like old times and Stick put all thoughts of law-suits and body bags, out of his mind. "I didn't consider him an enemy. But I didn't consider him a friend, either. He was somewhere in-between."

They kept things in the present and even looked into the future, talking excitedly about making some real music together. "It got to the point where we had actually discussed doing an album together, recovering some of the masters he had lost from the 70s and actually re-doing some of those. He seemed very excited about it. I bought some of the tapes off eBay. There was an unrecorded song called 'My Cloud.' I re-did it. I put new lines and drums on it and everything." Gil was as happy as he had been in years, in years. Stick says Gil went up and down Harlem telling people the two of them had a new cut and playing 'My Cloud' for them. "He was in heaven." He was so excited he talked about taking the cut to his record company at the time, TVT, a small independent label that had made Nine Inch Nails a big success, and getting some money to produce the song properly in a studio."We had talked about doing some tours and had actually begun to hook some up." But then, wouldn't you know it, just as they were about to begin talking about roadies and venues, Gil was arrested with a controlled substance and jailed. "That" Stick says, "was the end of that."

That wasn't quite the end of that. In January 2004, a few weeks after Gil went down for his second stretch, Larry Gold, the owner of SOBS, asked Stick to cover for Gil at the club's annual concert celebrating Dr Martin Luther King Jnr's birthday on January 15. "I said sure, this is great, I'll call up the guys and they can get paid. Gold said, 'how do you want to bill it?' I said, 'Brian Jackson and the Amnesia Express, which was the name of Gil's backing band. Larry gets a call from prison. Gil is irate, incensed because I'm using the name 'Amnesia Express.' Gil told him, 'He will not use that name, that name belongs to me. I said okay I'll call it 'Brian Jackson and the Midnight Band.' Larry says what if he gets mad about that. I said look, he's got to pick a name. He can't have two bands. He can't even have one because he's in jail. He said okay. To make a long story short, Gil didn't like that I went through with it. By the time the show happened, he had gotten out on bail. He paid off some of the Amnesia Express musicians, I won't name who they are, not to appear. The day of the show they're supposed to be at soundcheck, I arranged a car for them, they just didn't come." Stick was able, though, to get some musicians to appear, among them Abiodun Oyewole, Ladybug Mecca (Digable Planets) and MC Safahri Ra. "It snowed like hell and there weren't a lot of people there. But we had a fantastic show." Gil could have, but he chose not to come to the show.

"People want to blame the cocaine for that. I don't think you can. You can blame cocaine when you need some money and you rip somebody off. You can blame cocaine for making somebody erratic, for being unkempt, for disappearing for months at a time, for missing gigs. You can't blame cocaine for making a man vindictive." Cocaine is a hell of a drug. But even it ain't that powerful.

By 2006, he was back in jail, sentenced to two to four years for violating a plea deal on a drug-possession charge after he left a drug rehab centre where, he claimed, he was refused HIV medication. He got out early again, paroled in 2007. He got the Amnesia Express together and began performing again, mostly at SOBS, his home from home when he did not have a home. Later that year he was arrested again, but wasn't sent to prison. The new recording, I'm New Here, came out and that began the comeback; though he'd never been away.

Stick, has tried to get on with his life. In the 1980s and 1990s, after he and Gil split, he got into some new things with George Benson, Will Downing, Gwen Guthrie, Roy Ayers, Kool and the Gang, Phyllis Hyman, Masauko, and with Ladybug Mecca (of Digable Planets).

In 2000, Stick finally released a solo album, *"Gotta Play"*, which, interestingly, included a guest performance by Gil on Home Is Where The Hatred Is.

"No one could have told me when I was recording my first album, Pieces of a Man, that it would be the 21st century before I recorded a solo album. But this collection of music represents my offerings of new friendship, fresh perspective, and a new life."

Stick and Gil's last and final meeting was in November 2007. Gil had been in and got out and was celebrating his release, as usual, with a show at SOBS. Stick decided to go see.

"I didn't announce myself. In between sets, I went downstairs and hung out with the band and said hello to him. As the second show was getting ready to start, I hugged him, and I said I just want to tell you goodbye and I love you. I started to leave and Larry McDonald blocked the door. They wanted me to play. I said no I didn't come here for that. I just came to pay my respects and see you guys. Larry continued blocking the door, saying mock-threateningly, 'You wanna leave you have to get through me!' I sat down calmly and said, 'Larry, they just told you they wanted you onstage in 5 minutes. I can wait.' Gil almost fell down on the floor laughing. That was reminiscent of the old Gil and old Brian."

Peace go with you brother

Don't make no sense for us to be arguing now

Time is right up on us now brother

Don't make no sense for us to be arguing now

All of your children and all of my children

are gonna have to pay for our mistakes someday

Yes – and until then – may peace guide your way

Peace go with you brother; wherever you go

Epilogue

"Right ain't got nothing to do with it!"

Anon.

I'll end at the ending.

The other day – I'm not sure what day exactly – I went to number 530 West 144th Street, apartment 25, between Broadway and Amsterdam, to see Gilbert Scott-Heron. You know, the one who writes those songs about plastic pattern people and the protest and the rage and the people who gave a damn. I thought he might be able to tell me what was wrong with him.

"It ain't right and it ain't wrong" he said. "It just is."

The End

Notes

PROLOGUE

[1] The line, "the protest and the rage and the people who gave a damn" is from Gil Scott-Heron song, "South Carolina (Barnwell)," *From South Africa to South Carolina,* Arista Records, 1976.

[2] There are further references to Gil Scott-Heron songs, "Lady Day and John Coltrane," *Pieces of a Man*, Flying Dutchman Records, 1971 and "Home Is Where The Hatred Is," *Pieces of a Man*, Flying Dutchman Records, 1971.

[3] The terms "species-essence", "species-being", "estranged labour", "sensuous external world", "will and consciousness' come from Karl Marx, *Economic and Philosophical Manuscripts of 1844*.

[4] Letter written by Walter Gilbert Heron announcing separation and impending divorce from wife Lucille Heron published in the *Daily Gleaner* [Kingston, Jamaica] August 10, 1936.

BLACK FLASH IN THE PAN

[1] According to John Leonard, *Walter Mosley: Devil in a Blue Dress* the young Malcolm X said, "killer-diller coat with a drape shape, reet pleats and shoulders padded like a lunatic's cell." 45.

[2] George Martin, "Gilbert, The Broth of a Boy from Detroit," *Daily Record*, August 22, 1951, 3.

[3] The line, "the cleanest and beautifullest, and best built city in Britain, London" is from Daniel Defoe's *A Tour Through the Whole Island of Great Britain* (New Haven: Yale University Press, 1991).

THE PRISONER

[1] Henry Edwardes, "Get Set For the Superstars of Tomorrow," *New York Times*, September 21, 1975, 17.

[2] Gil Scott-Heron, "Home Is Where the Hatred Is," *Pieces of a Man*, Flying Dutchman Records, 1971.

[3] The lines "Fathers are stones" and "Their voices like gravel; their lips granite white" are from Charles Fishman, "Fathers Are Not Stones" *XY Files: Poems on the Male Experience* (Santa Fe: Sherman Asher Publishing, 1997).

[4] Quoted from Gil Scott-Heron & Brian Jackson song "The Prisoner," *Pieces of a Man*, Flying Dutchman Records, 1971.

HE WAS NEW THERE

[1] The line "of substance, and flesh and of bone, of fiber and liquids" is from Ralph Ellison's Invisible *Man* (New York: Vintage, 1995) 3.

[2] The lines "a flood nor yet an influx", "swamped the British character" and "foam with much blood" are from Enoch Powell's speech, "Rivers of Blood," 1968.

THE BABE RUTH OF SOCCER

[1] Glen Daly, "The Celtic Song," Clifford Music Ltd., 1961.

[2] Offside, "Maroons Face Wolverines in Soccer Today," *Chicago Daily Tribune*, July 28, 1946, 4.

[3] "Babe Ruth of Soccer," *Ebony*, July 1947, 18-9.

[4] W.E.B. Du Bois, *Souls of Black Folk*. (New York: Barnes and Noble Classics, 2003) 117. Du Bois quotes from Elizabeth Barrett Browning, *A Vision of Poets* (1844).

[5] Charles Fishman's poem "Fathers Are Not Stones," *XY Files: Poems on the Male Experience* (Santa Fe: Sherman Asher Publishing, 1997).

WE ALMOST LOST DETROIT

[1] *Ebony*, July 1947.

[2] Offside, "Night Novelty: Big Time Soccer Under Lights," *Chicago Daily Tribune*, June 7, 1946, 33.

[3] "Maroons Lose to Wolverines At Soccer, 2-1," *Chicago Daily Tribune*, July 29, 1946, 24.

[4] *Detroit News*, June 29, 1946 and July 14, 1946.

[5] Walter Byars, *Associated Press*, February 28, 1946.

[6] The line, "that great iron city, that impersonal..." is from Richard Wright's introduction to Black *Metropolis: A Study of Negro Life in a Northern City*, (Chicago: University of Chicago Press, 1993) xvii.

[7] The lines "the now years" and "the maybe years" are from Margaret Walker, *"For My People": A Tribute* (Mississippi, University of Mississippi Press, 1992).

[8] The line "packed up his old kit-bag" refers to Wilfred Owen's 'Smile, Smile, Smile', *The Collected Poems of Wilfred Owen* (New York: New Directions, 1965) 77.

[9] "Across Canada with Alan Harvey," *Winnipeg Free Press*, July, 28 1943, 13.

[10] "Centre Forward Kicks Five Goals in Match," *Daily Gleaner*, February 21, 1942, 13.

HUSH NOW, DON'T EXPLAIN

[1] Quoted in Gil Scott-Heron, "Tuskegee #626," *Bridges*, Arista Records, 1977.

[2] Quoted in "Jackson News," *Chicago Defender*, September 11, 1948, 18.

[3] Quoted in William Walker, "This World Is Not My Home" <http://ingeb.org/spiritua/thisworl.html>

[4] Deuteronomy 28:27 (New Revised Standard Version).

[5] The phrase "perfect idiot" is quoted from Jean-Jacques Rousseau, *Emil or On Education* and "one great blooming idiot" is from William James.

[6] Quoted in Billie Holiday & Arthur Herzog Jr., "Don't Explain".

[7] Quoted in Gil Scott-Heron, "Ain't No Such Thing As Superman," *Midnight Band: The First Minute of A New Day*, Arista Records, 1974.

[8] Quoted in Gil Scott-Heron song "Your Daddy Loves You," *Winter in America*, Strata East, 1974.

[9] Gil Scott-Heron & Brian Jackson song, "A Toast to The People," From *South Africa to South Carolina*, Arista Records, 1975.

[10] Nikki Giovanni, "The Women Gather," *The Women and the Men* (New York: Harper Perennial, 1979).

HOPE IN THE BELLY

[1] "New Celtic star – he's from Jamaica!" *Daily Record,* August 5, 1951.

[2] Tom Campbell. Interview by Leslie Gordon Goffe. Tape Recording. Edinburgh, Scotland, November, 2009. Campbell attended Gillie Heron debut for Celtic on August 18, 1951.

[3] *Daily Express*, August, 1951.

[4] "New Celtic star – he's from Jamaica!" *Daily Record*, August 5, 1951.

[5] "Heron's Fine Lead Atoned For Celtic Flaw," the *People*, August 19, 1951, 10.

[6] "Match of Day at Firhill." *Glasgow Herald,* August 20, 1951.

[7] *Chicago Daily Tribune,* August 19, 1951.

[8] *New York Times*, August 19, 1951.

[9] *Lethbridge Herald*, August 21, 1951.

[10] New York *Amsterdam News,* August 25, 1951.

[11] Baltimore *Afro-American* newspaper, August 25, 1951.

BROTH OF A BOY

[1] George Martin, "Gilbert, The Broth of a Boy from Detroit," *Daily Record*, August 22, 1951.

[2] Gilbert "Gillie" Heron. Interview by author. Digital recording. Detroit, M.I., December, 2006.

A MAN'S A MAN FOR A' THAT

[1] Robert Burns, *A Man's A For A' That,* Signet Press, 1959.

[2] "The Drought – Shooting Cases in Manchester," *Daily Gleaner* [Kingston, Jamaica] March 9, 1897.

THE SON OF NO ONE

[1] Billie Holiday and Arthur Herzog Jr., "God Bless the Child" Okeh, 1941.

[2] Genealogical details from Richard Mitchell, *A Heron Family Grew in Manchester* (Richard Mitchell, 2010).

A REVELATION OF OPPOSITES

[1] Gilbert "Gillie" Heron. Interview by author. Digital recording. Detroit, MI., December, 2006.

[2] Quoted in Richard Wright, introduction to *Black Metropolis: A Study Of Negro Life In A Northern City*, (Chicago: University of Chicago Press, 1993) xvii.

[3] Quoted from Carl Sandburg, 'City of the Big Shoulders' and "spiritual strivings" quoted from W.E.B. Du Bois' *The Souls of Black Folks*.

[4] Quoted from Margaret Walker, "For My People".

[5] "Babe Ruth of Soccer," *Ebony,* July 1947 18-9.

[6] "Soccer Babe Ruth is Jamaica Negro," New York *Amsterdam News*, June 14, 1947.

[7] *Chicago Daily Tribune*, June 28, 1947, 33.

[8] "Gil Heron is Outstanding in Soccer Circles," *Chicago Defender*, September 11, 1948, 11.

[9] *Chicago Daily Tribune*, December 25, 1947, 37.

[10] The Bible, Genesis 37: 34.

[11] "Spartas beat Detroit in Soccer 5-1" *Chicago Daily Tribune*, June 20, 1949, C4.

PIECES OF A MAN

[1] The line "Could not take a drink of water wherever" refers to Gil Scott-Heron and Brian Jackson song "95 South (All Of The Places We've Been)" from *Bridges*, 1977.

[2] The lines "The veil and strivings" and "spiritual strivings" are from W.E.B. Du Bois, *The Souls of Black Folks,* (1903).

[3] Quoted in Gil Scott-Heron & Brian Jackson song "Three Miles Down," *Secrets*, Arista Records, 1978.

[4] Athal Smith, "The Lanite," *Lane College Yearbook*, 1949.

FIRST MINUTE OF A NEW DAY

[1] Gil Scott-Heron "95 South (All Of The Places We've Been)".

[2] Gil Scott-Heron & Brian Jackson, "Rivers of My Fathers," *Winter in America*, Strata East, 1974.

[3] Gil Scott-Heron & Brian Jackson "Three Miles Down," *Secrets,* Arista Records, 1978 and "Must Be Something," The First Minute of A New Day, Arista Records 1975.

[4] Gil Scott-Heron "Better Days Ahead," *Secrets,* Arista Records, 1978.

[5] From Lillie Scott funeral document, Berean Baptist Church, Jackson, Tennessee, November 9, 1960.

WAITING FOR THE AXE TO FALL

[1] George Martin, "Gilbert, The Broth of a Boy," *Daily Record*, August 19, 1951.

[2] *Glasgow Herald*, August 27, 1951.

[3] *Daily Record*, August 27, 1951.

[4] *Glasgow Herald*, August 29, 1951.

[5] Gilbert "Gillie" Heron, "Grampian Mountains" from *I Shall Wish For You*, Aaron Peal Publishing Company, Detroit, Michigan, 1992.

[6] Robert Frost, "sigh, somewhere, someday" from "The Road Not Taken".

[7] *Daily Record*, December 1, 1951.

OH, ISLAND IN THE SUN

[1] Gilbert "Gillie" Heron, "Embrace you but cannot" from *I Shall Wish For You*, Aaron Peal Publishing Company, Detroit, Michigan, 1992.

[2] *Daily Gleaner*, February 12, 1952, 8.

[3] *Times*, January 9, 1950.

[4] Lindy Delapenha, Interview by author, Digital recording, Kingston, Jamaica, August, 2008.

[5] Roy Heron, Interview by author, Digital recording, Ontario, Canada, February, 2005.

[6] *Daily Gleaner*, February 14, 1952.

[7] Langston Hughes, "Big Sea".

[8] *Daily Gleaner*, July 5, 1939.

[9] "Father of Florist from BWI," *Cleveland Call and Post*, July 2, 1936, 7.

[10] *Daily Gleaner*, June 16, 1949, 4.

[11] Irving Burgie song "Island in the Sun".

[12] Louise "Miss Lou" Bennett, "Colonizing in reverse".

[13] *Daily Gleaner*, April 6, 1935.

[14] *Daily Gleaner*, February 14, 1952.

[15]"First Intercolonial Footer Match Today', Daily Gleaner, 28 December 28, 1935, 14.

[16] *Daily Gleaner*, December 24, 1935.

[17]*Daily Gleaner*, February 27, 1947.

[18]*Daily Gleaner*, March 3, 1947.

[19] *Daily Gleaner*, March 12, 1952.

[20] *Daily Gleaner,* March 11, 1952.

MOTHER AND CHILD REUNION

[1] Refers to Gil Scott-Heron, "Push Comes to Shove," *1980*, Arista Records, 1980.

[2] Arna Bontemps, "A Black Man Talks of Reaping" *American Negro Poetry: An Anthology*. (New York: Hill and Wang, 1963).

[3] *Jackson Sun,* January 25, 1962.

GONE WITH THE WIND

[1] *The People*, 19 August, 1952.

[2] Allen Iverson, Philadelphia 76ers Press Conference, May 7, 2002.

[3] Sean Fallon, Interview by author. Digital recording. Glasgow, Scotland, November, 2007. Fallon is a former Celtic full back.

[4] Gilbert "Gillie" Heron. Interview *Daily Record*, 19 August, 1951, "Gilbert, The Broth of a Boy."

[5] Phili Vasili, The History of Black Footballers, http://www.vasili.co.uk/

[6] Tom Campbell. Interview by Leslie Gordon Goffe. Tape recording. Edinburgh, Scotland, November 2007. Campbell is the author of *Celtic: The Encyclopaedia*, Argyll Publishing, 2008.

[7] Gilbert "Gillie" Heron, "Tell Me Sir" from *I Shall Wish For You,* Aaron Peal Publishing Company, Detroit, Michigan, 1992.

[8] *Alphabet of the Celts:A Complete Who's Who of Celtic FC,* (Polar Print Group, 1994).

[9] Gilbert "Gillie" Heron, "and as my predictable world collapses" *I Shall Wish For You,* Aaron Peal Publishing Company, Detroit, Michigan, 1992.

[10] *Daily Gleaner*, July 28, 1951.

[11] *Sunday Mail*, June 15, 1952.

[12] Gil Scott-Heron, "Winter in America," *The First Minute of a New Day*, Arista Records, 1975.

[13] Gil Scott-Heron & Brian Jackson, "A Lovely Day," From South Africa to South Carolina, Arista Records, 1976.

[14] *Daily Gleaner*, 12 July, 1952.

[15] Gilbert "Gillie" Heron, "the first time that I saw her" from *I Shall Wish For You,* Aaron Peal Publishing Company, Detroit, Michigan, 1992.

[16] *Daily Record*, 19 August, 1951.

[17] Gilbert "Gillie" Heron, "what is there left" from *I Shall Wish For You,* Aaron Peal Publishing Company, Detroit, Michigan, 1992.

[18] *Kidderminister Times*, 12 March, 1954.

THE SENSE OF AN ENDING

[1] Sean Fallon, Interview by author. Digital recording. Glasgow, Scotland, November, 2007. Fallon is a former Celtic full back.

[2] *Kidderminister Times*, 12 March, 1954.

MANCHILD IN THE PROMISED LAND

[1] The line "They were nowhere" refers to Ralph Ellison's essay "Harlem is Nowhere."

[2] Gil Scott-Heron, "The Bottle," *It's Your World*, Arista Records, 1976 and "Home Is Where the Hatred Is," *Pieces of a Man*, Flying Dutchman, 1971.

[3] Neal, Larry. "Malcolm X—An Autobiography" *Black Boogaloo*. Journal of Black Poetry Press, 1968.

[4] Melvin B. Tolson, "Hideho Heights" *"Harlem Gallery" and Other Poems.* Charlottesville: University of Virginia Press, 1999.

[5] Langston Hughes, "Dream Deferred".

[6] Brian Jackson, Interview by author, Digital recording. Jersey City, NJ, July, 2010.

BLOOD IS THICKER THAN MUD

[1] Gayle Heron, Interview by author, Digital recording, Detroit, M.I., December 2006.

[2] Nat Hentoff, liner notes for *Small Talk at 125th Street and Lenox,* Flying Dutchman Records, 1970.

[3] Leonard Feather, *Los Angeles Times*, 1971.

[4] Whitey on the Moon', "US Senate report on Equal Opportunity in Education," 1971.

[5] Amiri Baraka, "Black Dada Nihilismus" *Transbluesency: The Selected Poetry of Amiri Baraka/LeRoi Jones (1961-1995).* New York: Marsilio Publishers, 1995.

[6] The phrase "watermelon and mustard greens" refers to Gil Scott-Heron, "Small Talk at *125th Street and Lenox," Small Talk at 125th Street and Lenox,* 1970.

[7] Letter to Bobbie Scott Heron from Margaret Heron, 1970.

[8] Jamaican beauty pageant references from Consuelo Lopez Springfield ed., *Daughters of Caliban: Caribbean Women in the Twentieth Century* (Indiana, Indiana University Press, 1997).

[9] Gayle Heron, Interview by author. Digital recording. Detroit, M.I., December 2006.

[10] Friedich Nietzsche, *Thoughts Out of Season.*

[11] Gil Scott-Heron & Brian Jackson, "Hello Sunday! Hello Road!" *Bridges*, Arista Records, 1977.

[12]Gil Scott-Heron, Interview by author, Digital recording, New York, N.Y., March 2010.

[13] Gilbert "Gillie" Heron, "It's great to be an American" "it's been a very long time" "I sometime wonder" "so for future generations" and "The Mouths of Babes" from *I Shall Wish For You,* Aaron Peal Publishing Company, Detroit, Michigan, 1992.

[14] Book jacket of Gilbert "Gillie" Heron, *I Shall Wish For You,* Aaron Peal Publishing Company, Detroit, Michigan, 1992.

[15] Gil Scott-Heron, "Who'll Pay Reparations on My Soul?" *Small Talk at 125th Street and Lenox,* 1970.

[16] Gil Scott-Heron & Brian Jackson, "The Prisoner," *Pieces of a Man,* 1971.

[17] Gil Scott-Heron, "The Middle of the Day," *Free Will*, Flying Dutchman Records, 1972.

[18] Gil Scott-Heron & Brian Jackson, "The Needle's Eye," *Pieces of a Man*, 1971.

[19] Gil Scott-Heron "Your Daddy Loves You," *Winter in America*, Strata East, 1974.

[20] Gil Scott-Heron & Richard Russell, "Running," *I'm New Here*, XL Recordings, 2010.

[21] Gil Scott-Heron "The Other Side" *Spirits*, TVT Records, 1994.

[22] Pieces of a Man website, 15 April, 2009.

[23] Gil Scott-Heron, Interview by Leslie Gordon Goffe. Tape recording. New York, NY, March 2010.

[24] Gil Scott-Heron & Brian Jackson, "Hello Sunday! Hello Road!" *Bridges*, Arista Records, 1977.

ME AND BABY BROTHER

[1] Denis Heron, Interview by author. Digital recording. New York, NY, November 2007.

[2] Gil Scott-Heron, Interview by author. Digital recording. New York, NY, March 2010.

[3] War, "Me and My Baby Brother," *Deliver the Word*, 1973.

BRIAN'S SONG

[1] *New Yorker*, August 9, 2010.

[2] James Maycock, *Mojo,* December, 2003.

[3] Nikki Giovanni, "The Women Gather," *The Women and the Men* (New York: Harper Perennial, 1979).

[4] *Washington Post,* June 21, 1975.

[5] *Atlanta Daily World,* April 15, 1976. *Guardian*, February 20, 1976.

[6] *Washington Post*, 14 September, 1977.

[7] Jon Pareles, *New York Times*, November 5, 1984.

[8] Angela Terrell, *Washington Post*, August 27, 1974.

[9] Clive Davis, Interview in *Billboard* magazine, November 26, 1977.

[10] Gil Scott-Heron & Brian Jackson, "Corners," *1980*, Arista Records, 1980.

[11] Gil Scott-Heron, interview with author, The *Guardian*, October, 1988.

[12] "Gil Scott-Heron Has Staying Power," *Los Angeles Times*, April 11, 1981, D5.

[13] Gil Scott-Heron & Brian Jackson, "Madison Avenue," *Secrets*, Arista Records, 1978.

[14] Gil Scott-Heron, Gil Scott-Heron, "Home Is Where The Hatred Is," *Pieces of a Man*, Flying Dutchman, 1971.

[15] Gil Scott-Heron & Brian Jackson, "Angel Dust," *Secrets*, Arista Records, 1978.

[15] Gil Scott-Heron "Lady Day and John Coltrane," *Pieces of a Man*, Flying Dutchman, 1971.

[16] Gil Scott-Heron, Interview by author, Digital recording, New York, NY, March 2010.

[17] *Los Angeles Sentinel*, August 23, 1990, B.14.

[18] "Gil Scott-Heron's Rap," *Village Voice,* July 17, 2001.

[19] Gil Scott-Heron & Brian Jackson, "Peace Go with You Brother (As-Salaam-Alaikum)" *Winter in America,* Arista Records, 1974.

BIBLIOGRAPHY

Baraka, Amiri. "Black Dada Nihilismus" *Transbluesency: The Selected Poetry of Amiri Baraka/LeRoi Jones (1961-1995).* New York: Marsilio Publishers, 1995.

Bennett, Louise. *Jamaica Labrish*. Kingston, Jamaica: Sangster's Book Stores, 1966.

Bontemps, Arna. "A Black Man Talks of Reaping" American Negro Poetry: An Anthology. New York: Hill and Wang, 1963.

Berger, John. *Ways of Seeing: Based on the BBC Television Series.* London: Penguin, 1990.

Defoe, Daniel. *A Tour Through the Whole of Great Britain*. New Haven: Yale University Press, 1991.

Du Bois, W.E.B. *The Souls of Black Folks.* New York: St Martin's Press, 1997.

Ellison, Ralph. *Invisible Man*. New York: Vintage, 1995.

Daly, Glenn. "The Celtic Song," Clifford Music Ltd, 1961.

Drake, Horace & Clayton, St. Clair. *Black Metropolis: A Study Of Negro Life In A Northern City*, Chicago: University of Chicago Press 1945

Dunbar, Paul Laurence. *The Complete Poems of Paul Laurence Dunbar*. New York: Dodd, Mead and Company, 1922.

Ellison, Ralph. *Shadow and Act.* New York: Vintage International, 1995.

Fishman, Charles. "Fathers Are Not Stones" XY Files: Poems on the Male Experience. Santa Fe: Sherman Asher Publishing, 1997.

Frost, Robert. *Mountain Interval.* New York: Henry Holt and Company, 1916.

Giovanni, Nikki. *The Women and the Men.* New York: Harper Perennial, 1979.

Heron, Denis. Interview by author. Digital recording. New York, N.Y., 2007.

Heron, Gayle. Interview by author. Digital recording. Detroit, M.I., 2006.

Heron, Gil. *I Shall Wish For You.* Detroit, Michigan: Aaron Peal Publishing Company, 1992.

Heron, Gilbert "Gillie". Interview by author. Digital recording. Detroit, M.I., 2006.

Heron, Roy. Interview by author. Digital recording. Montreal, Canada, February, 2009.

Hughes, Langston. *The Big Sea*: An Autobiography by Langston Hughes. New York: A. A. Knopf, 1940.

Hughes, Langston. *The Langston Hughes Reader*. New York: George Brazilier, 1981.

Leonard, John. *Walter Mosley: Devil in a Blue Dress.*

Martin, George. "Gilbert, The Broth of a Boy from Detroit," *Daily Record*, August 22, 1951.

Marx, Karl. *Economic and Philosophic Manuscripts of 1844*, New York: Dover Publications, 2007.

Mitchell, Richard. *A Heron Family grew in Manchester*. Richard Mitchell, 2011.

Neal, Larry. "Malcolm X—An Autobiography" *Black Boogaloo*. Journal of Black Poetry Press, 1968.

Nietzsche, Friederich. *Thoughts Out of Season Part I*. Aeterna, 2007.

Owen, Wilfred. *The Collected Poems of Wilfred Owen, Chatto and Windus.*

Sandburg, Carl. *Chicago Poems*, Chicago: University of Illinois Press, 1992.

Scott-Heron, Gil. *The Vulture*, The World Publishing Company, 1970

Scott-Heron, Gil. *Small Talk at 125th and Lenox*, The World Publishing Company, 1970

Scott-Heron, Gil. *The Nigger Factory*, Dial Press, 1972.

Scott-Heron, Gil. *So Far, So Good*, Third World Press, 1990.

Scott-Heron, Gil. *Now and Then: The Poems of Gil Scott-Heron*, Canongate, 2001.

Scott-Heron, Gil. Interview by author. Digital recording. New York, NY, 2007.

Tolson, Melvin B. "Hideho Heights" *"Harlem Gallery" and Other Poems.* Charlottesville: University of Virginia Press, 1999.

Walker, Margaret. *For My People: A Volume of Verse.* Iowa: University of Iowa, 1940.

Wordsworth, William. "French Revolution" *The Complete Poetical Works of William Wordsworth.* Philadelphia: Troutman & Hayes, 1851.

DISCOGRAPHY

1970 Small Talk at 125th and Lenox	Flying Dutchman
1971 Pieces of a Man	Flying Dutchman
1972 Free Will	Flying Dutchman
1974 The Revolution Will Not Be Televised	Flying Dutchman
1975 The First Minute of a New Day	Arista
1976 From South Africa to South Carolina	Arista
1976 Its Your World	Arista
1977 Bridges	Arista
1978 Secrets	Arista
1979 The Mind of Gil Scott-Heron	Arista
1980 1980	Arista
1980 Realeyes	Arista
1981 Reflections	Arista
1982 Moving Target	Arista
1984 The Best of Gil Scott-Heron	Arista
1990 Glory: The Gil Scott-Heron Collections	Arista
1994 Spirits	TVT Records
1999 Evolution and Flashback: The Very Best of Gil Scott-Heron	RCA
2006 The Best of Gil Scott-Heron	Sony/BMG
2010 I'm New Here	XL Recordings

INDEX